UPON A SUMMER'S DAY

LAND MYSTERIES
BOOK FOUR

CELIA LAKE

Cover design by Augusta Scarlett.

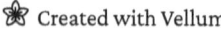 Created with Vellum

UPON A SUMMER'S DAY

Upon A Summer's Day is a direct sequel to *Old As The Hills*. I recommend reading *Old As The Hills* first.

On the Summer Solstice of 1940, Gabe made a solemn oath. Two parts of it were easy enough, he was already doing them. The third part has haunted his every choice since.

When he is asked a question that August, Gabe knows he must answer yes. His answer will change him, his family, and everything around him. There is no other way through but keeping his word and dealing with the consequences.

No one said he had to do it the way anyone else expects.

Upon A Summer's Day is a short novel that takes place in the autumn and winter of 1940 as World War II moves into a second year with the start of the Blitz Join Gabe, his wife, his family, and their allies in unweaving a tangle of ancient magics, turning assumptions on their heads, and refusing to follow destructive traditions. The fourth book in the Land Mysteries series, *Upon A Summer's Day* directly follows the events of *Old As The Hills*, and is best read in sequence.

CHAPTER I

G abe stared out across the clearing. He'd brought Meliora to a stop on the path, so he could think. He hadn't bothered to dismount and she was being exceptionally patient. Gabe had hoped a ride would help settle him, as it almost always did. This time, it hadn't.

It hadn't made things worse. But it also hadn't made anything better. There was still the looming, inevitable question he'd have to say yes to. He knew that, as he knew his own name and the shape of his magic. He'd given his word, and he could feel the oath tighten around him like vines and greenery and the shimmering coils of a serpentine dragon any time he even thought about doing the other thing, about saying no to the impossible task before him.

It would have been easier if he'd died a hair under a fortnight ago. Not that he'd wanted to die. But he would have understood that sacrifice of giving all of himself he could to one burst of magic, one casting of Merlin's Certainty outside the walls of the salle, feeling all the magic burn through him one last time. It would have left a gaping hole in the world, it would have shattered Rathna, their children, and his parents. A number of other people, most likely. It wasn't as if he'd wanted to do it.

It would still have been simple. Straightforward. It was the sort of simple and straightforward that Livia Fortier had done when she traded her life in battle for victory and glory and an empty Council seat that had to be filled. He had not liked the woman at all, but he could respect the elegant simplicity of her chosen death.

Though, to be honest, every single one of the people who loved him - and those who knew him well - would have said that he, Gabe, was never simple. Going out that way in one rush would not be like him at all. The rush, yes. The simplicity, never.

It made him laugh to himself. He knew he ought to take himself home. Somehow, while he wasn't paying nearly as much attention as he should have, the light had turned golden. He'd been out here for hours, then. His parents might be back by now. Rathna and Ferdinand, likely. Rathna had expected to miss supper, but not Avigail's bedtime.

That got him fumbling for his watch. Half-seven. He ought to head home. They'd be worried. The grooms, even if his family were still out. Still, he couldn't bring himself to shift his weight, to tell Meliora to head home. She'd be wanting her supper, and it was selfish of him to keep her from it.

He wanted to shy from that golden light, blessing everything it touched, even Gabe, even if he didn't want to feel blessed right now. His fingers clenched in Meliora's mane, the reins loose in his other hand, before he forced himself to relax them. That wouldn't do any good. Even if no one saw him, he couldn't afford that kind of thing. Not now. He couldn't risk anything showing when someone else was around.

It was only then that he heard something behind him. Off to his left, making him twist over the bad ankle, and it complained, as it insisted on doing. He ignored it, as he always did.

Sitting there, on her own mare, was his wife, hands resting loosely on the chestnut withers. "Ready to come back for supper?" Rathna's black hair was in a long braid down her back. She was wearing jodhpurs and short boots rather than tall ones, and the green linen blouse was the same one she'd been wearing that morning. She must have changed quickly, then, rather than fussing with things. Rathna asked it lightly enough, but Gabe knew full well she wasn't at ease at all. He hadn't meant to do that to her. Bad enough for one of them to be this tangled.

He spread his hands, the reins still loose. "Who's home?"

"Your parents are still out. Gil and Magni are in their rooms. Isobel was taking Ferdinand off for a distraction when I came out to the stables. She knows you entirely too well." Gabe's mouth quirked up. Yes, Isobel knew him well enough for that. She'd learned it early in her apprenticeship, and she only had a year or so to go. But Ferdinand had only been Rathna's apprentice for nine months, even if they were nine months packed with challenges. He'd been living here at Veritas for a bare six weeks, he was still learning the more private rhythms. "If we go back now, no one will bother us."

He sighed. They needed to get back, for the sake of the horses, if nothing else. "How's Madhup settling in with you back?" Her mare, named for honey as well, the honeybee, in this case.

3

"You're changing the subject. Or rather, you are completely and entirely unsubtly ignoring the previous subject. Come back. Sandwiches, coffee. Stronger drink if you need it, which I think you do."

He winced. He wasn't sure what it would do to his control if he did. Or if he took one of the potions. His ankle was definitely complaining now he'd noticed it again. His stunt during the duel with Alexander earlier had been needed, and that didn't mean it had been a good idea. Doing a back flip to avoid showing emotion was both stereotypically British and simultaneously a bit more showy than his body liked these days.

Rathna must have caught something in his expression. She usually did. "Come on. Home. What have you been doing, besides duelling Alexander?"

Gabe grunted. "Duelling Alexander. Thinking." Once round with magic, once round with words, and he was not at all sure of the outcome of the latter. The magic had been tidy enough. They'd come to a draw the last round, though Gabe had taken the first two bouts. Alexander had leant into all his skills, in a way Gabe hadn't seen him do often before. Alexander had certainly understood, somewhere, that Gabe had needed to throw himself against something implacable, and had offered himself for that. The question of what the man had seen in him, in his oaths, was one he desperately wanted an answer to. He was entirely certain he would not get it.

"And you've been out here since?" She tsked once. Rathna was, in fact, very tolerant of his habits when it came to food and sleep in the midst of something that needed doing. Not least because she could be nearly as bad. Now, though, she shifted her own weight in the saddle. "Come on. Staring at the field isn't doing any good, or you'd be done already."

Gabe had to laugh at that, and this, he let show easily. "Fair. Lead on, then." They made their way back to the stables in mutual silence. He could tell Rathna wasn't upset with him, but she was, he was sure, worried. That was entirely fair, he was being worrying. From the stables, they went up the side stairs to their rooms, and by the time they got there, a tray with sandwiches and such was already waiting.

"Go bathe, you. You've had a day of it." Gabe managed a bow. As he was making his way to their bathing room, she added, "Which potion should I get out?"

He grunted. "You want me to talk, you know which." Behind him, he heard her open the doors of the potions cabinet. Also their drinks cabinet, it wasn't like anyone could confuse which was which, and they needed both things handy on the regular. By the time he emerged, in a dressing gown and pyjamas, she'd changed into her own. She was settled on the sofa, with the food laid out on the low table.

"Food before we talk..." She looked him up and down. "Yes. Eat, then." There was no way he was going to duck this conversation, and he didn't exactly want to. For one thing, Rathna had every right to know. They were partners, in every possible sense of that word, for all their professions led them in different directions well before they met. He loved her with his whole heart, in ways he was still untangling.

His love for her made him think of the Penelope his profession was named for. Someone so steadfast, so complex, that she had plots within plots to keep her lands and her son and her people safe, even when they were beset by guests protected by all the magics of hospitality. He suspected he'd still be trying to make sense of what it meant to love Rathna properly if they passed their century mark together.

Now, though, he ate. And took the milder of the potions, he still wasn't sure he dared the stronger one, even when he went to bed. He didn't taste much of the food. At least it wasn't bitter in his mouth, or sitting in his stomach like a rock. Of course she'd chosen well, and it wasn't as if the staff didn't know these moments happened. They came around regularly, given Papa's role in the Guard, Gabe's in the Penelopes, Rathna's more delicate balancing act as a Portal Keeper, and all the intricate expectations of a landed family.

Finally, though, he'd had enough he could stop. He leaned back against the arm of the sofa, facing her. She nudged his knee. "Foot, please. I'll wrap it for you."

She did it better than he did. Part of it was the much less awkward angle, of course. But she had a touch to it. It was as if she read the flow of his magic, the way it silted up in the old break and the way the pain warped it. Rathna had a knack for laying the lines of the wrap where they'd do the most good.

"Thanks." He lifted his foot into her lap, tucking the other under the bad leg's thigh to prop it up better, and folded his arms across his chest. "Alexander asked the question. The one I told you about."

The one that had been lurking, waiting to pounce, since the Summer Solstice. Since he'd spent a night riding with the Fatae ladies of the Wild Hunt. They'd granted his request, but they'd required three things. He knew - as they must have known - that he'd have promised nearly anything, even his life. The cause was good. The cause was essential, in fact, a way to bring together the magical community - and the non-magical folk, by their standards, esotericists and occultists.

The Fatae queens had given him a ring. He'd not pried magically into how it worked, for all that was the bread and butter of his life. When he wore it, he could feel it warm against his skin when it was needed. As far as he could tell, it presented itself as whatever symbol would be persuasive to that person. At least twice, it had been some esoteric emblem probably from some secret society, and he'd had to do some quick talking to pretend he knew what it was. With the magical folk, his own people, it had been easier. He could talk about it coming from the Fatae, and they'd read the truth of it.

He'd promised to ride with the queens through the night. That had been easy, for all it had somewhat tainted every time he'd been on horseback since. He'd promised to do what he was already doing, convincing as many as he could to join their efforts in a great working to keep Hitler and all invasion on the far side of the Channel. So far, it had worked, though it had only been two weeks, and the bombing raids were increasing. Far too soon to tell, for any complex magical working. And Lammas night was as complex as it got, for all that the part he had personally been party to was a fairly simple ritual.

The last thing they'd asked him, though - told him, required of him, whatever way he put it - that was the one with the kick. They'd said that someone would ask a question he wanted to say no to, and he had to answer yes. Further, they had told him he would recognize the question in its time.

He'd known as soon as Alexander asked that this was what they'd meant. Now he had to explain it.

Gabe took a long breath, letting it out slowly, drawing on every fragment of his training. Also, drawing on Mama's gift for calm in these moments, for not acting out of season, conserving her energy, in particular. "They bid me say yes to a question I wanted to say no to. Alexander asked me that question today." Gabe held up his hand. "He didn't press for an answer. He must have seen something, in my oaths I think, that gave him pause. But I know what I'm going to say."

"We know what you're going to say." Rathna glanced up as she said the first word. "What, precisely, was the question?"

"Will I make the challenge for the Council." He could hear Alexander's voice, the precision of his chosen accent. Alexander was as much a master of words as he was duelling. More so, probably, though the two wound around each other so tightly in him it was hard to tell. "The new moon at the end of November."

Rathna's hands stopped moving, her palm cupping the curve of his ankle. Her fingers tightened for just an instant before she made them stop, the same way his hand had curled into Meliora's mane not too long before. "Livia's seat? They can't be serious."

"Livia's seat. I pointed out there were good reasons I didn't challenge eighteen years ago." Magister FitzAlan had raised the question then, when he knew he'd be retiring from the Council. Gabe had been gloriously in the first flourish of falling in love with Rathna. He'd absolutely known, as deeply as he knew his land, that he couldn't bring her among the Council as it stood.

Livia had been the most obvious problem - she'd made no effort to hide the fact she thought most people far beneath her. It was a tolerable sort of bigotry for people who were white and from the Second or Third Families, as Albion counted it. But Rathna's parents had been Bengali, neither of them had been of Albion as they counted it, and her early years had been spent around London's docks. She was not the sort of person admitted to the Council Keep in the ordinary way of things. Livia would have made every moment Rathna was near her agony, and Gabe wasn't having that. There were others on the Council who weren't a lot better, though they kept their disapproval much quieter.

But Livia had died, had gone out in one last burning flash of magic, two months ago today, in her own Certainty. Gabe had been there when her husband Garin, also a Council Member, had brought her back to the Council Keep, never mind at her funeral. It had shattered Garin in ways no one had expected. Alexander had been honest about that much, and Alexander had reason to know. He'd been on the Council himself for decades, nearly as long as the current Head, Cyrus Smythe-Clive. And he'd helped train Garin back in the day.

Alexander knew what he was asking. That was the curse of it. Alexander knew better than anyone else what he was asking Gabe to weave himself into. And if Alexander hadn't talked fully about what that had cost him over the years, Gabe was an expert in unweaving tangled circumstances himself. He could read enough of it in what Alexander so deftly avoided. The negative space it made, that was the proper word for it, even if he couldn't see the details.

He could also see that space in how the Carillons - Geoffrey, in particular, but Lizzie as well - had arranged things when they brought Alexander in among their intimates. That group included Gabe's parents, Gabe and

Rathna, Gil and Magni, Kate and Giles Lefton. And of course there were Aunts Mason and Witt, who'd mentored Gabe from the time he was nine or so. Not that he'd realised that at the time. He really was scattered, the way his wits were wandering into memory. They'd added others since: Thesan and Isembard Fortier, for example, who'd been close to Alexander for years.

But there had been something about how the Carillons introduced Alexander that had the undeniable trace work of magic supporting an old injury. Gabe knew well enough about that, given his ankle. And there was the way Alexander guarded himself, even when among people he now counted as friends.

"You're going to say yes." Rathna swallowed, then her fingers began moving, working on the wrap again. "There's no point in fussing about that. What does it mean to say yes?"

"That's the thing, I don't know. Alexander said I could keep being a Penelope, keep doing what I'm doing." He spread his hands. "I've had a chance to see more, this year, than most people."

"Tell me about that." She'd been gone for a lot of it, in the Netherlands and France, trying desperately to use her own magic, her own brilliance, to save just a few more lives each time. She'd taken magic and twisted it into shapes that would form a portal. Last he'd checked the count, dozens of people had found their way to freedom and relative safety because of her. Not as many as she'd wanted, but every life mattered.

"I've been up at the Council Keep more or less weekly with the project. Formal and relatively informal." They'd asked him, the Council had, blast them, to coordinate research. His task had been gathering up all the tidbits he could find about what magical measures and countermeasures might be needed, setting up walls that would hold against whatever Hitler and German magicians could bring to bear. That was important work, and Gabe was brilliant at it. Born to be brilliant at it, and trained to it, both. He couldn't do half of what he'd pulled together except for the fact he'd loved the land since he knew there was land to love. He'd made that his speciality among the Penelopes, and now where had that got him?

Rathna touched her fingers to the edge of the wrapping as she finished up, sealing it in place with a little pulse of magic. "What does it feel like when you're up there? Aside from the portal, we talked about that."

Gabe inhaled sharply. Then he looked up, meeting her eyes. "You wonder why I call you my bright lady. You always hit your mark." Then he answered, it wouldn't do to delay. "Not like Veritas does. But it shouldn't." He tilted his head, trying to find words that made sense outside his head, even if Rathna was far better at interpreting his incoherence than even Mama. "Curse Penelope's many threads, and all the many suitors." He grimaced. "It feels like it could be a place I held."

"We already knew you'd say yes to making the challenge." Rathna had a gift for taking the difficult part and flipping it around. She'd done it when they'd barely known each other - several times in succession - and she'd only got better since. "Does it matter if you win?"

Gabe shook his head. He could feel that constraint on the oath. He had to present himself, not succeed. Which suggested, now he thought on it, that whatever power made choices in the challenge, it wasn't the same as the Fatae queens he'd met. "Only. I can't walk in there - however it's done, I don't even know that yet - and not be willing to come out having won. Whatever that takes. But no. The question put to me is making the challenge. Alexander said some others. Giving the land the choice."

"Of course you can't." Rathna's voice had a tart note now, and Gabe looked at her directly again. She was half-smiling, though. "We know you will say yes. We know you'll give it your best. You've never been able to do anything else, not in your whole life. And don't say I didn't know you then. I get plenty of stories from your family."

Gabe held up his hands, conceding silently. She went on, her head now tilted to the side. "So what's the next step? Talking it through with Alysoun and Richard? Did Alexander give you any other information?"

"Rather a lot, for Alexander." Now that he'd had time to think about it, more information in a couple of paragraphs than Gabe had ever heard from the man at once. He ticked them off on his fingers. "I asked what I can ask him about, and he said anything that's already public. Geoffrey's pet alchemist is apparently already working on the usual run of potions people request, and if I don't want them, they'll go to good use somewhere."

Rathna nodded. "Which implies Geoffrey knew he was asking, doesn't it? Or Lizzie. Probably both of them." She talked more with Lizzie, on the whole, and Lizzie was as deft an analyst as Mama was, though on a somewhat different trajectory. "And?"

"He's thinking about less public information, but he said as much, straight out. He said, what was it?" Gabe paused to flick back in his memory. "They don't talk about much of it. And he's trying to figure out which things are permitted but never done, as he put it, versus what's not permitted and for good reason." His fingers twitched. "They've been intending to ask me since the day Garin brought Livia home, apparently. Cyrus and Mabyn let Alexander decide when."

"Huh." Rathna frowned. "I have a lot of questions, but I think we're at the point where I want Alysoun and Richard to hear them. Should I arrange that for tomorrow morning, before anything else?"

Gabe wanted to put it off. And he knew, as surely as he knew the investigative cantrips he used near every day, that he shouldn't and honestly couldn't. "Will you sort that out? Let the staff know, and Isobel and Ferdinand? Can you rearrange your morning?" Mama wouldn't be at her best in the morning, not if they were still out tonight. But Papa would have to get into the Guard Hall in Trellech sooner than later. And Gabe had work to do as well. They both always did. Those interviews in Christchurch, for one, and there were half a dozen other things on his list for after lunch, starting with a key conversation with Mason and Witt, because they needed to know.

"Can and will." She wriggled out from under his foot. "Let me go do that. You get into bed, take the potion you know you need. What did you do to the ankle?"

Gabe smiled sheepishly. "Vaulted over the wall from the observation area in the salle and did a backflip? It seemed the thing at the time."

That made Rathna turn back, laughing, and bend to kiss his forehead. "Serves you right. And it probably was the thing at the time. Now, though, is the time to take care of yourself. I'll be back up in ten or so."

Gabe waited until the door had closed behind her to move. He didn't exactly feel better about any of what was coming. But he'd told Rathna. She'd asked things that helped. The more complicated questions would come in the morning, the practicalities and logistics and lists of what he should put to Alexander in one form or another.

For now, well. She was right. Rest was the thing while he could. And the bed did look awfully inviting, even before the part where Rathna would be joining him very shortly. They'd make the most of all of each other they could, while they had the chance.

CHAPTER 2
AUGUST 13TH AT VERITAS

R athna glanced around the library, making sure everything was in order. Alysoun and Richard had their tea, she had her chai masala, Gabe had his coffee. Alysoun looked more tired than anyone liked. She had the dark smudges under her eyes. They hadn't got back until later last night than they'd planned, and both Gabe and Richard needed to be in Trellech soonish. Rathna hated dragging Gabe's mother out of bed, but needs must.

"Just the four of us?" Alysoun settled in her chair, wincing once. Gabe was standing by the French windows, looking out down the lawn toward the pond and the salle, but he turned around as his mother spoke.

"For right now. I've a meeting scheduled with Witt and Mason after lunch. And interviews before that."

Richard raised an eyebrow, leaning back in his own chair. "Out with it, then. Everyone else is decidedly occupied elsewhere." They were, indeed. Isobel had taken Ferdinand out for a quick course in foraging local plants, and Gil and Magni were consulting on something in London.

Rathna nodded. "Gabe?" They'd talked about this first thing this morning, once he was up and moving.

Gabe circled back, taking his place next to Rathna on the sofa. "I need to rearrange a number of plans, and I need your help, Mama and Papa, sorting out the full range of the implications." It was a curious way to put it - Gabe was forty now, an acknowledged expert in his own right. But in these circumstances, she'd have gone to her parents and asked for help if she could, just for the general sort of emotional support. Alysoun and Richard would have far more than that to offer, she was sure, but she also had no idea how they'd take this. Neither did Gabe.

"That's an interesting place to begin, Gabe." Alysoun's eyes had gone more focused. "Go on."

Gabe spread his hands. Rathna was proud of him that this came out in a reasonably coherent stream. "I told you both that the Fatae had placed three requirements on me. And about the question, the one that was still lingering." He waited just an instant to make sure they were following. "Yesterday, Alexander asked if I would challenge for Livia's seat at the end of November. I have to say yes. I promised." There was a note of anguish there, complex and ringing. Then he gathered himself and forged on. "The question is what it means."

As soon as Gabe put it that way, Rathna felt herself straighten, like she'd brushed the near-electric force of one of the strongest portals. Gabe, beside her, must have felt it, because his hand immediately settled on her arm. She half-nodded to acknowledge it, but focused on Alysoun and Richard's first reaction.

That was exactly what she'd expected. Alysoun's eyes widened, and then Rathna could see all the wheels moving. Her mother-in-law was exceptionally quick to spot the kinds of things they needed, even on a morning of a day her body was arguing with her. Richard was slower, but steady, and he had a deep knowledge of the structures of the Guard, the Penelopes, and the Ministry that would be tremendously helpful.

Gabe waited. Fifteen years ago, even five, he'd likely not have managed to hold his tongue for long. Now, she could feel one of his fingers twitching, but otherwise, he looked remarkably still.

"That's not the only question, surely. That you make the challenge, not that you succeed, yes?" Alysoun ticked off on her fingers as Gabe nodded. "A list, then. Richard, would you?" He reached over and snagged a notepad and the pen out of his breast pocket. "There is the challenge itself, but that seems to me, in the whole, either easiest to sort out or outside our ken and can't be planned for."

That, now, made Gabe relax a little, and he slipped his arm around Rathna instead of leaving his fingers dancing on her arm.

Alysoun went on. "The interpersonal implications, both of the challenge and of success. The current makeup of the Council. I have some notes, of course, and I'm sure Lizzie has quite a few more. Thesan, as well. And then the larger implications for Gabe. Did Alexander offer any information we should know about?"

"A surprising amount. He made it clear that they want me to make the challenge. Who wins is - well, they want to present a choice. That I could continue as a Penelope, though it might affect which cases I took. I am, of course, a tad dubious about that, but I need to talk it out with Mason and Witt before deciding anything else there."

"To be fair, you're spending most of your time on Council work as it is, and have been for months." Richard pointed out once he'd made his list and his pen had stopped. That was true, and Gabe had largely been enjoying it, even, figuring out how the various acts of magic tangled with each other. "Your original objections, many of which still stand, even if Livia in specific is not a factor." He added a few words to the list.

Gabe's mouth quirked into a smile. "Just so, Papa." Rathna remembered that particular conversation very well. That had been the first morning she'd properly talked to Alysoun and Richard. Gabe had been so fierce and firm about why he wouldn't challenge when Council Member FitzAlan asked. "And there's the larger question of Alexander, about what being on the Council has meant to him and for him and I don't know the word here, done to him. Except it obviously has."

Alysoun nodded at that. "Excellent point. Anything else for right now?" She rubbed her hands together briefly. "Right. The challenge itself."

That was the easiest to answer. Gabe explained what Alexander had shared, both the offer of information, and the current limitations. Alysoun raised an eyebrow at the comment about Alexander not being sure how much of some things he could share, that certain things weren't discussed. But she didn't press that point at the moment. Alexander had made the quite real point that after the other events of Gabe's summer, he should have expected they'd want him to challenge. Rathna couldn't argue with that at all. He'd done three impossible things that summer, and come through them remarkably well.

He'd thrown himself into locking one of the oldest portals in Albion, he'd ridden a night with the Fatae, and he'd come through a massive act of ritual magic in one piece. He kept giving everything he had when it was needed. She loved him for it and was terrified of what it might mean next. Continuing to go upward from there, that was the thing legends were made of, the sort that ended in heroic deaths. He had been all but certain that the ritual would have been such an ending, going in, and he had given his all even then.

Once Gabe had gone through the entirety of his conversation with Alexander, his mother nodded. "And you bring your own skill with duelling, if relevant, and an exceedingly creative mind when it comes to problem solving. I dare say you could fine-tune a few skills, and you might want some potions, but it isn't as if you need to cram for the meat of the exam."

"Mama." Gabe snorted.

His father nodded along. "You know your skills. Far better than most candidates, I suspect, actually. You've always had a clear idea of what you can and can't do. You do try for the impossible on the regular, but you..." He paused, rummaging for words.

Alysoun picked up evenly. "You know what's a reach, and generally how much of one it is. That is quite rare. And it's not the sort of thing that can be taught. Rathna, love, you had to learn how to reach. Gabe only had to learn how to measure and adjust on the fly."

Rathna smiled at that, leaning into Gabe's shoulder. "Fly, as it often seems like." He was slightly less inclined these days to fling himself off a horse at speed or rappel down from a cave or climb out of a window than he had been. But slightly less left quite a lot of scope still.

"Which brings us, I think, to the original objections." Richard peered up from the list. "Livia Fortier."

"Not just Livia, to be fair." Gabe said. "But yes. Alexander pointed out that they've been doing their best to diversify a bit. Vidya Archarya's a step in the right direction, but there's only one of her. And you know how we feel about that."

She and Gabe had had endless conversations about that, analysing the dynamics of whatever social circle they found themselves in. It had turned into a beloved party game, honestly, begun during the first year of their marriage when they were living in the London flat. They'd fallen in with an amiably bohemian crowd, but there was a vast difference between a multi-faceted community and being a token, and Rathna had had her fill of the latter.

"Who else besides Vidya?" Rathna liked Vidya, mind. She didn't know the woman incredibly well, but well enough to know she was made of goodwill and a sharp interest in Healing research, and both of those were worthwhile.

"The other two recent additions are Laodamia Noble and Godfrey Peran. Laodamia has Matthias Sisley's old seat. Poor man." Alysoun tsked. "Richard, could you grab my notes from the desk?" He'd had incurable cancer, and gave over his seat only months before his death, as it turned out, two years ago. Richard stood, pausing to brush a kiss on the top of her head before going off to her desk in the east alcove.

"Laodamia Noble has got a knack for sympathetic magic and materia. She's published quite a few interesting papers." Gabe said. "Very interested in the locational implications, Mason's consulted her a few times."

"So we know she's competent." Alysoun smiled at that. Gabe's Aunt Mason and Aunt Witt were the two senior most Penelopes, nominally somewhat retired, but still very much in the midst of everything, especially given the war. They had exceptionally high standards, even by this family's measure of such things. "And Godfrey Peran had quite a career in the Army, didn't he, before this?"

Richard came back, slipping the book into Alysoun's hand. "Well-respected, knows his work. And unlike a lot of Army men, he's gifted with both the martial and protective magics. I got the impression he'd spent some time with Gospatrick, on his way up the ranks, and did well by it."

"I can check on that." Alysoun said agreeably. "Or rather I'll ask Thesan and she'll know who to ask over there. And the others from the past decade are a similar mix. Skilled, obviously, but tolerable on a personal level."

"It's an interesting question if anyone would say they like Ulric Monkton, exactly. Rather dour. But he knows his work." Gabe agreed. "Papa, what's your take on Nonus Powell?"

Rathna knew Powell was a former member of the Guard, but he'd retired rather than moving into more sedentary work as he got older. Richard laid it out briefly. "Not as sharp mentally as his cousin Angharad. The family's a bit reclusive, even though there's quite a few of them. He was competent. Not charismatic, but that's not always what you want. He did a fair bit of logistics work. I'd expect that to carry over. And so far as I know, he doesn't hold me or our family any particular grudge, though also no particular warmth."

Gabe nodded. "I can work with that. I haven't seen much of him around. He's been working on other things when I've been up at the Keep and I suspect that was deliberate on someone's part. Rathna, love, Desmond Belling? He's an astronomer."

Rathna wrinkled up her nose. She was a full member of the Astronomer's Guild, all the Portal Keepers were, but she largely ignored their internal politics. "That's another question for Thesan. She'd know him better." As Astronomy professor at Schola, Thesan had excellent reason to keep tabs on everyone in their shared Guild. "He's interested in locational magic, mostly. So I suspect he'd be working with the warding and protective magics lot. He's never been rude to me, but I can't say we've ever had a particularly lengthy conversation?"

The portal magics that were her passion and vocation relied on locational magic, of course, and she was quite competent in those parts. But she'd gone to other people for confirmation of the calculations for her most recent efforts, and now she wondered if that was going to cause trouble.

Alysoun glanced up. "We can figure that out. I'm sure Thesan will be glad to be informative. That leaves, hmm. Alcesta Romilly. Diviner. Apparently quite good at it, but it's hard to tell with that kind of thing."

Richard tsked. "She's got a knack for finding people, actually. No idea if it's actually divination or some spark of reading the locational magic. I've seen her map scry, though, she was brought in for a couple of cases. Missing children, you know we'll try anything we can for those. She's easy to work with and she's measured about what information she commits to."

"All right. That takes us back a decade. Alexander is his own topic. So, I suspect, are Cyrus Smythe-Clive and Mabyn Teague." Her lips tightened. "Anyone else before we get into that?"

"There's Garin Fortier, but I think no one knows what he'll do. Even Alexander." Gabe said. "I get on well enough with Malcolm Rolls. He's got used to how I do my best work now, it helps."

Rathna snorted at that. "Which is to let you do what you were going to do anyway."

"I just said that." But Gabe was laughing now, and that was a fine thing. "Theo Carrington's a snob about background, and so's Rhoda Morwen, but neither of them is nearly so nasty about it as Livia was. All right, on those counts, my specific objection is, I think, negated."

Rathna hesitated, before going ahead and asking. "Would you really turn it down because of me?"

"Whatever else it involves, there's a certain amount of social obligation there. The Solstice rites, and all that, but other things as well. Making a polite show at public events, at the least. Besides, I don't want to be somewhere you're not welcome. And not treated with basic respect." Gabe shrugged one shoulder, as if dismissing it, but she could tell from the edge in his voice that it was something she'd never move him from.

That was when the thought hit her. "Has that happened often?"

"I've told you when it has." He shifted to look at her more directly. "I wouldn't make the decision for you. But I don't want to be where you aren't. Especially these days."

Rathna supposed that her long sojourn in nearly occupied territory would do that to him. It was an entirely reasonable reaction. And it wasn't as if she wanted him to be far away right now, even though they both had ongoing work that dragged them around the country. She leaned to kiss his cheek, just by his ear. "Fair enough." Then she asked, "Silvia Warren?"

Alysoun pursed her lips. "Something of an enigma. She married Hesperidon Warren. Mabyn Teague took her under her wing. I gather people were surprised she didn't challenge for the Head of the Council when he died, but ..."

Hesperidon had ruled the Council - and that verb was quite deliberately used, Rathna gathered - for decades, from 1890-something, until his death in 1932. Cyrus taking over had been rather like an earthquake, though now Rathna was wondering exactly what that had meant.

Gabe was thinking along the same lines. "Cyrus is solid there. Not that we know anything about how that gets decided. Maybe Alexander would tell us that much. He did mention that they're all tied in on a wheel and spoke system, the Head at the centre. I can see how that'd make someone a tad cranky, as I heard about Hesperidon, but Cyrus has been..." Gabe frowned. "I am inclined to take his orders, and there's a thing I don't say much about people."

Richard snorted. "No. Argue with orders, yes. Come up with better ideas, reliably. But there's a reason no one seriously considered you going into the Guard." He held up his hand, automatically. "Except me, and I've long since got over that. Why are you inclined with Cyrus, then?"

"We talked some about this, the day Livia died, and I've talked to Rathna a little about it." Gabe glanced at her.

"Not that, though." Rathna pointed out. To be fair, they'd had a tremendous amount to catch up on, and she'd only been back in Albion six weeks. And it wasn't as if their lives had got less busy.

Gabe grinned at her and went on. "For one thing, he's competent. And he - as you said, I know how far to reach. He knows his edges. And he's not shy about recognising other people's skills. He trusted Alexander that day, gave him his head. And Alexander gave me mine." Gabe sighed. "I'm talking myself into it, aren't I?"

"If you do it to yourself, maybe you'll grumble less?" Alysoun pointed out. "You do have moods. We could all stand to be spared that one."

Gabe grunted, but it was more a resigned amusement than anything else.

"Mabyn Teague." Alysoun glanced at Richard, as if measuring something. "You remember, Richard, when we were sorting ourselves out better, we got to talking about women in awful marriages?"

"I do. But that wasn't Mabyn, surely? Her husband was long dead by then. There was still gossip about it when I joined the Guard, but he died in, what? '95?"

Alysoun nodded. "But she had that sort of horrible marriage. And it continued until his death, well after she was on the Council. That's a question, isn't it?" She looked at all three of them, her eyes more than a little stormy. "Either they're incompetent, or they don't care. Both are awful."

Rathna sucked in a breath, but she couldn't argue with that at all. "Things are better now. She seems quite happy with Smythe-Clive. And his daughter Gemma, we know her a bit better, though not intimately. She seems very pleased with things. She likes Mabyn, from everything I've seen and heard, in her own right, and I don't think she'd do that just to please her father."

"And that is a telling detail, yes. Though, honestly, it'd be hard to be worse than the late Lord Teague. Not a pleasant man, by all accounts." Richard was rarely so blunt about someone else.

It did make Rathna consider something. She held up a finger to let them know and felt Gabe squeeze her by the waist. The three of them went on, going through the other practical details, and she largely tuned it out. She knew the names and the general background, of course, it was the sort of thing the family tracked routinely, for all sorts of reasons.

When she surfaced again, she thought it was near five minutes later. She felt Gabe's hand shift at her hip, and the others all fell silent.

"Gabe, what was it that was bothering you? About how they are together?"

Gabe frowned. "I hadn't said."

That made her snort. "You hadn't. Put it into words now, please." They could do something with it, in words.

"It's." Then he nodded, one of those moments where he flung himself into the unknown and trusted it would work out, letting the words flow out. "The Penelopes are collaborative. To a fault, we're in and out of each other's offices and workrooms, all the time, except if an interruption would be dangerous. We don't expect to be brilliant at everything, even if we're all brilliant at a number of things."

"Modest, too." Alysoun added that, laughing now.

Gabe waved a hand. "Know our own merits. But we're not on a, what's the word. High horse about them. Stuck on rank and all that. Isobel will argue with Witt and Mason when she's right, and that's the point. And she has." The pride in that shone through, clear as the sun outside.

Rathna nodded. "And the Council aren't." It wasn't a question. It was a triangulation, from all the shards she'd heard over the years, or seen herself. "Alexander's proof enough of that, even if he doesn't talk about it. Especially since he doesn't talk about it, because that goes to show."

Gabe leaned back a bit, rubbing his face with his free hand. "Geoffrey might. Might not. It's hard to tell. But he's the one who brought Alexander in. Or Thesan and Isembard."

Rathna nodded. "We can ask Thesan." Thesan's husband Isembard was heavily occupied now, making sure his brother Garin didn't do himself or anyone else an injury. "Tea, Alysoun, sometime, do you think?"

"Tea. She might be glad of a chance to get away. And we could have their two over?" Thesan and Isembard's son Leo was just Avigail's age, and they enjoyed playing together. Ursula Fortier was the same age as their Anthony. Their eldest, Rowena, was glad to spend time with both of them. Rowena took after Alysoun that way, Rathna had come to think, with a curiosity about people that certainly didn't come from Rathna herself.

That did remind her to say something. "Find a day that works on your end, and I'll make it work on mine." That kind of negotiation was the norm around here, at least, and in general, they deferred to Alysoun's schedule and current health. Getting Thesan to come here would be easier on Alysoun as well.

Alysoun nodded. Richard scratched a note or two on his pad. "Was that all, Rathna?"

She shook her head. This was the part she was less sure of. If it were Gabe's idea, she'd be sure it was right, but he hadn't come up with it yet. Which meant it was either her particular kind of good idea - she had done that before, more than once - or that she was missing something.

"Can you put your own requirements on it?" It came out in a rush, suddenly. "We all know you're going to say yes. But they don't know that you're going to. Or what would make you agree."

There was an utter silence in the room. Rathna could hear the clock ticking away. Finally, Alysoun's voice broke the silence, a note of strain in her voice. "Please, Rathna, say anything like that comes to mind in the future. You're quite right. Alexander might spot it, I suppose, but will he say anything?" She then frowned. "What would you say, if you could, Gabe? You'll need to present it as a, a matter of business. Ritual coordination."

"Collaboration. Sharing." Gabe was right there with his reply. "That's what hit me, talking to Alexander, coming back to it. They don't share. He didn't say so in that many words, but they obviously don't. I want the right to share. For what I share to matter. That whatever I learn there, in the challenge, that I'll tell them if I think they should know it. Not be bound by custom to keep it secret."

Richard cleared his throat. "Just you? Or for them to share as well?"

Gabe shrugged. "I can't force them to share. It would undo all the possible good of it, to make them. But I think I have enough standing to make it clear this is a desperate weakness for them. It's going to cause even more problems if they don't deal with it." He waved a hand. "I've seen enough for that, and they know it."

Alysoun snorted. "There's not been a Penelope on the Council in what, two hundred years? There might be a reason for that. They're overdue, by a long shot, for your particular blend of problem solving."

That made Gabe laugh, far more relaxed now. "Well. Untangling the impossible is what we're for." He then glanced over at the clock as it chimed. "I really should get on. Papa, are you coming?" He shook his head. "And I've got behind on my reports again. I really need to find time for that tonight."

Richard tsked. "You are always behind, and it's always a scramble." It wasn't scolding, just resigned to the way Gabe was. "Give me a minute. I've a meeting at ten, and I need my notes." It was coming up on half-nine. "Collect Isobel, then. Meet you at the portal." There was a flurry of getting things together for the day until Rathna and Alysoun were left alone in the library with the remains of the tea and coffee.

"Can you spare half an hour, Rathna, help me sort out notes and perhaps write the one to Thesan? Then I'll go back up to bed, and you can get on with your work." It wasn't quite a question, certainly not an order.

"Gladly. I've got a few minutes still." And Alysoun was right, the invitation would come better from her. Besides, whatever she could do so Alysoun could rest a bit more would be welcome and appreciated by a number of people.

CHAPTER 3
AUGUST 21ST AT THE COUNCIL KEEP

"Y̲ou heard Churchill's speech last night?" Alexander let Gabe into the green meeting room. It was what had become their regular appointment to hear Gabe's report of his work. This week, however, Gabe had made it clear he'd like to discuss the question Alexander had posed. Not beforetime, either, there were only three months left. He'd taken his time about it. Alexander and Cyrus had expected that particular conversation last week, honestly.

Today, there had been a scattering of messages from Gabe all morning, catching up on pieces Gabe had dropped by the wayside. Usually, he was better than that at presenting himself as having some semblance of order. None of them were urgent, but Alexander had a strong sense of a whirlwind, flinging things out not quite at random. Fortunately, most of the chaos had come to him. The message that had included Cyrus was a great deal more orderly.

Behind him, he could hear Cyrus and the distinctive

rustle of Cyrus's notes and pen, as he leaned over to say something quietly to Mabyn. Cyrus - or perhaps Mabyn, Alexander wasn't clear on the originator - had asked Silvia to sit in today. Without, Alexander suspected, giving her much warning of some of the topics.

Gabe nodded. "The Royal Air Force deserve every bit of praise they're getting. 'Never in the field of human conflict was so much owed by so many to so few.' True enough, indeed, and the man does have a way with words, one that's desperately needed. But of course, in so many places, much of the work of the few goes utterly unacknowledged."

"For good reason, including our oaths on it, but yes. We all serve, though, in our ways." Alexander gestured at the free chair before taking up his own. Cyrus was at the end of the table, as usual, with Mabyn to his left and Silvia next to Mabyn. Alexander took the seat to Cyrus's right, automatically putting himself between any potential danger and the Head of the Council. He wondered if Cyrus noticed. Hesperidon wouldn't have. Alexander was sure of that now. If he did, he would have just taken it as his due.

Not that he expected Gabe to pose any actual danger, mind you. It was the principle of the thing, not letting his guard down. Whatever Gabe said, wherever the conversation went, the challenge would be words and not magic or threats. Gabe was too much of a professional and entirely too well brought up to do otherwise.

Gabe nodded agreeably at Silvia, not commenting on her presence. Usually it had been Malcolm, or a couple of times one of the others with a particular speciality. It had been Lucas Holder, often enough, who had talents in both ritual and illusion. Both of those were relevant when people started talking about broader applications of esotericism and occultism, and the many and varied groups doing their bit. He slid into his seat, propping his cane next to his chair so it wouldn't be in the way.

Once he was settled, though, he wasted no time. "To begin, I've my usual report, of course. There's still nothing definitive. While the bombings by air have increased dramatically in the last week, there are still no real signs of any attempt to cross the Channel by other means. We can take that as something of a victory, perhaps, at least if it holds. The various esoteric groups seem to be trying to find their feet. No particularly articulate pamphlets or letters."

That carried them through perhaps twenty minutes of discussion. Cyrus had a question about a letter in the *Times* the week before, and whether it might or might not be a coded message. Certainly, the title had a particular note to it, "Snakes and Apricots". Gabe read it out, clearly and distinctly, and Alexander watched his face. He knew Gabe had particular opinions about snakes, but none of that showed now, just his commitment to reading the letter neutrally, exactly as printed.

It was, in fact, one of those letters where he had to wonder why the *Times* spared the ink, especially in these days of paper rationing. The letter was not long, describing a man looking at his apricot tree, finding a single large apricot fallen to the ground, with a hole all through it.

When he and his gardener examined where it had been, they had found a quite small - two foot - grass snake twined around the vine. It made a rather interesting symbolic picture, even if one weren't inclined to let one's mind wander in that direction. One other apricot had the same hole, but apparently none of the others had been touched by bird or wasp. That, at least, could have been chalked up to decent protective charms, perhaps on the gardener's part.

Gabe had anticipated the question, as he pulled out three pages of analysis from a reliable cryptographer. Giles Lefton, almost certainly, not that Gabe named him. If Gabe did join them on a permanent basis - as Alexander both hoped and worried about - their meetings would at least become more informatively entertaining. Gabe didn't lecture, he didn't grandstand. He simply thought everyone should know as much of everything as possible. It was an entirely novel approach, given the way so many in the upper echelons of magical society - and the Council in particular - wanted to hoard their knowledge.

Silvia ventured a comment, perhaps ten minutes into the broader discussion of what to be alert to, and Gabe took it well. She hadn't exactly challenged him outright. For one thing, Silvia knew a dozen ways to do that in any given setting. Not that Gabe wouldn't have spotted it, also, if she tried. His mother knew at least two dozen, from all Alexander had picked up over the past five years. But Gabe also didn't have any difficulty respecting the places Silvia had quite real knowledge and expertise different from his own, without budging on his understanding of the underlying realities.

In the end, Silvia admitted she was over her head on the specifics. Gabe brought things to a close, though, with a twist. Gabe set his notes aside, and added, almost offhandedly. "Mind, Eric Parker, the writer, is a noted naturalist. Eton and Merton College. The hunting and shooting sort, but he and his wife were also quite involved in getting the Wild Birds Protection Act passed in 1933. That's been good for a number of the magical birds, too, especially the smaller ones. But one does have to investigate everything curious, doesn't one?"

Cyrus raised an eyebrow. "Every time I think I've a measure of your expertise, you surprise me."

Silvia stiffened and murmured something before getting up to refill her tea from the tray by the bookshelves. Alexander noticed, of course, she was subtle but he was excellent at spotting that sort of thing, he'd needed it far too often to keep himself out of too much trouble. It gave them a natural break in the flow. Mabyn tilted her head. "That all from your report then?"

Gabe nodded once, and Alexander saw the minute shifts. He wouldn't have spotted it, except that by now he'd duelled Gabe dozens of times. If Gabe had been standing, he'd have leaned very slightly onto his front foot, an almost imperceptible angle in his torso. Now, it was his eyes that gave him away, as much as anything, the way there was a gleam in them that Gabe got most reliably in a duel.

"May I speak freely, in regard to a question Alexander posed on the twelfth?" The question was - quite properly - addressed directly to Cyrus. Gabe didn't look at Alexander beyond the simple angle of the thing. On the other hand, Alexander was quite sure Gabe was entirely aware of every small movement Mabyn or Silvia made. Alexander himself certainly was.

"You may." Cyrus inclined his head. Cyrus had a notable amount of personal gravitas that did well in these moments. He made the ordinary agreement look appropriately imposing.

Gabe didn't sit back as he had been, but he angled himself - again, a small precise movement, barely notable - to include both Mabyn and Silvia. "A week ago Monday,

Alexander asked if I would challenge for Livia Fortier's seat in November. I would like to discuss that before giving my answer."

"Discuss?" Alexander had expected a question or two, but not a discussion, per se. Discussions were not how this was done. "I told you then what questions I was open to, and which I was contemplating."

"You did, Alexander." Somehow, Gabe put a note of warmth there, where it had no right to be. Again, it was utterly not the mode in which one conducted conversations about a challenge. "This is a broader question. The sort of thing the Head of the Council would need to decide upon."

Definitely not what Alexander had expected. He flicked a finger at Gabe, indicating the younger man should go on. That youth hit him then. Alexander himself was seventy this year, and Cyrus and Mabyn were five and seven years older. Silvia was in her mid-fifties. Gabe was nearly young enough to be her son. And yet, here was Gabe, absolutely sure of himself, absurdly certain he had every right to come to this table as an equal.

To be fair, that was precisely why they needed him to make the challenge. Over and over this summer, he'd thrown himself into the impossible with a due amount of caution but near enough no hesitation. It was why the three of them - Alexander, Cyrus, and Mabyn - had agreed the night of Livia's death that they needed him to make the challenge, whatever it took. The outcome wasn't up to them, quite possibly wasn't even up to Gabe. But they had to get him through that doorway into the challenge chamber at the top of the keep.

Trust Gabe to make it his own, as he'd done everything else. Alexander shouldn't be surprised. Whatever part of this he could bring back to Geoffrey and Lizzie, when all was said and done, he expected Geoffrey would laugh. The last few moments put Gabe in an elite company - with Geoffrey himself - of people who had wrong-footed Alexander with a handful of sentences.

Gabe took his time, reaching for his tea before he went on. "Let me lay out my question, then. I know, of course, that there are - there must be - particular protocols for the challenge. Before, during, and in the enduring after. That there are things I will make oath not to speak of."

"Just so." Cyrus said. "And Alexander has my full permission to tell you whatever is not so bound." Not that Cyrus would try to forbid Alexander at this point. That would go decidedly badly, and they both knew it. So did Gabe, almost certainly.

"Can you tell me, then, here and now, before I give you my answer, if anything forbids me sharing my experiences in the Challenge with you of the Council? Whether I am successful or not, mind."

Silvia sucked in a breath, an unusual show from her. She normally made an art form of being unflappable. Beside her, Mabyn folded her hands firmly in her lap. Or perhaps sat on them. It was hard to tell from Alexander's angle, and with all his focus on Gabe himself. Slowly, Alexander turned to look at Cyrus, who was doing a far better job of looking unruffled.

"It is not done. It has not been done." Cyrus hesitated, the only outward hint of how unsettled he also was. "Why?"

The question made Gabe smile again. Alexander caught it as he turned back. It was the kind of smile Gabe got in a duel when he'd pulled off something particularly clever that would be a problem in a few exchanges. Alexander still only had a one in two chance of spotting what it was when Gabe was duelling, before it landed. "Have you looked at the patterns of who has joined you? Laying it out, in terms of background and expertise?"

Alexander blinked at that. He'd looked at the charts, of course. All of them went by the encoded map of the keep often these days, and the tokens there mostly reflected someone's Schola house or particular magical skills. It was Mabyn who asked the question, "Yes, but clearly not in the way you mean. Would you explain?"

Gabe nodded, reaching into his bag, and pulling out a rolled set of large papers. He unfurled one end, sending the end down to near Cyrus. He added a near-wordless charm to make the end stick flat to the table, before he did the other corners the same way. "The names of the current Council Members." He gestured. "In order of their challenges, of course. What follows is a crude representation, to begin, the Houses. Not that you have anyone who didn't attend Schola."

Then he flicked his fingers, and colour began to spring up, as he named them all, one by one. The first half of the names were predominantly the Fox House purple. Cyrus, Alexander himself, for all that was an increasingly ill-fitting robe these days, Theo Carrington, Livia and Garin Fortier, Matthias Sisley. There were a few exceptions. Mabyn was of Owl House. Then there was a period where it was Owl with a smattering of others in alternation. Troilus Watts was the lone member from Horse House, Lettice Fowler from Seal.

It was the more recent years, the last fifteen, that got interesting. They were a veritable riot of colour. Silvia was the only Fox among what was that, four from Bear House, three from Seal, two from Salmon, and even one from Boar. Gabe let them look, then another flick of his fingers brought up dots representing their specialities. The more recent to join them ran heavily to enchantment, warding, protection, and martial magic, as well as a good dose of the ever-useful sympathetic and materia magics. Even, for the first time in a very long time, a Healer.

"You'd think that the Land had noticed there was going to be a war." Gabe's voice was a shock when he spoke, both for the comparative lightness in his voice and the way it cut across everything like the sharpest knife, where the pain just wasn't felt for an ageless time after.

Alexander barely resisted the temptation to bury his face in his hands. It was there, staring them in the face, and none of them had talked about it at all. The Land chose, yes, the land that Alexander loved more than anything else. The pattern was stark when laid out this way. He knew Cyrus had been working hard to broaden the list of candidates, but it had been an uphill struggle. All had gone to Schola, it was true. But until fifteen years ago, for more than a century, only the narrowest sliver of Schola had any real representation.

Cyrus spent a good several minutes looking at the chart before he lifted his eyes. "Expand on your point, if you would? How did you come to notice this, in particular, and how does it play with your question?"

"Patterns are what I do." Gabe leaned back, looking entirely relaxed now, and that was worrying in and of itself. Or it would have been, if Alexander weren't increasingly sure that Gabe was actually on their side. Or rather, he was on the side of the Land, of her magic, and that's what mattered. "You've seen my work. This is the simplest form of it. You need a Penelope. You know that. I know that. But I need my head to do this."

"And that means sharing your challenge?" Cyrus was feeling his way through it, the way Alexander had felt his way through fields studded with mines and explosives in the last war. It had to be done, and any step might change the terrain forever, if it didn't kill you too.

Gabe nodded once. "The Penelopes work collaboratively. We always have, I gather, I stole an hour to go through some of our oldest histories on Saturday. It's the only way we can do our work." He turned his palm up. "All my ability to see patterns, what you have given me glimpses of the past year, means I can tell you don't share much at all. Not if you can possibly help it."

Alexander felt the hit of it, back to a conversation in a forest near Berlin. He remembered the way Geoffrey had cut him off at the knees with a precept so basic that all of them had been ignoring it for as long as Alexander had been alive. Longer, certainly. Gabe wasn't the only one who'd looked at history.

Cyrus looked down at the chart again. "And you being able to share is the price of your agreement?"

Gabe shrugged. Gabe notably didn't say anything else, and that silence caught Alexander's attention immediately. He focused, just slightly, trying to read the man, trying to guess what the next sortie would be, and saw the vivid iridescent green shimmer rippling through the pattern of his oaths, the same shine he had seen flare so sharply when he had posed the question in the first place. At the time, he had thought it best not to press. He had no idea what that colour, that pattern, meant.

If Cyrus noticed anything at all, he didn't give any indication, but instead asked another question. "Do you require others do the same?"

"I hope they will. If anyone wishes to, I will treat it as the gift and sign of trust it is. But no, I do not want anyone to be forced to it. I can bargain with my own magic, not anyone else's. All I ask is, how do I put this, respect for what I learn from the experience in turn."

It hit Alexander like the fall of an ancient statue might, and instinctively and immediately, he pulled close all the magics that might hide his reaction. From Gabe, but also from Silvia and Mabyn and even Cyrus. What had Gabe spotted, then, of Alexander's own disasters here? Quick as lightning and tinged with sharp heat, Alexander could barely count the ways he'd been used as nothing but a tool for the decades that flashed through his memories. He'd never talked about them with Gabe, he'd barely talked about them with Geoffrey and Lizzie in any detail, and yet somehow, he knew Gabe had seen enough.

That kind of vow, decades ago, would have saved his heart. He would not have wandered, alone in a desert, for year after year, never really having a home to come back to, certainly not one that he trusted. He had that now, he had somehow built it and found it, and been welcomed into it, but no part of that had come from the Council. He'd thought that impossible.

Cyrus let out a long breath, but he didn't take more than that to come to a decision. "If that is your condition, then, agreed. You are permitted to speak of whatever you wish from your challenge, among the Council, as you see fit. And if you choose to do so, I will make sure that the conversation is conducted with respect. Fair?"

Suddenly Gabe was smiling, a broad honest smile that was letting all of his coiled intention loose in the room.

"More than fair. Thank you." He inclined his head once, then finally glanced at Alexander. "Alexander?"

Alexander needed to talk to Geoffrey, that was what Alexander needed, and he wasn't going to have a chance until at least tomorrow. Tonight's Council meeting was already packed, and this little wrench was going to add to it. But he couldn't fault either the desire or the way Gabe had set it up. Now, he did his best to make his reply easy, almost casual. "You make excellent points. Not that I'd expect you to do anything else. I agree."

There were murmurs from the others, though rather muted from Silvia. Cyrus nodded. "If that's the case, then may we formally have your word?"

Gabe had obviously done his research here as well. He hadn't asked Alexander about it, certainly. "I Gabriel Anthony Edgarton, Heir to the demesne of Veritas, Penelope, and Master of Incantation and Materia, swear on my magic and on the Silence that I come willingly to the threshold of the Council. I likewise swear I will present myself on the 29th of November or whatever other date may best suit, to make my Challenge and let the Land make her choice, holding secret and private all that must be so." Alexander watched the magic ripple through him, moving like a swift snake. He had guesses about what Gabe saw, the gasps of his great fear. But while he could see that the oath took well, he couldn't be sure of the rapidly shifting details of the form the magic took. He saw that green flash again, now more like the brief visit of a hummingbird than a dragon, so quick that he almost missed it, and he filed it away as one more piece of the puzzle.

"Well said, and your oath to challenge is accepted." Cyrus cleared his throat. "We have a bit to discuss. Do you mind showing yourself out?"

Gabe shook his head, gathering up his things and rolling up the chart before tucking it under the flap of his satchel. "Let me know if there are any other questions on the report. Alexander, I would now love a chance to talk to you in more detail, at mutual convenience. I'll send a note with times that might work on my end, assuming no crisis."

"Always assuming no crisis." Alexander agreed. Not until he'd talked to Geoffrey, though. He needed to sort out his head before going deeper with Gabe.

The four of them waited while Gabe let himself out of the room, hearing a brief muffled conversation with one of the staff. Cyrus kept his eyes on the charm lights above the door while everyone refilled their tea. Alexander poured himself two fingers of brandy, and another glass for Cyrus at his nod. Two minutes later, Cyrus cleared his throat. "He's gone through the portal."

Unsurprisingly, Silvia was the first to speak. "You just agreed? It's not done, Cyrus, you know that. Even Mabyn and I've barely talked about it."

Cyrus spread his hands. "Mabyn and I have talked about our respective challenges. But you're right, the Council hasn't. Not in a very long time, I think. If people did, it's only in fragmentary references in the notes I have. Guesses. It's not forbidden, though. We'd know if it were."

Silvia got up in something of a huff, swirling off to the sideboard. "Why, Cyrus? Do you think you know better than everyone before you?" Including her husband, and that was tricky to navigate.

"I've come to think each Head is chosen for our own reasons, just as with every challenge that brings someone to the Council." Cyrus's voice was remarkably even, though Alexander could hear the edge of strain in his voice. People thought Cyrus was easy-going, and he was. It was a mistake to think that meant he wasn't quite competent in his own right. Dangerous and ruthless when that was called for, even. All of them were.

"You didn't even discuss it." Silvia turned back.

"You can't have it both ways, Silvia. Either I'm in charge, or this is an actual democracy. And in this case, there is nothing that forbids what Gabe wants. He is not requiring the same from any of us."

"He has more sense." Alexander pointed out. "Cyrus, decent chance I'm going to write you a journal message at three in the morning realising what he told us without making it obvious. Pardon, Mabyn." Since it would almost certainly disturb her sleep as well.

Mabyn snorted. She, at least, was reasonably calm about it. "Apology accepted. And the warning is much appreciated." She considered, speaking more to Silvia than Alexander and Cyrus now. "I thought Gabe was flighty, originally. But the more I've seen of him, the more I'm sure there are deep roots there. Well, we know there are, even if I'm sometimes not sure what sort of plant grows in that ground. Maybe, though, we need to find out."

Cyrus shook his head, relaxing a little. Silvia returned to the table, sighing. "I'm overruled, obviously. I don't care for it, though." Alexander could see all the tension running through her, and that was going to need tending at some point. At the same time, he was the worst person to try to do anything useful with it. Silvia would not listen to him and he would only spoil the fragile moment of balm. She thought of him, Alexander was sure, as her husband had. By their lights, Alexander was made for fierce things that took skill, he would follow orders, he was for competence, not leadership. "Any specific reason, or is it about the break with tradition?" Mabyn asked it.

"I don't know, and that's the tedious part." Silvia tapped her fingers on the table, thumb to pinkie in quick succession. "Why can't he do it like everyone else has done, and be grateful for it?"

Mabyn shrugged. "Because he's not like everyone."

Alexander couldn't let that pass. "He was asked before, and refused it then. Expecting him to greet the offer with cries of delight or false humility is lying to ourselves. That won't do. And we're lucky he didn't make us ask three times." Geoffrey had taught him that the Owl house magics required ruthless honesty with himself, and it rather pleased him to bring that to bear here.

Something in that amused Mabyn and made Silvia frown even more, though she did not speak. Mabyn glanced at her, then went on. "Look, Alexander, can you lay out the paths from here? You're best at it."

It figured she'd ask. Though it wasn't as if Mabyn was wrong. "Simply put, assuming he makes the challenge - that nothing happens to him in the meantime." He knocked on wood and flung his fingers into the gesture to avert misfortune, one after the other. "He makes the challenge, and he succeeds or he fails. If he succeeds, he is our peer and colleague, and we do need his skills. Desperately. And we need his willingness, not his grudging agreement. If he fails, perhaps we'll learn something from whatever he does share." He lifted a finger. "You note he didn't promise to share everything. Just what he thought was needed."

It didn't mollify Silvia much at all, and she made a small harrumphing sound. Mabyn stretched. "Come up to my office, Silvia? We can talk it out there. Cyrus, you wanted a few minutes to get your notes together. Should I check about sandwiches?"

"Please." Everyone in the room knew the sandwiches

would be sorted, and the tea cakes and the tea itself and the coffee. It made a good excuse, though. Cyrus waited until the two women had left the room before sighing. "I hoped that part was going to go better."

"I assume Mabyn will fill you in later." Alexander leaned his elbows on the table, and his cheeks in his hands. "That was—"

Cyrus snorted. "Now I feel better. He got you too, then? I was wondering if it was just me." Then, more cautiously, Cyrus asked. "What do you think of my decision?"

"It's the right one." Alexander looked up. "I can't tell you all of why now. That's for three in the morning. But he's got reasons for asking, he's got reasons he didn't talk to me about it first, and what really matters is he agreed to make the Challenge. Everything else will sort itself out. He was as careful in how he asked as any master of ritual magic could be."

"And that's a curious thing, isn't it? We are. He isn't. Though I suppose he sees a lot of the precise language in his line of work." Cyrus let out a long breath. "And he's right we don't collaborate. You and I have, more recently, and every time we do, I think I've learned to do better. And then I turn around, and there's another place we're falling short."

"And as Gabe pointed out, we had every sign there was going to be a war that needed a host of people with specific skills. Including healing, and I hope to all the gods and powers we don't need too much of that directly." Alexander sighed. "I'm glad you agreed. And it is your call, fundamentally. Silvia needs to get her head around that fact."

Cyrus snorted, then stretched. Alexander could hear several joints crack. "I think I need a bit of fresh air before we move into the meeting. Want a walk?"

Alexander shook his head. "You go on. I want to write up my thoughts now, so I can come back to them more easily. I'll be in my office."

They parted at the door to the room, Alexander turning to go upstairs to the Council halls, while Cyrus went to the outer doors. Alexander settled in the chair in his office, and began writing down everything he could remember, so that he could talk it through properly tomorrow.

CHAPTER 4
AUGUST 22ND AT YTENE

Thursday, August 22nd at Ytene

Geoffrey was in the library, finishing up a bit of reading before supper, when the door opened after a bare, rhythmic knock. He carefully put his bookmark in the book as he said, "Alexander." Setting the book aside, he looked up, and then did a double take. "What happened?"

"That obvious?" Alexander went immediately to the decanter, pouring himself a glass of wine. "I need to talk it through with you. And Lizzie, if she's available."

"Urgently, or after supper?" Geoffrey stretched. "She's changing and reading to the children. She'll be down in a few minutes."

"After supper." Alexander sighed. "Do I need to change?" It wasn't like him to ask. Alexander used a change of suits or robes as deftly as Geoffrey himself did, the minute signals of the mood of the moment, what to expect, for those who knew how to read them. Right now, he was in what Geoffrey thought of as his working clothes, a neatly tailored suit of a deep charcoal grey, with precise details of the deep blue he favoured.

"Just us tonight. Cassie and Benton had something in Trellech, some charitable event, how you can creatively make over frocks. He's lending his service for the lists and organisation. And Rufus is home for once for the evening, and Ferry wanted some time. Don't bother to change."

"Good. Right." Alexander twitched - very unlike him indeed. But now was not a time to fuss over that. He'd give Alexander the time he needed, without jogging his elbow. Lizzie came down a minute or two after Alexander had taken a chair to flick through the pages of the day's paper. Lizzie raised an eyebrow when Alexander's greeting was polite, but brief. Geoffrey tilted his head, adjusted his monocle. He lifted one finger, trusting she'd read it correctly as a matter for later; that Geoffrey was concerned, but that it did not seem to be an emergency from the available information.

By the time they went in to supper, Alexander had progressed to being reasonably conversational. It helped that Lizzie had several intriguing stories from her afternoon of obligatory social engagements. She'd taken a lead role in several volunteer projects, both to lend a hand, and because they really were an exceptional source of information. This afternoon had been packaging up materials to go to various alchemists and apothecaries for supplies for the Temple of Healing.

Geoffrey had spent much of the day on war business. There had been bombs dropped at Bournemouth and Southampton yesterday, and while Southampton wasn't his responsibility, magically speaking, Bournemouth was at the moment. He'd had to check on that several ways around.

The rest of the morning had been occupied with a conversation with the local air raid wardens. The afternoon had been a review of the Ashley Walk bombing range, which ran south and west of Ytene's land. He was none too thrilled about a bombing range for exercises and testing on his immediate border, but it wasn't as if he could object. He'd already worked with half a dozen people to mitigate the effects on the barns and the property. Thankfully, magic could do a fair bit to muffle and buffer the explosions when they tested, and they had several wooded areas to help with that and anchor the enchantments.

As they finished up with supper, Geoffrey raised one eyebrow. "Library, Alexander, or your rooms?"

Alexander sighed, rubbing the bridge of his nose. "My rooms, I think. I want to get drunk. I shouldn't, but better there than down here."

Lizzie looked him up and down. "Headache potion, certainly." She decreed it. "Let me get that out of the still-room. Would you like me to stay for the conversation?"

"Please. Though I don't know how much of it I'll get into words." Alexander stood, more than a little creakily. "My apologies, Lizzie. I'm abominable company today." Geoffrey had to smile at that. Alexander had at least learned not to apologise to Geoffrey himself for that sort of thing.

"I'm sure there's good reason." Lizzie went off. Geoffrey shepherded Alexander upstairs, into his rooms, and into a dressing gown and pyjamas by the time she joined them again. He'd really got rather efficient at the process. They eventually settled with Geoffrey and Alexander on the sofa, Lizzie in the chair, all of them with drinks. Alexander drained the headache potion and set it aside, then let out a long breath.

CELIA LAKE

"Gabe's agreed to make a challenge for Livia's seat." It came out flat, in the sort of voice that meant there were a dozen things going on in Alexander's head, and it was their job to figure that out.

"You'd hoped he might." Lizzie tilted her head. "And yet?"

Alexander waved his hand, a general negation, or perhaps an uncertainty. "We need him to. And yet." He nodded at Lizzie. "And yet, I wonder what we're asking of him."

Ah, that would be a knot of it. "You put the question to him, what ten days ago? And this is yesterday, then, that he agreed?"

"With a condition." Alexander snorted, drinking a long sip of the wine. Geoffrey had chosen the bottle for drinking more quickly than most of his cellar deserved, thankfully. No need to insult the grapes. "He asked for a condition. No one's done that in - Cyrus is still figuring it out. Centuries, likely."

"Can you tell us the condition?" Lizzie, bless her, was on the questions. This was the tricky part. Talking about any part of the Council's work was complicated. Alexander spun between the threads of it like someone dancing with unsheathed steel at the best of times. This seemed even more threatening than most, for whatever reason.

And it wasn't as if Geoffrey were entirely rational about the Council. He loved Alexander; he trusted that Alexander was doing all he could to do what needed to be done to protect Albion's land and magic, as the Council were sworn to do. But the Council, an earlier iteration of it, under a different Head, in a different time - though less than twenty years ago, still - had killed Geoffrey's brother, for reasons Geoffrey still barely understood. Lizzie asking was easier, and Geoffrey was sure she'd set things up this way on purpose.

Alexander coughed. "He asked to be able to tell us what happens in his challenge, whatever the outcome. To share what he learned. To have us listen. With respect. Not to share ourselves. He didn't ask that. We'd have said no, reflexively. Even me."

"Maybe especially you." Geoffrey said it gently, to get a trembling shift from Alexander, then a minute nod. He didn't touch that vulnerability just yet. "What did you decide?"

There was a stillness, the kind Geoffrey had learned how to read well enough. Alexander closed his eyes, then opened them, nodding once to indicate he was admitting just how much that would have changed his entire life. Then he went on, as if nothing significant had happened; Hesperidon had taught him that lesson far too well.

"Cyrus agreed to the condition. Gabe made oath to make the challenge. Nicely made, too. You'd appreciate the delicacy of the ritual language." Alexander shook his head. "Silvia didn't like it one bit. She near enough challenged Cyrus's authority. It's the first time I've heard her slip so far."

Lizzie tsked. "Well, that's telling, isn't it?" An understatement, if Geoffrey had ever heard one. "Start at the beginning, would you? Yesterday, if we need to go back further, we'll ask."

That was a sensible way to do it. Alexander did better with a structure for it, walking through the meeting from the beginning, including the discussion about that letter in the *Times*. Something had struck Lizzie as odd about it too, but they agreed it was likely nothing. People were permitted to write odd letters, even in wartime. Not everything was a ring of spies or a sign of some misdeed. Probably, anyway. And Gabe's comments about the author, that this was precisely the sort of thing he'd write about, were a help, even if Geoffrey did have a comment about the foibles of Merton men, never mind Eton.

Bit by bit, they worked through the conversation. Geoffrey had to admit Gabe had been deft in all the ways he - and his parents - might well be proud of, as annoying as it was to be on the other side of it. They were certainly missing something, but like Alexander, Geoffrey couldn't put his finger on it. Nor could Lizzie, though to be fair to both of them, they were missing a fair bit of the details. No matter how well someone explained something - and Alexander really was quite forthcoming - there were all the things that got noticed without realising, in the midst of a conversation, and thus could not be repeated.

More importantly, Alexander seemed a little better for talking through it, even if they didn't have any particular epiphanies. As that bit of discussion wound down, Geoffrey glanced at Lizzie and got her nod. "Would you like me to stay tonight, then?"

Alexander blinked, as if that was a shock. "You were..." He gestured feebly with a couple of fingers.

"The question, Alexander, is if you'd like me to stay."

"I'll probably wake you up at three in the morning. Having realised something." Alexander shrugged, leaving it up to Geoffrey.

"In which case, you'll have someone handy to talk it through with. Come on. You're gnawing on this like a dog with a bone. I'd a book I wanted to read to you. It will likely make you laugh."

Alexander, by this point in their time together, knew when he was outnumbered. Lizzie stood, coming to give him a kiss on the cheek before she gave Geoffrey a longer one on the lips. "I also have a book, love. I'll be fine. See you at breakfast."

They stood as she made her way out, which made it easy for Geoffrey to shoo Alexander off to the bedroom without further active complaint. He took some trouble to make sure the bed was comfortable, that the air was circulating well, before they settled into bed. He did not sleep here often. The last time had been their once a year celebration of the lusty May and the dance of the lady of the land and her beloved. Geoffrey treasured every time, though, because of what it meant to be trusted.

By the time they fell asleep, Alexander had consented to a shoulder rub, as well as having the book read out loud. It was a rather ridiculous bit of magical theory from the non-magical, and its premises wanted interrogating. The author had a delightfully purple turn of phrase, too, which made the whole thing better. Well, better in one sense of the word. It got Alexander laughing several times, however, and that was all to the good. By the time Geoffrey slid the book onto the bedside table, Alexander was lying on one side. Geoffrey could curl up against him, and at least make sure he was not left alone with his puzzle.

The next thing Geoffrey knew was Alexander sitting up in bed, flinging the sheets wide, swearing at the top of his lungs in a running string of Arabic. Geoffrey had picked up enough bits and pieces to understand this was a particularly florid and detailed bit of cursing. Even if he hadn't, the length, volume, and range of pitch could have told him.

When Alexander finally ran down into a near-sobbing breath, Geoffrey cleared his throat. "Realised something, then? Water on the dresser."

Alexander waved a hand at him in the moonlight that

filtered through the windows, but stood. He went to pour himself a glass of water before saying anything. Geoffrey rearranged the pillows so he could sit propped up in comfort.

"Figured something out, then?" Geoffrey repeated the question, mostly for the amusement of it.

Alexander made an incredible face at that, screwing up his nose and mouth before he suddenly laughed. It was the barking laugh of someone teetering between tears and laughter, the edge of bitterness of not having spotted whatever it was sooner. Geoffrey patted the bed. "Do you need wine to go with your water? Fresh out of miracles, at least of the vintnerial kind. Is that the word I want?"

Alexander managed a snort. "Port. Let me. There's some on the drinks cabinet. Want some, as an apology for waking you?"

"Please." It would at least already be decanted, so very little fuss involved. Alexander came back inside of two minutes later, bearing two glasses. Once he was back in bed, he offered his toast, with a "To Gabe being who and what he is, long may he flourish."

Geoffrey echoed the last phrase, then added, "My." As dryly as he could. "Care to explain that toast?"

"He set the whole bloody thing up." That, now, was not a swear Alexander pulled out often. "And I swear, I hadn't told him this, though I suppose it's possible he got it out of Thesan or Isembard."

"Your antecedents are decidedly invisible, Alexander. I'm excellent, but it is three in the morning." Geoffrey pointed this out evenly and got a more relaxed laugh for his trouble.

"Fair, fair." Alexander took a slower sip of his port,

respecting the glass properly. "He set the whole thing up like a duel. I spotted that. I told you as much."

Geoffrey nodded. "And you have sufficient reason to know." They were going over ground they both understood, and Alexander was quite aware of it.

"Here's the thing I realised. He walked into that room, knowing he was going to agree. He didn't give a hint, didn't slip up in so much as a word or a gesture, until he'd got what he wanted. I saw something in his oaths, but I didn't know what it meant in time to guess. I still don't know, but I know it's connected." Then, more softly, unable to meet Geoffrey's eyes, he added, "What he wants would have kept me safe. Not that I'd have dared ask for it."

Geoffrey blinked at that, his hand moving to rest on Alexander's thigh, a comforting touch that acknowledged the second half of it, while his words focused on the first. "You're sure? No, of course you're sure. Even if you didn't realise it for what? Twelve hours."

Alexander laughed. "Bet you Mabyn and Silvia won't catch it. Cyrus might, but he doesn't know Gabe nearly as well. Or not enough ways." He shrugged. "I'll tell him later today. At a reasonable hour. No need to wake him, since you're here."

"The many-gifted." Geoffrey nodded, then laughed. "See, I have done you a service. You and Cyrus."

"And Mabyn. I'm sure she's glad not to be woken by Cyrus shouting." Alexander looked decidedly amused now, shaking his head. "Just. I wish." He let out a long breath. "I wish we didn't need him so desperately."

There was the tiny thread that Geoffrey had been looking for, a way to begin to unravel this particular problem. "Talk to me about that, would you? It may be there's something else there worth a light on it."

Alexander wriggled slightly, to get more comfortable against the pillows and headboard. "It nearly broke me. I thought it had, until you. Until that conversation in the forest, where you were so offended we never even offered each other vitality. All of us our own little stars in the firmament, doing our work, but solitary."

Geoffrey snorted. "You've been spending a lot of time with Thesan. Your metaphors have gone astronomical again. But no, fair. And I was angry. Still am, that you don't."

"Gabe called it out. To the four of us, to our faces. He made the point that the Penelopes are collaborative, down deep. It's part of them from the start. And here's the thing. I've barely ever heard of one going astray. They have tremendous skill, and they turn it to solving things. Not to scrabbling for power, or their own personal benefit. It's not like the Guard oath. Though now I say that, I have no idea what their oaths are, except when it comes to formal evidence and such. And I don't think Gabe would tell me right now."

"They're, on average, all competent ritualists by our standards, even if that's not their focus." Geoffrey said, after a moment's consideration. "They have to be, given that it seems like half their work as Gabe and Mason and Witt tell it is walking into a room and figuring out what idiocy people have got up to now. And a fair bit of that has ritual as a component."

"Just so. But it's not the mastery Gabe named. Incantation and Materia, for the record, but not Duelling, though he could certainly claim that."

Geoffrey grunted at that. "And what do you think of all of that, now you've had some space?"

"We could break him. I think of him walking into the

Council meeting after he comes through the Challenge. I think of the wall of disapproval that would face him. I think of what it would do. He comes to the land as a lover, though I don't know that he'd put it in the terms you or I do. But it's in his every step, the way he looks, the way he takes in space."

Geoffrey exhaled. "The way you did. Until they broke you. You've told me enough of that." How Alexander had come into the first Council meeting after his challenge. Hesperidon had barely acknowledged him then sent him off as an attack dog on someone's relatively minor indiscretion.

That wasn't where Geoffrey stopped, though. "Gabe certainly gave me chapter and verse about the Knightwood Oak after the Lammastide ritual. Down to what's nesting nearby." Geoffrey thought back to that. After Gabe had recovered from the immediate aftermath of the ritual, he'd insisted on going back out there. Geoffrey had gone with him, in his position of Lord of the northern New Forest and temporary regent of the southern half, where the tree herself was.

It had been one of the more educational hours of Geoffrey's life. Gabe had known just what he was looking at. He'd spotted effects that Geoffrey would have needed days to notice, and a number of diagnostic charms besides. "He looks at things differently than we do, doesn't he? Unchained. No, that's not the right word. He runs in deep channels, too, at times. He calls out what matters and ignores the rest."

"Fair enough." Alexander ran a hand through his hair, smoothing a bit back from his face. He took another sip of the port, then he started laughing, quick enough on the drink he almost spluttered. He kept laughing, even after

Geoffrey reached to slap him on the back a couple of times.

When the laughter finally settled, Alexander reached to put his glass on the night table. "He - maybe we needn't worry too much." He let out a breath, as if trying to catch up with himself.

Geoffrey set his own glass aside, raising an eyebrow. "Well, for one thing, he'll have you waiting to greet him." It was possible this had slipped Alexander's mind. Just barely. "And others who want him there."

"Oh, I suppose." Alexander waved it off. "It wasn't that, though it's a good point. It's how he - he figured out how to overset every single backstabbing impulse we might have, through sheer honesty. Or at least, I'm pretty sure he can carry it off. Maybe not today, but in three months? By then he'll have figured out how to say just what he wants, to get the effect he thinks is needed."

When Geoffrey didn't say anything - because he wasn't sure what to say here, honestly, Alexander went on. "I'd thought we'd need to protect his heart, his love of the land. But no. I think we're the ones who need protection. The ones that will have to shed old skins like a snake, if they can."

"He didn't ask you to commit to doing the same, though." Geoffrey frowned, following through the logic.

"No. But we will. Not all at once, I'm sure. The old habits will die hard. And I suspect Silvia will go on kicking her feet for a bit. Several of the others, too. Garin, likely, when he notices. But there's a way in which it's inevitable. When that's the thing that makes sense. When honesty, when the love of the land and the magic disarm everything else."

"When we give ourselves to the land, and she rises to

greet us." Geoffrey said it quietly, near enough a prayer. The two of them had found their way to that, somehow, and Alexander was right. Once touched by that gift, it was near impossible to turn away from it for good.

"And all of us, every single one of us on the Council has that moment to look back on. Maybe only the once, some of them. I don't know, I truly don't. But I think maybe once is enough, given time. Example. And Gabe's solid in himself, in a way I never was, and for him, it's not just once. He lives in it. He doesn't need us. He doesn't even want us, I'm entirely clear, even if that offends Silvia to the tips of her toes. We desperately need him. That's what woke me, I think, being sure of that."

"And the others, who might not agree?" Geoffrey leaned back a bit more. He wasn't sure this was the time - or perhaps the place - to have this conversation. But he was also rather sure that if they didn't now, he wouldn't bring it up again. It touched on the tender places.

"I hadn't thought of it exactly until Gabe brought out that chart. It wasn't just the swap from being two-thirds Fox House or better, it was the mix of the houses. Salmon and Seal, more than the others."

"Creative thinking. New ideas. Different solutions. Not the way you've always done it." Geoffrey saw that one easily enough. It was a conversation he and Lizzie had fairly frequently. He was, as they had come to say, for logic. Lizzie was - coming from Salmon House, like Gabe himself - made for the mental leaps and range of skills that turned the knowledge and logic into something useful.

"And oh, that's going to be hard for those who are used to Fox House being the cream of the crop, always assumed to be the best." He began chuckling, and it built up, rolling over, until he toppled to lean against Geoffrey's shoulder, completely trusting. Geoffrey shifted his arm just in time, letting him lean.

When Alexander subsided, he let out a sigh. "Silvia's still young compared to us. She'll sort it out. I hope. If not, that could get entirely messy." Then he yawned. "Problem for a different day."

"Sleep. In the morning, you can fill in Cyrus. And we can amuse Lizzie. She'll be glad she got her sleep, though." He twisted to kiss Alexander's hair, just the once, before Alexander rearranged himself in bed. "Do you have time for a ride before you go off tomorrow?"

"Probably. If we can be done by ten. It'll put me in a better mood, so - probably best if we do?"

"Grand." Geoffrey nestled up against Alexander's back again. "May sleep touch you kindly this time."

It got him one more chuckle. Geoffrey stayed awake, listening, until he was sure Alexander was truly sleeping, then finally let himself drift off as well.

CHAPTER 5

AUGUST 28TH AT THE GUARD HALL IN TRELLECH

The meeting on Tuesday morning ran long, as it often did. It was a necessary evil, Richard knew. There was nothing quite like getting everyone in the same place for an hour or two to coordinate everything. It helped the more common back and forth of memos and notes and scribbled comments in the journals, depending on the formality and urgency of the question. And he was, of course, master of swinging by someone's office or desk, timing it just right. He'd had decades of practice.

Today's meeting, however, was not optimistic at all. The bombing raids had picked up, for one thing. So far as they could tell, the Luftwaffe were currently focusing on airfields, which were at least a military target. On the other hand, they sometimes had gods-awful aim.

The RAF had a number of advantages, even if that didn't seem like much when the bombs were coming down. They were over home territory. The briefing had made sure to mention that had dual benefits. They could refuel or make repairs very quickly if needed, and if they did have to bail out of their aeroplane, they landed over friendly territory.

The Luftwaffe, in contrast, were getting picked out of fields and the open water on a regular basis, to be taken off as prisoners of war.

There had also been a remarkably reassuring amount of international support. The briefing got derailed for a couple of minutes about pilots from Czechoslovakia and Poland who'd been coming on to help. Remarkably efficiently, apparently. Richard could have told anyone who listened that when you had competent skilled folks, let them at it. They'd sort out the language barriers, and besides, it was a relatively limited set of necessary vocabulary. But even so, the RAF and their allies were barely holding back the tide, and there was no telling how long they could keep it up.

None of that was, on the whole, specifically the Guard's duty. Most of it was handled through the Army proper, the Home Guard, or whatever local constabulary was handy. Albion's Guard were only brought into it if there was something odd going on. They were treated something like one of the Intelligence services. Certain criteria popped up, one of them would get called in and left to their work.

On the other hand, the Guard were responsible for everything relating to Trellech or the magical communities in other places. And London was certainly a target, a dozen ways over, as were a number of other cities. Every single one of them had been called out every night they were on duty, and some they weren't, to do what they could to get people to safety. That was where magic sometimes bought lives, by being able to calm a fire just a little longer or hold up a caved-in roof until others could pull the survivors to safety.

But it was exhausting to keep going, without any hope of a pause or a break. They might get one if the weather got bad, but even that wasn't a sure thing. And bad weather brought its own challenges, what with flooding or freezing or all the other possible dangers. They talked through a bit of that, which bridges were dubious, what places to keep an eye on, and then were dismissed to the rest of their days.

Richard had just turned away from a conversation with Ibert Morris when he felt the tap on his arm. "Got a few minutes, Richard?" Kate Lefton stood there, smartly in her uniform, despite the fact he was sure she'd been on call all night.

He didn't see nearly as much of her as he liked these days. The two of them near enough split the more delicate sorts of cases between them at this point. It wasn't as if fraud or dangerous magic or distressingly human impulses around hurting other people took a break for the war. That meant they were rarely free at the same times right now, bar the very occasional social event, and those were scant and becoming more and more so. Richard cleared his throat. "For you? Of course. My office? Yours?"

She tilted her head, sharing that slight pause of evaluation. "Mine, please. My warding's better." It was one of her particular specialities, so likely yes.

"Let me tell Simons I'll be up in a few minutes so he won't wait on me." He stepped aside to tell his aide, and then joined Kate again, letting her lead on. It would be a change of pace, and a different view of the world. He spent far too much of his life these days either in his office documenting and filling out paperwork or in the midst of things, with no time to think or breathe.

She nodded as they went past a handful of people in the hall. Kate paused for a moment to check on something with one of the Guards who was waiting for her to return. Watching her - a few steps back, he didn't want to loom - Richard was pleased all over again. He'd spotted her relatively early in her career, and she'd blossomed over the last twenty years. She was sure of herself, confident in her decisions, and not at all grasping at authority. Most of it was her own work. But Richard was proud of her every time he saw her rise to the moment and make things a little better than they'd been before.

Once she'd dealt with that question, she pressed her hand on the panel by her door, and gestured him into the office. As always, it was remarkably tidy. Richard himself kept things neat, but Kate was precise about it, at work and at home. It made things easier for her husband Giles, who'd been blinded by gas in the last war. What should have been actually the last war, the war to end all wars, and wasn't. She made it look natural, but he'd caught her a few times aligning something, testing the distance against the width or length of her hand, even here, where Giles was unlikely to be.

She waved him into the guest chair, a comfortable seat with a cheerful blue cushion, a brighter complement to the Guard blue. She shrugged out of her jacket, hanging it up, leaving her in blouse and split skirt. Richard took in her overall body language. "Something up?" Then he flicked his fingers. "How are Artemis and Theodore doing?"

"Complaining about not being at tutoring school yet, the both of them. They go off on Sunday." Thanks to a chance of birthdays, they were nearer two years apart in age, but only a year in schooling. "Artemis can't wait to get back, and Theodore wants everything she knows right now."

Kate laughed, her fingers moving to brush the pair of photographs on her desk. Artemis looked remarkably like her mother, with tumbling waves of hair, though a darker red-brown than Kate's own. Theodore - no longer the

Teddy of his childhood - was dark-haired, serious in expression, and looked up to his sister no end.

"Not that any child of yours would whinge," Richard said, amused. Kate was made of good humour - and so, honestly, was Giles. But they didn't tolerate much in the way of complaints, at least not without excellent cause.

"Thesan and Isembard gave them a run through last week on what to focus on this year if they want to go the directions they're talking about." Kate leaned back in her own chair, then asked, "Mind if I bring up the warding? She mentioned something I wanted to run by you."

"Of course not. I assume you have some reason for the extra wards?" The ordinary run of warding in the Guard Hall was normally fine for quotidian work, and they both knew it.

Her mouth quirked up. "More than one, even." She shifted her hands, and he felt the dampening effect of the wards spring up, the slight itch at the back of his neck that it always caused. Only then did she rub her palms together briskly and sit in her own chair. "Partly about some starting duelling training for Artemis, partly about another matter."

"Not Schola's warding, then. I thought Isembard still had that well in hand." Richard had a guess or two about where Kate was heading, but he'd let her do it and not anticipate.

"He does, though he wanted my eye on a couple of pieces of it. I do like that about him. He's not grabby about his expertise. And he gave me a couple of ideas. Easier to reinforce at a distance, and that'd be a help right now. We've several people who could do the monitoring work, but travel would be a trick, especially around the portals we're worried about."

"Dover." Richard agreed. "Southampton. Well. Any of the ports and shipyards, for one, and London as well."

"Just so." Kate flipped her hand palm up. "That wasn't it, either. It was something Isembard mentioned, though of course it's technically public, isn't it?"

Ah, that was where she was going, yes. "Gabe." Once someone declared their intention to challenge for a Council seat, anyone could find out who if they knew to look for it. Kate wouldn't have had any trouble with access, it got passed through to the Guard library as a matter of course.

"Gabe." Her mouth twitched up, and now she finally leaned back. "You hadn't mentioned it."

"I've barely seen you in three weeks, other than larger meetings." Richard pointed out. "Alexander put the question to him on the twelfth, and we've been just a tad busy since then. Busier than usual."

Kate's mouth quirked further up. "Still." She shrugged. "Anyway, when I told Giles, he said Gabe had had a question about a bit of cryptography that hadn't come to anything obvious. But he hadn't mentioned anything about it either. So I'm asking you. Can we be of any help?"

Richard let out a slow breath. "The thing you'll find about children, though you've likely figured it out already, is that they don't stop being your children when they're grown - with children of their own. That doesn't mean you actually understand everything about them."

Kate snorted. "Isn't that a blessing and not a curse? God forbid we might be bored."

"There you go, sounding very like Gabe." Richard pointed out. "Gabe's not gone out of his way to tell anyone outside the immediate household - and, of course, the Council. Alexander put the question to him on the twelfth. We talked about it the next morning, the four of us. All the hells broke loose that night, but I gather he filled in Magni and Gil within a day or two. Magni's been running him through drills a fair bit, in whatever scraps of time Gabe finds. He told Charlotte not too long after that, but I only know because she asked Alysoun something about it." Their daughter had her own life, a delightful one, and with any luck Richard would manage lunch with her tomorrow. But she was far less entangled in politics, oaths, or, for that matter, complex magics outside of her husband's alchemical perfume work.

Kate grunted, and now she'd shifted into thoughtful mode. "Alexander, obviously. We can assume Geoffrey and Lizzie know?"

"Likely, yes." Richard shrugged at it. "And I assume Isembard found out from Alexander?" He could run the trajectories of that as easily as Kate could.

"Thesan, actually. She had tea with Alysoun, she mentioned. And something about checking the house affiliations and some other details of a number of people." Kate looked up. "Are - no. That's the wrong question. Of course you're at least a bit worried."

Having someone say it out loud made it real, and conversely easier to get a grip on. "Yes. I don't understand half of it, and that's a problem for me. And also, I'm worried. Anyone sensible would be. As skilled as Gabe is, as competent, in ways I can only trace with both hands and a labelled map, anything could go wrong. Stupid, tiny things. I can't get that out of my head."

"We spend our lives sorting matters out when something tiny has gone wrong. Except when it's someone deliberately doing something awful," Kate agreed. "What does Alysoun say?"

That made Richard chuckle. "Very patiently, she says

that Gabe has done any number of absurd things. There are at least three this summer, and I'm sure dozens we barely know about. And he's come through well enough. Better than that, most of the time. And she pointed out that while Rathna is taking the whole thing seriously, she's not. What's the word she used? Panicked about it. Cautious, doing her underlying maths, talking the permutations through with Gabe, but not panicked."

"Huh." Kate took her time considering that. "And you've never really understood how Gabe makes things work. You've said as much."

"Many times, and to his face. He gets results, and far more often than he should, he gets them elegantly, even. That doesn't mean I understand it. I understand Anthony. I more or less understand Rowena, though the longer she leans into the Seal House magics, the more I know I'm missing things."

Kate nodded at that. "But Gabe has always been his own self. The highest possible standards. You set those, over and over again. That one, I understand." Her mouth settled into a proper smile this time. "You did the same thing with me. Uncompromising standards, but fair ones. And Gabe's always risen to the challenge."

Richard rubbed his face. "You think he's doing that here? That he's doing it because he thinks he has to, to - meet my expectations."

"Oh, I'm sure it's his expectations, too. That it has been for ages. You are a model, Richard. You are not a dictator. But he's had your example in front of him. And Alysoun's, for all she has exceptional standards in other areas than yours. Of course Gabe wants to match that."

"Huh." Richard swallowed, letting his eyes close for a

long breath, willing to let Kate see that. "All right. Fair enough. I certainly can't find a good argument."

"There probably isn't one. I did try this out on Giles before today." Kate's hands reached toward a biscuit tin on the shelf behind her. "Biscuit? You look like you could use a touch of restorative. Mrs Meredith's shortbread, very much the thing."

"Thanks." Richard leaned forward to take one, taking a bite and appreciating the chance to gather his thoughts. "What's your advice, then on - how to support him?"

"Besides being yourself? Laying out your expertise, your knowledge of people." Kate frowned. "I did ask Isembard this. But for all there are multiple challenges, best he knows, they're independent of each other. They do whatever it is they do to make challenge on their own. It's not that they're all in one room and only one of them can triumph. It's not that simple."

"Well, also not that destructive. I can just imagine how badly that would go, if you had any sort of personal enmity in play." He sighed. "Particularly for replacing Livia, who was certainly better-known as a duellist than an alchemist. People will take notions about that sort of thing."

"Quite." Kate's voice was dry, now. "You've seen the others who've challenged? I gather there might be a couple more, though Isembard didn't know who."

"Lilac Powell. Fox House, of course." Richard said, promptly. "She's a skilled duellist by most standards. Magni thinks she cheats herself, and I'm inclined to agree. But neither of us has ever seen her duel full out, just public bouts under Gorham rules. Decent enough human, I gather, so long as all you want to talk about is duelling."

"That was my impression too, on the duelling. I don't

trust anyone who only duels Gorham, honestly." Kate nodded. The Gorham rules were three touches, no charms that would do lasting damage. That not only limited the options quite a lot, but it wasn't the right sort of impulses for anyone who might actually need to fight for their life. Richard had begun his life duelling under Gorham under most circumstances. Gabe had expressed a strong preference for Richardian, one of the oldest formal duelling forms, as soon as he'd learned to use a staff to brace his bad ankle. Richard had come to prefer the fluidity and flexibility. "And Lycus Sisley."

"Cousin to Orion, and nephew to the late Matthias, though his father married in and took the Sisley name. Also Fox. Making a play for what they think of as the family seat." Not that Livia's seat was meant for a Sisley in specific, just that there had been a Sisley on the Council for going on three centuries now with only brief breaks. "What did Isembard say about that?" Isembard knew Orion Sisley rather well. He'd had the training of Orion and of Claudio Warren, early on in his time at Schola. Richard knew they were still close, even though those two were well out of their apprenticeships and into their early thirties. Now both serving near the front lines, if he remembered the most recent summaries right.

"Hot-headed - Lycus has definitely got the family temper. I gathered there's no chance Orion could get back in time to make an attempt." Kate considered. "Lycus is also a duellist. As Gabe is, actually. Which made, what's her name, Herana Phipps an interesting contrast. Owl House, and her talents are largely Incantation. She's done some interesting work around mood and performance. I read one of her articles a year or so again, on methods for settling down an angry crowd."

"Huh. Do you remember which one? I'd like a look."

Kate nodded, absently, then reached for a volume on her bookshelf and pulled it out, flipping through it and then writing down a title, author, and the publication information. "Guard library has a copy, or did." She passed the slip of paper over. "I'd be interested in what you think of her other work, if you get a chance at it. She hasn't actually crossed a line herself, but some of her work might, if people put it into practice." Kate lifted her hand. "Already raised it in private with the relevant parties, of course."

"Of course." Richard inclined his head. "Who else. Alysoun heard Adrastos Rix was planning on it."

"Transformation, isn't he? He was a year or two behind me in school. Rather a weasel at the time. Honestly, I didn't care for him much. Seal House, and one of the more secretive types out of there." She glanced up again, amused. "Though maybe Rathna would know more? He'd have been a few years ahead of her."

Richard nodded. "I'll ask." He shook his head. "Usual range of suspects, then. I expected a wider spread, somehow."

"Gabe is rather unusual by their standards?" Kate offered it a little diffidently.

That made Richard laugh and laugh, his hands coming down with a thunk on the wood of the desk. "Oh, you have no idea. He trotted out a chart for them. One of three he's made. Showing the houses and specialities of the people who challenged a while back, and then last fifteen years or so."

Kate tilted her head, running through the lists mentally. He knew that look. "Plenty of Fox, smattering of, what, Bear? I know there's Bear in there." It was her own house. That was the sort of thing that was held up as something to emulate. "A few Owls, too, right?"

"Just so. And more recently?" Richard loved watching her think, honestly. She had all the information, or at least most of it.

"Bear, a few. Salmon. Seal. Huh, yes. By those standards, Gabe's not quite so unusual. All Schola, mind, but Schola's been doing a good job diversifying. And in supporting people who don't come from the Great Families." Kate had, Richard knew, been a help with that. She'd visit to talk to students who'd found themselves dumped into a set of unspoken rules and expectations they had no clue how to navigate. She'd made it through herself, but Richard strongly suspected it had nearly done her in once or twice, from her reactions later on. Certainly it had left her with a tendency not to admit a disadvantage unless she absolutely trusted someone. "One of the charts?"

"The second one was about the people who challenged and didn't succeed. Quite a lot of Foxes in there. There hasn't, in fact, been a successful challenger from Fox since Silvia Warren, who was something of an exception in a couple of directions. Certainly, she had a better idea how to prepare."

"Quite." Kate frowned. "That's something they don't talk about much, no one does. And I don't think it's just that I'm not around those conversations."

"Alysoun did get that much out of Alexander, via Lizzie. The Council doesn't talk about it either. There are plenty of theories about who succeeds and who doesn't, and when, but as far as Alysoun could tell when she looked at what's published about it, every time someone else challenges, the theories go out the window. It's not about house, it's not about magical skills. Someone can not succeed the first time, and succeed later - Garin Fortier, for example. Sometimes people die, and no one's got any idea why them, why that time. Mostly they don't, but there have been strings of challenges where no one succeeded or someone died, like it's some sort of twisted fad."

Kate's mouth twisted up; this was in fact the kind of puzzle she particularly liked, even if it was rather outside her usual scope of society. "I'd like a copy, actually, if he can do one. I'll write if that wouldn't cause you problems?"

"No, please do. Offer whatever help you'd like, or Giles too. Gabe has to know people will sort it out, and it may just be he's been juggling so many other things he hasn't got in touch himself." Richard wouldn't pretend he understood it, but he was sure Gabe wouldn't be upset by Kate mentioning she knew. "The third chart's more complicated. You probably need him to explain it in person, but it's a trajectory of what people do after they either succeed or fail. He'd worked back twenty-five years last I saw it, it needs layer charms to make any sense of it."

"Where on earth does he find the time? I know he at least goes to bed regularly. Rathna would have comments, otherwise." Kate ran her fingers through her hair.

"I don't know either. Alysoun says he's putting all the frenetic worry into something he can see. She thinks he'll have some epiphany in a week or so, and settle down to whatever preparation he decides he actually needs. I have been told not to fuss at it. Just let him take over a library table. Which, I note, I was already doing." Richard rubbed his face.

Kate laughed. "Fair, fair. And you do keep enormous tables around for a reason." She was about to say something else when there was a knock at the door, still muffled by the wards. She cleared her throat. "I need to see what that is."

Richard gave a nod and felt the warding drop away.

Kate stood, going to the door for a quick low-voiced conversation, before she turned back. "I'll be out for a bit. Got something that needs my delicate touch, apparently, and a woman who's not too obviously terrifying."

"You do manage to hide it well enough," Richard said, amused. "You know where to find me. Thanks. I'm glad we got the time we did."

Kate nodded, but Richard could see she'd entirely shifted trains of thought. Time to go back to his own office and see what new lists needed his own attention.

CHAPTER 6
SEPTEMBER 10TH AT VERITAS

"Not too much of a bother to have you out here?" Alysoun was stretched out on the chaise longue, with a decent view of the lawn down to the pond and salle. Every last joint felt like it was aching, not least because she'd spent most of last night in the warded great hall at the centre of the house. More comfortable than an air raid shelter dug into the garden, certainly. The hall was reinforced magically so that nothing would come down directly on top of it, but that didn't make sleep any easier.

Lizzie shook her head. "Of course not. Tea? Shall I be mother?"

"Please." Alysoun leaned back. "How are things at Ytene?" With most other women, certainly most other Ladies of the Land, there would be a dance to these pleasantries. There were specific modes to be obeyed, lest the entire social structure collapse in a heap. Or so Alysoun's mother had had it. Richard's, too, when she had deigned to speak to Alysoun on any matter of relevance. With Lizzie,

Alysoun needed to do none of that dance, but she did still actually want to know the answer to the question.

"Last night was not good. Nothing like London, of course, earlier in the week, but bombs at Ringwood and Somerley, six miles southwest of us. And I gather several on the coast, down at Highcliffe."

"Gabe will want to know about that, and check in. Or to ask Geoffrey, at least, how they're doing."

Lizzie's mouth quirked up. "For someone who keeps protesting that he's got plenty to keep him busy already, he does pick up new people to take an interest in."

"He pointed out, quite reasonably, that significant acts of magic draw people together. Even if he never sees the Lammastide ones again, that doesn't mean he wouldn't want to help." Alysoun spread her hands, then stopped when her wrist objected. Lizzie brought her the tea at that point, and she wrapped her fingers around the cup. Not the done thing, but she was at home, and she wanted the warmth.

Lizzie took her own seat. "The bombing range next door isn't helping. But we check the wards, there are muffling charms to keep the horses steady, all of that." Running a breeding and training stable in the midst of this Blitz must, indeed, be a particular kind of challenge. Though one grace of this war, if it had any, was that they were no longer emptying every barn in Britain for horses to send into the gaping maw of the battlefield.

"Canterbury took several hits last night, and Dover. And Richard was called out to London, quite early on." She shook her head. "Hundreds of dead, maybe. They were still looking for survivors and hoping for more." There was nothing she could do for them, other than the charitable donations and sorting supplies.

Alysoun forged on. "Richard heard this morning that the Levetts, in Sussex, had quite a few around their lands. They were still sorting out just how badly off people were. Ditton, up north of us. We had the sirens twice? I think it was twice. Of course, we were in the Great Hall, under the best of the warding, by then. But nothing near here."

Lizzie nodded. "We've worked out how to make sure all the staff have space. It's not too awkward, and it's not as if we're doing much entertaining in the great halls, is it? The gift of an old estate, drawing on the history to help keep it standing a bit longer. And I suppose it's going back to the time where the entire household lived in the same hall, with a great central fire. I'm just glad we could get both Kate and Isembard to look at things before they were entirely swamped for different reasons."

"Quite." Alysoun let out a long breath. "So. What did we want to make sure we get through before one or the other of us gets called away for something?"

"I hope me, so you can get a bit more rest," Lizzie said, agreeably. "The various family first, before Gabe?"

"How are the children doing?" Alysoun agreed with that order.

"Edmund's liking being a second year at Schola. Rather more than being a firstie, I think." Lizzie smiled at that. "He's found enough of his sort of people. They're in one of the libraries until all hours, but of course we think that's entirely ordinary. And it's early yet, but Merry's settling in at tutoring school. I'm glad to have her out of the New Forest. Honestly, she's well up north. Rosie misses them both, but her governess keeps up with her well."

Less chance of bombing. That was a calculation they'd have to make at some point, especially if Kent kept getting more than most places. On the other hand, she was fairly sure that if they did try to get Avigail out of the house and away, she'd just sneak back in by whatever means necessary. And she did take the risk of the air raids properly seriously. She was often the first one down in the Great Hall, blanket pulled around her and a book in hand to keep herself distracted.

"Avigail's glad to have her mama home. And we're all very glad Rathna's back safely, too. She's gone a lot, with Ferdinand, picking up his training, and doing a lot of work on portals nearer the bomb sites, as needed." Alysoun let out a slow breath. "I feel better that if something happens, we stand a chance of knowing immediately."

"There is that. Not that I've the strongest sense of it yet myself. And it's not as if Geoffrey is very close to his extended family, often for very good reasons."

"But Geoffrey - and Alexander - will keep going off and doing dangerous things."

Lizzie snorted. "Very competently on the whole. But here we are at Gabe, aren't we? Who is cut from much the same cloth, isn't he, even if it comes out differently?"

Alysoun chuckled. "Entirely different sort of colour or style or whatever the metaphor of choice is, but yes." she considered. "I suspect there are things you can tell me, and things you'd like to but feel you can't. I understand, of course."

As she expected, Lizzie didn't hide her relief at that. They were good enough friends - and had been for, what, fifteen years now years now - that they didn't cloak things with each other. But there were still times and topics like this one, where things were more uncomfortable than the norm. "I knew you would, but people do get touchy. And that's where I wanted to start, actually."

Alysoun raised an eyebrow. "Oh? Someone new?"

"I've got a few notes on Lilac Powell and Herana Phipps. Less on the men. Though I'm curious why Lycus Sisley isn't serving somewhere. You'd think he's the sort who'd be somewhere active. Geoffrey has his suspicions about where Adrastos Rix is serving." Which meant some sort of Intelligence work there, but not directly with anyone Lizzie knew.

Lizzie went on. "But yes. I've heard rumours - through Cephus and Bertram, actually - of another challenger, something Michaelton. An Alethorpe man, on the line between apothecary work and alchemical research. They think he knows his actual work, but he's been chasing theories that are somewhat more dubious. And I'm trying to track down another one, quite interesting, a Maisie Wallace, who went to Dunwich." Cephus and Bertram were Geoffrey's pet alchemists, as he usually put it.

"Curious." Alysoun frowned, trying to recall the various of Gabe's charts. "The last three challenges had people from outside Schola, didn't they, but not a lot of success? Though I don't know how you measure that sort of thing. One person succeeds, the others don't. But that would make seven candidates, wouldn't it?"

"Just so. But we do like our sevens, as a society, don't we?"

Alysoun considered her options here, and in the end went for asking. There were only three real options. Either Lizzie knew and would tell her, or she knew but wouldn't answer, or she didn't know. One out of three was actually fairly good odds. "What has Alexander said about how the challenges actually work? He and Gabe talked, and I'm glad to share what Gabe told me."

Lizzie laughed. "We might get a better picture at that. So the piece I know that you might not is that the Council can encourage people to challenge, but Gabe was, of course, unusually so. Often a given member of the Council might suggest it. Even more or less sponsor someone, help them prepare, all that. But it's usually just one."

"And that is like and not like what Gabe was presented with. He did not describe it as a suggestion, for one thing. And for another thing, I gather it was a mutual conversation between Alexander, Cyrus, and Mabyn."

Lizzie nodded, peered at her cup, and frowned at the patterns in it. "How's your tasseography?"

"Mama was much better at it, but I can have a look. Why?" Lizzie stood, bringing Alysoun the cup, which Alysoun set up properly, with the handle toward her. "What was the question?"

"I was thinking about what we should pay attention to, in order to be of the greatest help." Lizzie came around the chaise to lean over, but not block Alysoun's light. She was attentive to that, in a way few people were.

Alysoun nodded and considered. "I think that's an apple tree on the side. That's the nearer future. But there, look, the same shape again, at the further future." She turned the cup slightly to get a better angle. "Mountains. Multiple mountains. And that's to the northwest, functionally the Council Keep. One mountain means powerful friends, but more mean you also have powerful enemies." She snorted. "Tell us something we didn't know. Though to be fair, it's not so much Gabe having personal enemies, as having annoyed rather a lot of people in his line of work."

"At some point, as Geoffrey keeps telling me, it doesn't so much matter why they started being an enemy." Lizzie tilted her head. "Is that a knife or a dagger?"

"Dagger. It's got the cross guard, see? That's at the rim, that's what's going on right now. Again, nothing we didn't know. That's a favour from a friend."

Then she considered what had immediately caught her eye. "That's a snake, a serpent. Normally, they're bad luck - spiteful enemies, a bad omen, something like that. But seeing as it's Gabe." She frowned. "And would you call that a long coil, not a separate wave?"

Lizzie peered into the cup. "Yes. You can see how the line traces, what, that's two-thirds of the cup. An extremely large snake." She paused. "Can you tell me about the snake?"

That was an interesting question. There were, in fact, relatively few things Gabe was actually private about, but this was definitely one of them. It had taken him years to tell Alysoun and Richard - or even Mason and Witt, who had, if anything, more right to know. Mason and Witt had mentored him, taught him near enough everything he knew, and his magic was woven through with theirs in a hundred ways.

She'd seen them, now and again, in professional mode, how one of them - or Lucy Doyle, who'd been Gabe's actual apprentice mistress - would start a sentence, one of the others would finish, someone else would chime in a particular detail. It was like watching one of the best bohort matches, where everything ran seamlessly.

Not long after he'd turned eighteen, in the tail end of the last War, he'd had a tremendous fall from his horse. They'd been incredibly worried in the aftermath. Not so much about the physical injury, which had actually mended quite well with potions and bracing and all that. But he'd been entirely unlike himself for weeks. Months, though it had not been a static thing.

And something in it had changed him. She'd seen that, again, later, with Charlotte, whose life had made an entirely different pivot, nearly as unexpected. At the time, all she'd been able to do was to be near, to offer what help Gabe had seemed willing to accept. Seeing her son hurt was bad enough, knowing that she, herself, could do very little of use had been far worse.

Eventually, bringing all of his skills to bear, he'd finally given her enough information. Enough of his nightmare of a great black snake, the night before the fall. Enough of what he remembered from the fall itself, and the days afterward. She was, when she was not so caught up in the moment that she lost her perspective entirely, a skilled analyst herself. Gabe got that from both her and Richard. They'd agreed on that long ago. Alysoun remembered the moment when the pieces had clicked into place, and she understood enough of how he was now using an entirely different map than anyone expected. Even, she was quite sure, Gabe himself.

The ankle still pained him, rather like how Alysoun's body pained her. She'd worried over that in the sleepless nights for many a year now, if she'd given him that particular poison inheritance. Only in him, it wasn't all over his body; it was concentrated in his ankle around the injury. He could forge past it in ways she couldn't. As he said, almost dismissively, it just hurt. It didn't mean anything, not anymore. It didn't generally fog his mind, or blur his reflexes, as her own hurts did, though some of the potions he took when the pain was worst certainly did both.

Which brought her to the question of the snake again, and what she could tell Lizzie. Lizzie was one of their particular web of allies, with skills of her own. Alysoun trusted her, near as much as she trusted Richard, or Gil or Magni, Mason and Witt. Lizzie had a knack for spotting the precise detail among a thousand that was relevant. Besides everything else, if Alysoun diverted from the question,

Lizzie would know there was something there. She wouldn't be rude about it, but she'd keep looking for the answer, as Alysoun would in her place.

Gabe's life had hinged on the curved fang of a snake, once. And for all that snakes were considered bad omens, dangers, ill luck, a hundred other wrongs, he had turned all the assumptions upside down. And gone remarkably blithely on his way to all outward appearances.

None of that was simple to explain. Finally, she said, carefully. "Snakes mean something different to Gabe. From before he met Rathna. And while he's a child of Albion, back through the centuries, he isn't bound by our symbols. Not that one, anyway."

He'd come back from India having learned the proper prayers, the way the offerings were made. It wasn't like her customs, nor was it like Richard's family, but Gabe made his own way in this, as in everything else. He'd added to where he'd started.

Once, Alysoun had asked him what the offerings were for, what they hinged on. Gabe had been sprawled on his back on the sofa, entirely unable to sit in one place for more than a minute or two at a time that day. He'd shrugged, rolled off the sofa, come up on his feet, and said they were powerful, dangerous, the guardians of treasure, and the givers of blessings. That the twist of their bodies turned fate. He'd said that it had taken something that weakened him, sapped his balance, to something that was strength and flexibility and a new perspective.

And then he'd plucked a book off one of the shelves, presenting it to her with a bow. When she'd worked through the text, she'd been left with even more questions. No book that took the reader through a series of fantastical problems that needed logic and orthogonal thinking simultaneously would do anything else. But they were exactly the sorts of problems he solved day in and day out, and that way of thinking, from every angle, was what he needed to be himself.

Alysoun had always wanted that for him. More than anything else, even more than love, and she wanted plenty of that for him as well. She'd done as her parents wanted, and she'd been happy, more than happy. But for Gabe - and for Charlotte - she'd always wanted to see what they would be if they could do anything they chose. It would be churlish now - and cowardly - to back away when that was what happened. When that was what Gabe was making himself in the world, whatever the reasons for it.

Lizzie, thankfully, didn't pry further, but waited for Alysoun to finish running through her internal rumination before returning to the teacup. "The mountains are interesting, then. I've heard a few flickers - nothing I can substantiate to the degree I'd like - that Silvia Warren's not happy he's challenging. She's backing Lilac Powell, but she's also had Herana Phipps to tea."

"How do you know that, then?" Alysoun kept peering at the cup. She didn't see the things she'd been more afraid of. An hourglass, with its indication of imminent peril, for example, or a falcon, a persistent enemy. It wasn't pessimistic, except there wasn't much indication of what sort of enemy action to watch for.

"Oh, Benton trained her under-butler. Naturally." Thomas Benton had been Geoffrey's man through and through since they'd met in the trenches and Benton had been assigned as his batman. They'd spent years in Intelligence work, and Benton had settled into being an impeccable steward for Ytene, including training up a number of junior staff. By now, he had quite the network of information whenever it was called for. "Of course, there's discretion involved, and besides, he didn't actually know what they discussed. But it was an unusual visit, notable, and so he noted it."

"I appreciate the information. Anything on the others we haven't already discussed?"

"Not really, though I'll have another round of the gossip papers in summary for you on Monday. You'd asked what Alexander had said about the challenges. Let's get back to that." Lizzie moved away, after taking the cup back to refill it with tea, then Alysoun's to top it off. "There's a door at the top of the Council Keep. You go through the door, whatever happens happens, and everyone knows if you are successful or not. Some people are injured, a few are killed, and from what he said, there are good guesses why, but rarely any certainty."

"All at once?" Alysoun frowned.

"Everyone enters, one after another, but Alexander allowed that you don't see anyone else. Or at least generally not. I gather there are exceptions to everything. But it's not a pitched duel, whatever the popular lore suggests. He said most of that's complete tripe, of course."

"I still can't decide if I'd feel better if it were a pitched duel. Gabe would have a good chance there." Alysoun would prefer that people she loved didn't get into dangerous fights, on the whole, but both Richard and Gabe were, in fact, exceptionally skilled at it. Watching them do something they were that good at - as good as she was at analysis - was something she treasured.

"People apparently come out in different orders. Sometimes quite quickly, sometimes after hours, and there's no real rhyme or reason there either. It takes as long as it takes, he said. With that shrug, you know the one."

"Where there's at least three things he's not telling you, almost certainly more." Alysoun agreed. "Gabe said he's being remarkably informative, actually, but no details about what that means."

"You're very patient." Lizzie said, leaning her elbow on her knee. "I think I'd be tearing my hair out."

"Mostly," Alysoun said, "It's knowing that Gabe had done dangerous things since he apprenticed. Many of which I don't actually know about until they're over and he's come home. The difference about this one is the lead time - months. It's ridiculous. But I'm not sure me fussing over it is going to do any good, so I sit on my hands and I don't. I swear, no one warned me about this part of being a parent."

"To be fair, you were a very different sort of child. Neither of us went directly into the dangerous things ourselves, though my mother worried over me being on ships far from land in who knew what weather. But she also knew she couldn't keep me home." Lizzie let out a small sigh. "One day, again, I hope. I'll let you know if I hear anything else."

Before Alysoun could say much more, there was a knock on the library door. At her reply, their housekeeper came in. "Pardon, m'lady, there's a message on the phone from Ytene. Could Lady Carillon go back as soon as possible. There's a need to bring some supplies through the portal, and everyone else is out. Something for healing, I think."

"I'll go at once. Can't keep that waiting." Lizzie waved a hand. "Don't move, Alysoun." She came over and bent to kiss Alysoun's cheek. "And I've got a couple of novels I'm done with. I'll pass them along next someone's coming this way, or have someone stop in if it's the other way round."

"Of course. My love to your family, in all their scattered places."

Lizzie laughed at that. "And mine to yours." She picked up her bag smoothly, striding out of the library briskly, as she did when she wasn't putting on the fussy sort of manners. It left Alysoun to stew over the tea leaves and what shards of information she could add to her own analysis.

CHAPTER 7
SEPTEMBER 25TH AT THE COUNCIL KEEP

"So. Why is Silvia still in such a snit?" They'd retreated to Cyrus's office after an unreasonably contentious meeting, even by ordinary Council standards. It had started with an hour of argument over the division of labour on various necessary tasks. Then it had foundered entirely on the shoals of coordinating matters relating to the declared challengers.

Mabyn had made a circuit of the Keep, making sure everyone else had left. Cyrus and Alexander had caught up with their respective journals, paperwork, and decanting a scrap pile of notes from the meeting into a single location. Now, though, she'd come back, which allowed Alexander to ask the question that had been burning him since twenty minutes into the evening meeting.

"You expect me to know?" Mabyn closed her eyes, letting her weariness show much more than usual. Then she waved her hand. "Drink, please. Bribe me."

It made Cyrus laugh as he put a glass into her hand. Alexander was not cruel, he let her get a good swallow or three before he cleared his throat hopefully.

"Good grief, Alexander. You're a dog with a bone." Cyrus settled back, crossing one leg over the other. "Do we need food?"

"You're putting me off." Alexander glanced from Cyrus to Mabyn, then back to Cyrus. "Mabyn, you know her better than anyone else. I can tell you've talked about it too, if you wish to calibrate."

It got another snort from Cyrus, but he let Mabyn answer. "She is still in a snit about Gabe, in specific. It's not a reaction I'd seen before, and I don't know, what's the word. It's one of those potions with an ingredients list a mile long, half of them cloaked in historical inaccuracy, and you can't tell what the active parts are anymore."

Alexander nodded once. "That seems a fair description. Tell me what you can, if you would? You've far more to draw on than I do." Flattering someone like that was not a skill he brought out often. He was sure it wouldn't work on Mabyn at this stage in their long knowledge of each other, except perhaps to get a smile out of her, which would be worthwhile.

"Keeping with our metaphor, let us say there are four groups of ingredients: Hesperidon's opinions, common opinion about the Penelopes, that Silvia is absolutely of Fox House in ways I do not at all understand, and Gabe himself."

Cyrus tilted his head. "That's better put than the last time we wrestled with it."

Dryly, Mabyn lifted her glass. "That was a fortnight ago. I've had somewhat more sleep, and despite a far too tedious meeting, no one has actually done anything truly idiotic in my presence today." She shrugged. "I have kept thinking about it. Because you're right that it's obvious, and it's going to be a problem if we don't sort it out and Gabe succeeds."

Alexander inclined his own head.

Mabyn opened her eyes, peering at Alexander. "You're sure he's going to triumph, aren't you? Not just make it through, but come through, I don't know. Whole-hearted."

"I have some theories. And I have some history in my head I do not wish to repeat." Alexander spoke quietly, looking somewhere between Cyrus and Mabyn, not directly at either of them.

"Trade you." Mabyn was, at times, entirely too quick. It was easy to forget she could be. She had all the appearance of the sort of feminine softness that meant people ignored her. She, of course, had used that to her own advantage - and Alexander had gathered more recently, her own protection in her younger years.

Alexander spread his hands. "Fair." He considered. "I'll even go first." He waited for the shock to ripple through them both. That was part of why he'd offered. He wanted to keep them off-balance, not asking the questions he really didn't want to answer.

"Go on." Cyrus leaned forward now, entirely focused on the conversation. He wasn't predatory about it, not the way some from Fox House could be. More like Mabyn's Owl, an open gaze taking in the entire field, looking for the faintest twitch of movement.

"For one thing, all the reasons we asked Gabe to challenge in the first place. He has skills we need, but he has skills we don't even know about. I'm certain of that, and I've seen more of him - and Mason and Witt - than you have. Informally, when they're throwing half a sentence of a reference of some case into the conversation. The way we do, about things that happened twenty years ago. Every so often they'll explain things, especially right now, since Gabe has his own apprentice at the moment. But often, no, it's just a mutual shorthand."

"All professions have those," Mabyn pointed out. "And as you said, we do too."

Alexander shrugged. "I don't know how to describe it, except that they'll dance across half a dozen fields. Then you turn a corner in a sentence and suddenly there's an entire structure laid out, fit for use. I don't know what he'll bring to the challenge chamber, in any sense, but I strongly suspect it's more than the rest of us did. More flexibility."

"Some of us are flexible." Cyrus pointed out. "I don't mean me. Though honestly, I'm not sure I could tell you, still, exactly what I brought to my challenge, beyond a rather fatalistic impulse."

Alexander had not dared ask about this, before. He knew the outline, they all did, how Cyrus had come to his challenge deep in grief at the death of his wife the previous year. From the tidbits Cyrus had mentioned over the subsequent decades, Alexander knew he'd half expected to die in the process.

The death hadn't been his. Childeric Fortier had gone into the challenge chamber that same night and not come out. Alexander had read the notes, years later, when he was sure no one else was in the Keep. He'd read them because it was the Fortiers, and it was the year Phillip and his mother had died, and any scrap of information might matter. Childeric had been the golden child of his generation, older cousin of Garin and Isembard, and while he had limits to his skills, they shouldn't have killed him. No one had an answer, not then, not since, and that bothered Alexander a great deal.

Into the silence, Alexander pressed forward. "All three

of us felt we had to, for reasons that seemed decent at the time. And we got lucky, if that's the word."

It made Cyrus bark, sharp amusement mingled with darker emotions. "Luck." Then he turned his palms up. "There are days I think better me than many people, and then I turn around and wonder what I just said. But we are here, for what good that might do anyone."

Before he could lose his nerve, Alexander took a deep breath, let it out, and forged ahead. "If he succeeds, I plan to talk about my challenge. My challenge, and about walking into that first meeting. I'm not asking permission. I'm giving you fair warning."

Cyrus made a noise deep in his throat that was half a growl. "Two months worth."

"Just so." That said, Alexander leaned back, and now he waited.

"Why?" Mabyn picked up, though now she was just as sharply focused.

"That is not the question we traded for, Mabyn." Alexander let his mouth quirk up. "But because he's right. I can't put all the ways he is into words yet, but he is. You know it too, both of you. And I rather think Silvia does as well, and that's why she's fighting so hard."

"Ah, well." Mabyn leaned back, taking a sip. "I can tell when you're not going to budge. As I said. Four points. Hesperidon's opinions are the easiest, probably."

Cyrus grunted. "That the Penelopes are eerie, they do not fit into civilised society properly. Their women are undecorous and their occasional men, effeminate. The Guard, he could deal with the Guard well enough, even if he mostly left it to FitzAlan or Malcolm. Their oaths are straightforward. We know what they are, and the bounds it puts on them."

"The Penelopes are committed to truth. And that is deeply uncomfortable," Alexander pointed out.

It made Mabyn look up suddenly. "That's a part of it, yes. I think - I've been coming to think this month - that Hesperidon didn't want them close, to see what he was keeping hidden. Sylvia has the same instinct, though I haven't been able to figure out if she has it for the same reasons, or if it's a borrowed cloak."

"And some of that gets tangled in the common perception of the Penelopes. They don't fit in boxes tidily. Two-thirds women, but not remotely feminine in the sense that would reassure the egos of men like Hesperidon. And half our colleagues, I think."

Mabyn snorted. "Male and female. And the male Penelopes, well. Gabe's a fair example here. Given to suitable outdoors pursuits, a skilled duellist, but manly isn't the word you think of when you look at him. Lithe, yes. Slippery, quite possibly. Flighty, I certainly did, until I saw him at the portal. Not solid, or sturdy."

"I'd say looks are deceiving in this case, only I don't think that's what's going on. My impression has been that they just don't care about the social norms, as a group. I've heard Mason say more than once that the uniforms are at least half so no one has to make any decisions when getting dressed quickly. That's besides being useful when they're actually assisting the Guard or the courts."

Mabyn nodded slowly. "That's the other thing, too. They don't mingle in the same sorts of society. Oh, we've seen Gabe at various things, with Rathna and his parents, but he doesn't go to parties often, the Great Families ones we'd expect."

"Some of that," Alexander pointed out, spreading his hand out palm up. "Is because he's cramming thirty hours into the average day. Some of it's because a number of your peers in breeding are bigots, and some of it is that they're just boring. And Gabe has a low tolerance for boredom. Rathna too, actually. But you saw him this afternoon. Once we were through with the things he found interesting, he was just done." More obviously so than Alexander had seen in him usually, he'd made note of it because it seemed a sign of strain.

"She's seemed to defer to him, the things I've seen them at," Cyrus said.

"I've come to the conclusion that Rathna thinks on a vastly different time scale than most of us. Years. Decades." He'd wondered, once he'd learned her maiden name, Stone, if there were some family line there, but she'd never talked much about her parents and their magic when Alexander was around.

He shrugged once and went on. "It makes some sense. Portals run for centuries, and they take years of steady work to grow in the ordinary way of things. And Gabe bounces back and forth between being entirely in the moment, and having a well of historical context to draw on. The references, earlier? Some of those are their own direct experiences, but it's just as common to hear one of them cite something from 1820 or so, well beyond their own lives. Entirely as if it's a book they all read last month for an agreeable argument." Alexander wanted to know what Gabe would see when - for he was sure it was when - he got his hands on the Council archives.

"Huh." Cyrus was frowning, the expression he got when he was working through the permutations. "Go on, Mabyn, what else while I think?"

"That brings us to Silvia. I hadn't seen this as clearly before. It hasn't been a visible issue, though now I see it here, I wonder about other places. Silvia doesn't understand his lack of ambition. She's a Fox through and through, and even if she hadn't started that way, she was shaped to it." Mabyn hesitated. "Her marriage."

"Yes?" Alexander made the question as even as he could.

"You know most of it, honestly. She married, quite young, to a man thirty-five years her senior, for the express purposes of having an heir. Which she then didn't do for near four years. And only the one child, though I gather that particular failing can be put at Hesperidon's side, not any lack of willingness on her part. She set aside her own apprenticeship for it, even if she came back to it later. Alchemy being particularly tricky that way."

"I am scarcely Hesperidon's partisan," Alexander pointed out, glossing over decades of his own isolation and resentment. "But I had the impression they were, if not in love, in comfortable union with each other."

"Remarkably, yes. Given the beginning of it. But that is in large part because Silvia shaped her aspirations around what Hesperidon would approve of. Not that they aren't also her own ambitions, but she chose from a set of those he would support, rather than going her own way."

"And now he's dead. Her son's a grown man with a marriage and two children of his own." Alexander tilted his head. He'd heard from Isembard that that marriage was cordial, but no more than that. It had been made as a political agreement. Claudio had done his part, and no one was actually desperately unhappy. It counted as fine, even to be expected, among a certain sort of family. That very much included the Warrens.

"And she has made her own Challenge, come through it well, found her feet. And then remade herself when

Hesperidon was no longer taking up all the space in whatever room they were in." Mabyn twitched one shoulder. "I do know what it is to make yourself acceptable in that way."

Alexander snorted. "Though not as much remaking as might be, given current circumstances. If she were able to be more flexible, we would not be having this conversation." His own impulses held that that sort of rigidity was destructive in a far different way than change was, and should be broken down regularly.

As for Mabyn, her own marriage had been difficult in far more overt ways. Alexander didn't know - he'd never quite dared ask, it was presuming too far - if her husband had actually hurt her physically. But it wouldn't have surprised him if the answer was yes. Certainly, the unlamented late Lord Teague had cowed her and controlled her emotionally, for all she had strong and capable magic of her own.

"I can see how that might make Gabe a difficulty. He has things that were never on offer to her." Cyrus was working through it out loud, and Alexander felt the little shiver of pleasure at being included that way. He suspected that would not become normal for him for a long time to come, if ever.

Alexander spread his hands. "Here's the other piece to think about. He has been very clear - in private with me - that he knows we need him more than he needs us. He has a full life, he loves the land, he has a family he adores, and who love him right back. He does not need our approval or our permission, he does not need our praise or our welcome. But we desperately need what he can offer."

"Desperately, Alexander?" Mabyn's chin came up as she stared at him.

Cyrus cleared his throat. "Alexander's right. We've mended some things, but there are others I do not know how to touch. We—" He gestured at Alexander. "We are ritualists. But you can't build a ritual if you can't find the shapes to build it with. Alexander's strengthened walls that were crumbling, made an oasis out of desert, helped me see the ways we're connected as a group better. As you have, Mabyn, differently. How I think of it as a garden, with each having different things they bring."

"How then, is Gabe a replacement for Livia? I'll grant you the skilled duellist, but..."

"I do not think having someone with Livia's sharpness and hardness - never mind her lack of tact - is actually something that's required. We worked with it, because she was good at what she did. Superb, in fact. Because she'd come through her own Challenge, and that counts for a great deal. But Gabe will not replace her. He is, however, something we need. A whole set of tools we need, I suspect. And are going to need more, the longer the war goes on." Alexander knew the lines of theories about how the seats passed from person to person, and he was increasingly sure that near all of them were wrong. Gabe's charts had just brought that niggling feeling into sharp focus.

Mabyn let out a slow breath. "Silvia's not going to budge. She's got her back up, now."

Alexander shrugged. "That's hers to deal with. Me, I'm thinking about a war, about the amount of land being turned to agriculture and the implications. Also thinking about what bombing's doing to the land magic, a few bits of tracking down what might be espionage or what might be fools courting the Fatae. There's been a good handful of spies picked up in the last month. If she wants to keep throwing a snit, she can cope with the consequences."

"Which are?" Cyrus cut in smoothly.

"Dealing with Gabe." Alexander let both of them work through their visible discomfort at that thought before he went on. "You saw him in that meeting with her, same as I did. He doesn't need to be liked. Not by her. He doesn't need to be right, he needs the right thing to happen. She's got no idea what to do with that, does she, Mabyn?"

There was a long pause. "No. We're back to how she's entirely of Fox House. I don't know how to translate. Cyrus goes at it differently."

"And Gabe's parents are both firmly Foxes - far more than me, as we've talked about. But their ambitions run differently from Silvia's, too."

Mabyn tilted her head. "But it means Gabe's used to being around that."

"Any number of other people, too. You know what our upper Ministry and the Courts and all look like. Not so much the Guard, certainly not the Penelopes or many of the crafters. But just because he's fluent in navigating those expectations doesn't mean he'll let someone pull his strings. She has no power over him, and he knows it."

There was an even longer silence now. Finally, Mabyn said, "What do you know about Gabe's preparation? Change of subject, I know, but you're so certain." She added after a moment, "I gather the others have all been making the expected sorts of appointments for protective robes and potions and talismans and amulets, and whatever else might be useful. I haven't heard about any of that on Gabe's end."

"And you asked?" Alexander asked it casually, though he knew where he wanted to go with this.

"I asked. Better me than Cyrus." She lifted her chin. "What do you know, Alexander?"

"Many things I'm not telling." This time, though, he was smiling. "Come on. Here we are again at needing him. For one thing, I'm quite sure that whatever protective gear or tools or amulets or whatever Gabe might need, he already has on hand. He walks into unknown magical situations a couple of times in the average week. Rather more often than those of us actually on the Council who do our fair share, I might note."

It made Mabyn chuckle, at least. Alexander had got much more comfortable judging when he could tweak her nose and amuse her - and Cyrus - than he had been a few years ago. Then he shrugged. "And he's seeking out advice, just not from the Council. Not mine to tell."

That was in large part because he knew Gabe was talking to Geoffrey about some of it. Or rather, Geoffrey had wanted to talk to Gabe about it. He was being particularly closed-mouthed on the matter, and Alexander had decided not to press. It would take a bit. Both Gabe and Geoffrey had land obligations on Michaelmas Day, this coming Sunday, and various other things they had to tend to. Within the fortnight, probably, the way Geoffrey was circling something, very much in his more falcon mode.

"Will you tell us if there's something we need to know?" Cyrus had leaned forward again, elbows on his knees.

Alexander considered his answer here carefully. "In my judgement, yes. Do you trust me?"

"Gods help us, Alexander, but yes. Just." Cyrus waved a hand. "We're in deep waters, and uncharted ones, in several ways. I will take every bit of navigational help I can get."

"You are serious." Alexander leaned back. "You've broken out the nautical metaphors."

Cyrus grimaced. "I suppose. And I'm not trying to hide things from you."

"We come back to the fact that we have habits of hiding things, rather than sharing. And I'm just as bad as the rest of you. I'm not putting myself on any pedestal."

"Right. We are now officially going in circles. Can we talk through that petition on opening up the fields nearest the Penrith holdings for agriculture, and what petitions we need to put together?" That had been their other unsolved wrangle from the meeting. "If we have a proposal next week, we might actually get somewhere."

Alexander stood, refilling glasses while Cyrus and Mabyn set out the maps. This was at least a problem that had several possible answers to it. Those were a pleasant change from the greater and lesser mysteries.

CHAPTER 8
OCTOBER 11TH AT YTENE

Geoffrey waited with the kind of patience he hadn't felt in entirely too long. He could feel the magic he intended to use coiling in him. Beside him, he knew Alexander was intensely curious, but also not asking what Geoffrey had in mind. He had just been told that Gabe was meeting them here for something that would take the rest of the afternoon. It was just about three, which would give them three hours before the light went in the covered ring.

Gabe was a quarter hour late. He'd written an hour ago saying he'd managed to double schedule himself slightly. He'd be at Ytene no more than half an hour late. Geoffrey had sighed, and settled in on the bench by the portal with a book, Alexander doing the same beside him. He'd set aside the afternoon for this, and he was sure Gabe had some good reason for the delay.

The portal flared, and Geoffrey waited. Gabe emerged on the other side, wearing country clothing. Geoffrey was in breeches and boots, as if he'd spent the afternoon riding - which he had. Gabe had trousers instead of the breeches, but those were boots on his feet, rather than shoes, and the suit was cut for easy movement. He had his staff in one hand, his satchel over the other shoulder.

Gabe made a small bow, not the formal sort, but a proper acknowledgement he was on Geoffrey's land.

"Gabe." Geoffrey turned his palm up, indicating his welcome. "Be welcome."

Gabe glanced from Geoffrey to Alexander and read something informative there. He settled into an easy resting pose as the portal closed. "Pardon my tardiness. I'm doing worse with time than I'd like to be this month." Then he launched directly into the question at hand. "I'm interested to see what you have in mind. You didn't give much indication."

"No." It could have been sharp, but Geoffrey couldn't keep the smile out of his voice. He had a dozen reasons for this afternoon's work, but he would find pleasure in almost all of them. At least if Gabe was as skilled as everyone said he was. "Come down to the covered ring?"

Gabe nodded without saying anything further. Geoffrey turned, feeling Alexander take his place on Geoffrey's right, then a moment later, Gabe on his left. He set a quick pace down to the covered ring at the far end of the paddocks. All the mares were out in the pastures on the other side, well out of the way.

Gabe glanced around the ring. It wasn't the first time he'd been here. Geoffrey had used it a number of times when they were trying out new horses for Gabe himself, for Rathna, and ponies for their children. This time, though, was different. Gabe paused in the broad doors at the entrance. "You have something in mind." It wasn't a question, and Geoffrey was delighted to see that Gabe wasn't letting his guard down.

"Alexander, if you'd stand there, looking in through the smaller door. Stay on the outside of the building, not on the threshold."

Alexander raised an eyebrow, but simply nodded, taking his place in his own easy rest pose. Weight balanced between both feet, slightly forward on his toes, one foot just a hair back, allowing for easier turns or movement from a standstill, if called for. Geoffrey bowed Gabe further into the ring and moved to close the great sliding double door, sealing the warding as he did so. He didn't ask Gabe to put down his bag or anything else. That was part of the point.

Gabe glanced around, considering. The other end was closed off, a solid wall, with the only entrances where they'd come in. It was an ordinary covered ring, that way, with the supporting beams rising up to an angled roof. After a moment's consideration, Gabe took a few steps to one side, never turning his back on Geoffrey. He left about ten feet between where he stood and the double doors meant for horses and carts.

It made Geoffrey smile more broadly. Good. Gabe's instincts were excellent, even here where Geoffrey had long since sworn he was welcome, a guest, to whom no harm was meant. Balancing that bit of oath was about to get a good bit trickier for Geoffrey, but he'd had time to think this through. He took up his own place facing Gabe, far enough back he could see Alexander's face as well. Oh, he wanted to see Alexander's face.

"In a forest outside Berlin, I made a point to Alexander." He waited a beat, to see if Alexander would catch it before he said anything, and he saw the slight jerk of Alexander's chin, a cautious anticipation. "I said that no one made it through the kind of isolated, dangerous work we did in the

CELIA LAKE

last war who wasn't both incredibly competent and tremendously lucky."

Gabe inclined his head just slightly, not taking his eyes off Geoffrey. "I did not fight in that war, but that was also my understanding." His fingers flicked once. "I do not know your skills, but I am quite sure you have them. I've been sure since my parents invited you home for chats in the library."

Geoffrey laughed. "They had the advantage of information from Giles, I'm sure." This was going to be a pleasure, absolutely. "There's a question Alexander has asked me a number of times, and that I have not answered."

"You don't duel." Alexander said it again, perfectly on cue, not that Geoffrey had given him any warning of this. "Not so long as I've known you, or any of the information I could get out of anyone since your university days."

Geoffrey made a slight bow, taking in both his companions with it, though he also didn't take his eyes off Gabe. "I do not duel. I fight." He waited those glorious seconds, letting the silent beats of an owl's wings fill the space in his head.

Three heartbeats later, Alexander was laughing. Truly laughing, his head thrown back, like this was the best joke he'd heard in a decade. "Nekheny." Alexander shook his head. "How long have you been planning this?"

Geoffrey shrugged, but he didn't try to keep the grin from his face. "All things in their seasons. I did give you all the information you needed." He had, too, and quite early on in their particular mirror of a partnership. None of this took his attention from Gabe, who shifted his weight slightly.

"I do know how to fight, as well as duel." Gabe's voice was even, the sort of deceptively calm even that made Geoffrey sure he was pushing on this point just the right amount. He had his reasons for this, for skirting this close to the lines of his hospitality oaths. "I may not be of the Guard, but I'm more likely than most to be on the wrong end of someone up to no good."

"I know." Geoffrey kept his voice easy, refusing to let the strain of the balancing act show. Alexander might spot it in his magic if he paid attention, but he didn't think Gabe would know for certain. "I can offer my alchemist and my library in support of your challenge."

"And you have, and I appreciate it a great deal." Gabe said. He'd mentioned he was still making up his mind about the potions on offer, but was inclined not to take them. Geoffrey found that interesting, too.

"The last gift I can give you is testing your skills. You know a great many things, Gabe, but I know different ones. Let us test each other and learn from it."

That, that hit as Geoffrey had hoped, a slight shiver through Gabe's body. He adjusted the staff. "Rules?"

"Only whatever rules might apply in your challenge. And I gather there aren't so many relevant there."

Alexander coughed. "I, however, would take it as a personal favour if you didn't do anything immediately fatal to each other. So awkward to explain to your families."

Geoffrey snorted. "I believe we can manage that. You'll find a tack trunk next to the door, Alexander. It has various supplies." He and Benton had made sure of that this morning at the same time they'd checked all the wardings and protections on the space. He ran through his paces with Benton once a week, at least, even if he'd not needed his fighting skills for a good decade now. One never knew when one would. That was the hell of it.

Gabe nodded. "And we end when one of us has decisively won? The other down, incapacitated, and so on?"

"Just so. I'd appreciate it if you'd avoid damage to the roof, and any terribly loud bangs. Scares the horses and all that." Geoffrey laid it out almost diffidently.

"I'll do my best." Then there was that quiver again, as Gabe hitched the satchel strap over his far shoulder, hugging closer to his body. "Count of three?"

Geoffrey stamped once on the ground, clapped his hands, and called the warding up in a glow of light, waiting for it to settle for just a moment before he nodded. "On go. Three. Two. One. Go."

They were both bringing up their own protections by the end of the count. He'd seen Gabe duel a dozen times now, more a courtesy than anything else, since he did not engage in much discussion of such things either. It was too easy to slip up. He had the advantage two ways round, having seen Gabe's duelling, and the fact he was on his own ground here, and Gabe was not.

Gabe was appropriately cautious. Geoffrey could feel him getting a sense of the land beneath his feet. No. More of a sense. It certainly wasn't the first time Gabe had been to Ytene, nor was it the first time he'd connected with the New Forest's particular strands of magic. If Geoffrey weren't busy setting up his own plans, he'd lean back and watch how Gabe went about it. Gabe was pulling threads of light and power out from the air, the ground, the space around him, on the edge of visibility. Not something he'd seen Gabe do before.

Before the younger man could get too comfortable, Geoffrey settled into a harrying chase, pressing him to move away from the doors, into the broad expanse of the rest of the ring. He wanted to wear Gabe down, to see what he did when his resources were dwindling.

Also, he might have cheated just a tad. He'd taken the opportunity to shape the magic in the space just how he wanted it. He kept the twisting jabs that drove Gabe in a broad circle going with his right hand, before he held out his left, hand in the perfect curve, thumb to the top, tucked in. A great bird swooped down out of the rafters, landed on his hand for an instant, and then launched off, harrying Gabe from the air. Another gesture, and small dark shapes came out of the corners, yipping and tearing toward Gabe's feet, doing their best to foul his steps.

Behind him, he could hear Alexander's laugh, bubbling across. He'd got the joke, then, excellent. The great owl, for who he was, and how he so often saw the world, metaphorically and magically. And the foxes, for what everyone assumed of him, unless they knew better. He let them do their work, he'd shaped them well, and they would do what they were made for.

It gave him time to lay out several other lines of magic. A spot here that would bog down anyone who stepped on it, this one that would snare magic like a trap, another one that would suck it down like a free-flowing drain. He laid them out with quick precise flicks of his hands, calling the incantations under his breath. He never lost track of Gabe, just took advantage of the time he could get.

It did, however, take him a titch longer than it should have to realise Gabe was glowing.

The light was like the sun rising on summer solstice, not at full strength that burned the eyes, but growing every moment. Gabe wrapped the light around him, a pillar that swirled and shifted, clouds of light. First the owl swooped away, back to one of the dark corners, and then the foxes retreated, their yips and barks tumbling over each other in their audible confusion.

It was a kindness, to drive them away with light rather than pain, and Geoffrey made note of it. Effective, all the same, and he didn't have the heart to press his constructs into the fight again. Not when they'd bought him the time he'd wanted already. As Geoffrey gathered himself, the light around Gabe swirled brighter for a moment, obscuring everything within that circling column. Then it began to fade out, and Geoffrey could see that Gabe had drawn a wand from somewhere, his staff at full length in his left hand.

The staff came down across his body, on the diagonal, as Geoffrey loosed a charm that would bite sharply if it connected. Instead, the charm bounced off as if it had hit a thick stone wall. Before he could send another chasing it, Gabe was on the move, using the staff to fling himself over one of the enchanted spaces, pivot, then drive his wand down to the ground of the ring. He felt the quiver of the earth before he saw anything, and then he felt the pop of all three of his enchantments disappearing, as if they'd never been there.

That was a trick he hadn't known, and oh, he wanted to know it. He wanted to be able to do it that quickly, even more. Neither of them had made a serious attack yet, but they were back on even enough ground again. Gabe had dealt with the distractions, and Geoffrey needed to step up his attacks.

He considered his choices in the split second he had, and he settled in to snipe at Gabe. Stinging, burning charms that would hurt like a bullet did, without penetrating. He did not, of course, actually wish to do serious injury. It would be awkward. Alexander was quite right about that, even if the supplies included a wide range of potions and other materials that would handle anything up to an instant death.

Gabe danced through them. Not literally. Not quite. But he twisted and shifted. One brushed by his shoulder, another by his hip, nothing quite connected. Twice, there was that staff deflecting the magic to shoot off into the protections. Once, there was a shooting light from his wand, meeting Geoffrey's charm in mid-air and making it sputter out. They went on like that for minutes, a challenge to stamina and focus, but not much else. Geoffrey could keep this up for quite a while, but Gabe had the advantage of relative youth.

When he thought he might have worn Gabe down a bit, Geoffrey pressed again. He called up a coiling rush of air, the kind that could buffet someone to the ground and toppled massive trees, loosing it toward Gabe.

A moment later, Gabe wasn't there. He was dancing away, or bouncing might be a better word. He'd used his staff to vault himself backwards, landed, and done it again, putting yards of space between the two of them. It was the kind of space that meant he needed the distance and not just for protection. The wind chased him, pulling up a cloud of sandy dust from the floor of the ring, obscuring the lines of sight between them. Geoffrey didn't relax. He knew far better. Instead, he drew his own wand from inside his jacket. He waited until he had a clear line of sight, sending a shot of warning through the dust here and there.

As soon as the kicked-up dust dispersed a bit, he could see Gabe's shadowy shape in the back third of the arena, partially illuminated by his magic, but his features invisible. Geoffrey sent out a bolt of white-silver light, sharp and edged as a lightning bolt made into a perfect arrow, and waited for it to strike home. Gabe shifted, the staff moved, and then there was the immediately identifiable position of the second of the Triadic protection charms.

Geoffrey's shoulder suddenly ached in the mirror to it, the way it contracted and lifted the left shoulder, while the right hand braced against the impact to shift and deflect the magic into somewhere, anywhere, not lethal. His charm shattered against the protections, splintering off like shards of glass, going everywhere, deadly fireworks until they hit one of the wards and were absorbed.

Gabe did not move, did not shift, and Geoffrey was moving forward when, all of a sudden, he felt something coiling around him. Before he could react, there was the hard tip of a wand against the back of his neck, at the base of his skull, then a hand reaching around to pluck the silk pocket square from his jacket pocket. In his ear - he could feel the breath - came Gabe's voice. "Yield?"

Geoffrey's hands immediately went up, wand pointed well away from either of them. "I yield."

The pressure immediately dropped away. He could feel Gabe take two steps back. When he turned slowly, over his right shoulder, he could see Gabe wiping dust and sweat from his face with the pocket square. "Do you think I'll do?"

Geoffrey took a long breath. Then he was grinning. "You'll do. Teach me how you undid the ground enchantments, would you? I've never seen it done so smoothly and quickly."

"Oh, that's a Penelope trick. I'll show you." Gabe lifted his chin. "Alexander, if you could find a suitable potion from that kit. You'd have what, Geoffrey? Hemington's Elixir, or whatever your alchemist has done to improve on it?"

"The blue bottle with the gold cap, Alexander. It's got a

label." A painkiller and muscle relaxant. Geoffrey called out, "And a restorative for me, please. Or I suspect I'll fall on my face before we're halfway back to the house." He heard Alexander chuckle as he disappeared behind the wall in the outside. Geoffrey called the extra warding back to him, then let it flood through his body to renew him a little and feed and strengthen the standing wards.

"What did you do at the last?" Geoffrey asked, as Alexander came to join them, holding out a bottle to each of them.

Gabe took his first with a gesture that was simultaneous acknowledgement of the question he was not answering, swallowing it in the kind of eager, needy swallows that made it clear he couldn't have gone on at that intensity for too much longer. Well, neither could Geoffrey. That was fair enough.

It gave Geoffrey a chance to drink his own, and feel the renewal rush through him, the way a clean cool rush of water felt on a hot day, washing away all that ailed him. He looked Gabe up and down. "Come sit outside. Alexander, there's a bit of refreshment in there, wrapped up. I thought we might talk a little before going back to the house."

A seat was decidedly a good idea, and by the time they got to the bench that overlooked this bit of paddock, Geoffrey desperately needed to be off his feet. Alexander handed around the biscuits and bottles of lemonade, and waited until they'd both had some. "I could have told you you'd have a fight. In fact, I seem to remember doing so."

"Yes, but what kind of fight? That was what I wanted to know." Geoffrey snorted, recovering a bit now. "You prefer deflection to attack, but you did well enough with that, too. Especially at the end."

"You did set me up well for it. Use the dust as a cloak to

obscure the other charmwork, create a shape like me, anchored to me, and make myself near enough invisible. It wouldn't have worked without the dust in the air, the scent of it." Even the best invisibility charms couldn't entirely mute someone's smell.

"And enough magic in play I didn't feel that, either." Geoffrey nodded. "The downside of an enclosed space. Well done." He gave the praise readily. Gabe had more than earned it.

"I did like your owl and foxes. And I do get the joke." Gabe inclined his head, lifting the lemonade in toast. "And I know Alexander did." He'd been tracking well enough to notice that, even in the midst, then. Not that Alexander had been subtle, for once, but it was an interesting measure of how much Gabe had had mental space for. "I'll teach you the unweaving of those kinds of traps on the ground, but it does take a lot of practice to do fast." He shrugged. "I use it every week or two, in the usual run of thing, so I've had plenty."

Alexander snorted. "I did point out a few weeks ago, to Cyrus, that you walked into dangerous magical situations quite often. I expected you had suitable skills for it."

The conversation went on like that for another minute or two, the amiable discussion of particular charms and approaches, until Geoffrey cleared his throat. "Two things, Gabe. Related, but one is personal and the other's ..." He paused. "Both personal, but in different ways."

He felt, more than saw, how Gabe shifted, getting his full attention again. On his other side, slightly behind him now, he felt Alexander's hand shift, resting on Geoffrey's lower back. A particular sign of attention and affection, then, and not one Geoffrey got often outside the most private spaces of the house.

"Have you given a thought to the damage to the land magic in Germany? I know you've thought about here." They hadn't talked much about it, not directly. They hadn't needed to.

Gabe tilted his head. "I saw the reports." He waited a moment to read something in Geoffrey's eyes before he went on. "I gather you get the same information. I know Alexander does."

"That last night, the RAF conducted the heaviest raid on Berlin to date?" Geoffrey let out a small breath. "Berlin is a beautiful city. Was. And I have memories there." He didn't know how much had been damaged yet. Those reports would be slower, but he knew what bombs had done to London, to too many other places of Albion. His memories of Berlin held Alexander now, first and foremost, but other pleasures and trips before that, going back years. Of art, and music, and people who should have good lives, if at all possible.

Gabe held his tongue, and Geoffrey went on. "What do you know about the land magic there?"

"You don't need the formal explanation from me. I could give you the precis I wrote up when I started my current project. A great deal of what they talk about is blood and soil. The people and the land, and they're twined so tightly in the cosmology that even a Penelope couldn't pull them apart at this point, not without damage." Gabe considered. "But you're not just worried about the bombing. Though I agree, it's a problem in a number of ways, there as well as here."

"No." Geoffrey let out a slow breath, and leaned back slightly against Alexander's hand, finding it a necessary reminder. "I would like to ask you a favour, beyond keeping that in mind. If, as we suspect, you are successful in your challenge, will you investigate something for me, when time allows?"

"I expect to be quite busy for a while." Gabe said, carefully. Geoffrey noted, with some internal amusement, how he didn't humbly suggest he wouldn't succeed. He might not, but it wouldn't be a lack of skill or speed of wit that held him back.

"This particular question has been waiting since 1922. It can wait a bit longer." Geoffrey made himself go on. "We know that my brother Temple was working on a project in the latter part of the Great War. It had something to do with the land magic, not gasses or munitions, but something more far-reaching. He was killed when he would not yield on the matter. What I have been able to learn since suggests that something broke his ties to the land magic, as surely as being in the trenches did for too many. I know how death came to him, but I do not know what led to that death."

He was dancing through who he'd learned it from, or what else he'd learned. His brother had been executed by the Council, or next thing to it. He didn't know whose hand had done it, though he had his guesses. Two of them - Garin Fortier and Theo Carrington - were still alive and on the Council. Two were dead, Livia Fortier and Hesperidon Warren. One was retired, Paulus Watts. And then there was Silvia Warren, who had not been on the Council at that point, not yet, but who certainly knew more than she'd ever let on.

What Geoffrey had also learned - thanks to Alexander, almost entirely and all of that in the last five years - was that it had been something of a mercy killing. They'd wanted to drive Temple back to Ytene and the demesne estates. When he would not go, they did what was needed to preserve the land and its magic. It didn't make it any better to think they might have run out of options. Not knowing what had broken his brother, though, that stung. More to the point, how could they avoid doing the same thing again, bringing the same burning grief to others?

Gabe had tilted his head, his eyes half closed, as if furiously working away at some duel in his own head. "And you want my skills at sorting out what happened? Working backwards."

"I do. I'm aware it is a large and complex favour. In exchange, you have my full support, leading up to your challenge. And if you succeed, I will exert myself - and so will Lizzie - even in Council spaces. Make a presence, help shape things as would be useful to people who are devoted to protecting Albion and her magic." There, that had brought Alexander to some reaction other than reactive quiet. Geoffrey felt the fingers tighten on his back, then relax.

"It seems to me that is exactly the sort of question that someone on the Council should deal with. I am sure they have reasons they haven't. They might even believe them." Gabe looked past Geoffrey to focus on Alexander. Whatever he saw there made him arch an eyebrow and leave off burrowing for more details. "If I succeed, I will do what I can. Starting with finding more of the lay of the land."

"That will do very well. And as I said, it is both relevant and not directly urgent at the moment." Geoffrey let out his breath completely. "Everyone ready for a larger tea? We should reassure Lizzie we are all in one piece still." There. He could lay several subjects to rest now, for the time being.

CHAPTER 9
MIDDAY ON NOVEMBER 15TH AT VERITAS

Richard had to lean against the doorframe before he could summon up the energy to make his presence known. He'd managed to write, let them know he was safe, he'd be home, well, sometime. But that had been hours ago.

Before he could figure out his next step, the door opened. He nearly fell across the threshold, but then there was an arm offering support. One of the footmen, James. Alysoun stood there, pulling a knit shawl around her shoulders. "Bath's ready for you, love. Want me to come and talk?"

"Make sure I don't fall asleep in it, please, yes. Is there?"

"There's food and tea. You can have more information when you've had some." Despite his utter exhaustion and despair, Richard managed a faint snort at that. It was a good bribe, and they both knew it. James helped him stagger along to the baths at the centre of the house. Richard inhaled deeply when the steam hit his lungs. James nudged the stool out where Richard could half-collapse on it once he'd got most of his clothes off.

"Do what you can with them? I'm on duty tonight starting at…" He closed his eyes, trying to remember the time. "Half six."

"We'll have your uniform waiting, sir." James glanced at what was in his hands. "The other like this?"

"Yes." It was the modified Guard uniform, suitable for wearing around people without magic. He strongly preferred the Guard's blue to the current uniform of khaki, but there was no denying it was a help in being taken seriously. He'd needed that, dozens of times in the last night alone.

James turned on the shower. "Do you need me to stay, sir?"

Richard shook his head. "I can make it to the bath. My thanks, and my thanks to Cook and all." James nodded, and went out, bringing the clothes with him, leaving Richard alone with Alysoun. He let out a breath. "Are the others back?"

Alysoun tsked at him. "Shower, in the bath, eat food, drink tea, and then I will tell you." He wasn't going to get more out of her, but he thought that there was no immediate worry, which was the information he really cared about right now. He turned the faucet for the shower, at least spared cold water still in the pipes, because it came from the same cistern as the soaking bath. The water hit him, flooding everything away for a minute.

Once some of the dust and worse had washed off, he began to work on scrubbing. It turned the sponge dingy, then grey-brown, but by that point, he'd got most of the grime off of him. He soaped up again, washing his hair as well as he could. Then he washed the rest of him one more time, almost all of it sitting on the wooden stool that was usually Alysoun's aid in such things. And Gil's, who found it hard to balance on one leg in the shower space, when he'd taken his prosthetic one off.

Finally, he looked up to meet Alysoun's eyes. Surprisingly, she had not got into the bath herself yet. She was perched on the steps up to it, entirely naked, just waiting. He knew then how exhausted he was, that all he could rise to was a brief moment of aesthetic appreciation, before worry took over. "You'll get cold." It came out automatically. His body was still remembering the sharp contrast between the heat of the fires and the chill of the November night air, the way he'd been back and forth between the two extremes over and over.

"Not with it all steam like it is, my love." Her voice was very gentle. "Can you make it over here, or do you need an arm?" Hers, by implication, and he would do a great deal to avoid that. Alysoun was tremendously strong in a number of ways, but her body gave her more than enough trouble, and he refused to add to it if he could help it. He'd rather go on hands and knees if he had to, but he thought he could manage the ten steps or so to the raised soaking bath.

"I see." There was a faint smile that flickered across her face, then she moved to perch instead on the far corner, giving him room to manoeuvre. "It's no wonder we have stubborn children and grandchildren."

Richard took a deep breath, then levered himself up, using one of the grips on the wall to make sure he didn't overbalance. Step by step, he focused on getting into the bath. He'd likely need help getting upstairs. Richard suspected Alysoun had already made that calculation, and someone would be ready with a dressing gown and an arm when he needed them. He could feel all the aches hitting him now, on top of the exhaustion. The soaking bath could only do so much.

Finally, he was sitting on the edge of the bath, then slipping into it. He landed on the seat with a mis-judged thump that sent a brief moment of agony up his spine. He had done something to himself last night, a pull in his back trying to get a buckled door open. Before he could hide the reaction, Alysoun slipped in next to him, then pulled over the tray at the side of the bath. Tea, huffkins with cheese and others with jam, and two potions. She'd pulled from Gabe's collection of them, which made Richard raise an eyebrow.

"You're on duty in seven hours. Half dose of that one, and take the other when you get up. And there're restoratives upstairs, but I didn't know which you'd already taken." Alysoun's voice was clear, precise, and she'd obviously been weighing those choices since she knew he'd be coming home for however little rest he could get.

"Cheese?" Richard frowned. It wasn't rationed, not like bacon. Not that he could have faced bacon today, not after the smoke from the fires. "And jam." Which was rationed, though at least the portions were fairly generous, and they made a fair bit from their own gardens. "And the good tea." Now tea was rationed, the family had mostly devolved into herbals from the kitchen garden, given the amount of it they went through on the average day. He quite liked the taste of mint, fortunately. But the black, here, might carry him through long enough to stagger to bed.

"Cook did her magic." She gestured with her hand. "And you need something you can eat by hand, so huffkins." They were the Kentish variety of bread. Cook put things on and in them, with little indentations in the top made with the thumb. "Hard-boiled eggs and nuts, too." The chickens on the home farm were still laying remarkably well given the season and the circumstances, so they could draw more on eggs than many people. A bit of the sweet, from the jam huffkins, to keep his strength up. He couldn't bring himself to argue with it at all.

Besides, it was Alysoun who managed the household, along with Mrs Broadly, their current housekeeper, and with Cook. Between them, they somehow managed all the various ration books of everyone who lived here, family and staff alike, plus the necessary entertaining. Richard knew when not to interfere, especially in the current circumstances.

He managed to get an entire cheese huffkin into him, along with half of a jam one and half a mug of tea. Finally he had to lean his head back against the side of the bath and close his eyes. The hot water was restorative, though he was sure now that Alysoun had added some of the bath oils that made it more so. After perhaps half a minute - not that he trusted his sense of time right now - he felt her hand on his thigh. He covered it with his own, then sighed. "Information now?"

"What should I know to pass on?" Her voice was soft, as if she didn't want to disturb or startle him. That was - well, it was considerate, but it was worrying. After a longer pause for consideration than it should have taken, he shifted, offering to settle his arm around her shoulder so she could lean against him. Alysoun rearranged herself immediately. It wasn't something they did often, the way she had to lean and contort a little wasn't kind to her aches, but right now, they obviously both needed it.

Only when she was settled did Richard go on. "Coventry's still burning. Hundreds dead. Hundreds more injured. I don't know how many incendiaries landed, but the Coventry cathedral's a hollowed out wreck. It started at half seven last night, and we didn't get the all-clear until half-six this morning." And then they'd needed the day's light to begin digging people out from the wreckage.

"And the portal at Allesley, what, two miles away?" Alysoun could do the maths on portal locations easily.

"Yes. It meant we could get there in good order once we knew. Not that we were able to do as much as..." Richard let out a gasping breath. The fire brigades had been caught up short. Not only had all the phone lines and other communications had gone down, but so had the water mains. And Richard and the other Guards couldn't show their magic. He'd used his over and over again, to keep fires from growing when he could get away with it, to make pockets. Anything to give people a chance to get dug out, but that only went so far. He'd given far beyond sense, and he didn't regret that. Only that it hadn't remotely been enough.

"And you're on duty tonight."

"Need everyone we can get. Need double everyone we can get, to be honest, but we'll make do." Richard sighed, then at least got his eyes open, nuzzling at Alysoun's hair for a moment. He needed to remind himself she was safe here, that they'd reinforced the warding and the supports. As safe as anyone was in England these days, which didn't feel like it was saying much right now. And he needed to remind himself why they went out and gave everything they could. So that so many people could live and love and smile and be with their families.

She gave him the space for his thoughts, though eventually, she cleared her throat. "You must have gone by Rathna and Ferdinand. They started in London, but she sent a note saying she was going out to stabilise the Allesley portal. With the Guard bringing in more people and equipment, they weren't sure it would hold." Ferdinand had been her apprentice long enough now - and in quite dire circumstances, this past spring, and summer - to be quite a bit of use with that, Richard suspected.

"Gabe?" His voice almost cracked there, and he swallowed.

"Southwark. London wasn't hit as badly as those two nights in September and October, but it didn't look good. He thought dozens, they were still counting. But one of the alchemical labs next to that tanner's shop on Gryphon Lane took a glancing hit. No one was sure exactly how dangerous it was going to be. He and Isobel are there. He thought it would take them most of the day when he wrote an hour ago. Mason and Witt were coordinating from Trellech."

So Gabe would come home exhausted, too. A different kind of exhaustion. He'd be using the fine point of his magic and all his wits, where Richard had been using brawn and the sheer force of his magic and experience. Richard nodded. "Gil and Magni were organising things at the Guard Hall." Magni was firmly retired, but that didn't - as he'd pointed out - stop him from being able to run communications and keep people going in the useful directions. And Gil could keep up with the lists while seated. It freed up other people for the field, and all the too-many things that needed to be done.

"And tonight?"

"Tonight, we see where they need us. Possibly not Coventry, it's too awkward if we come and go, and by this evening, all the help we could have done with magic will have been done. The local Guard can help with location, but most of that is - well." Most of that would be clearing buildings and preparing people for burial by this evening.

Alysoun nodded once. He could feel her movements

against his shoulder. "Eat a bit more, please, then." Food couldn't actually substitute for sleep, but food, the best sorts of restorative potions, and a bit of care could do a lot. The problem was he'd already been relying on that night after night, with scarcely a break. They might get a bit of a breather if the weather turned too stormy to fly, but that seemed a very thin hope to lean on.

He reached for the other half of the jam huffkin, chewing it slowly, making himself eat, though he wasn't remotely hungry. He had experience in that, at least, in the demands of a crisis. Richard wouldn't be foolish about it. He would do what was needed, and get up and do it again. Alysoun just leaned her head on his shoulder, breathing quietly, and he let himself enjoy that for as long as he could.

Finally, though, he could feel himself starting to drowse. "Bed for me. Can you check my journal starting at six, and wake me if there's a call?"

"Let you sleep if I can?" It was a good question.

After a regretful moment, he shook his head. "I should be ready to go where they need me. And I don't have it in me to get moving fast enough."

She shifted to let him work his way toward standing. She levered herself out of the bath, snagging her cane from the hook near the base of the steps. She shrugged into her own dressing gown, before touching the charmed panel that would summon one of the staff. By the time James appeared again, Richard was out of the bath, more or less towelled off, though his hair was still damp. James held out Richard's own dressing gown and then waited. Richard took a step or two, then nodded. "If you'd get the doors, James, please."

They made a slow procession upstairs, but Richard desperately wanted his own bed, not one of the guest rooms on the ground floor. He let himself fall into it, not bothering to change into night things. It would make getting up easier, anyway, and every fragment of ease would count today. The curtains were already closed; the room was lit only by the charm lights.

Alysoun came and perched on the bed, a reversal of how this usually happened. She was about where his hips were, making it easy for her to rest her fingers on his hand. Often, she was the one who needed a daytime nap, and he'd sit and read to her for a few minutes while she drifted off. She tilted her head. "More to talk about? Take your potion, if you would?"

Richard snorted, more amused now. "Are you going to nag Gabe when he comes home to do the same?" He pushed up on one elbow to take it, draining the small vial in one gulp. He could feel the magic spreading through him near enough immediately.

"It depends on if Rathna's back yet. But yes, if it's needed. I can't do what you're doing. But I can send you off in the best shape we can manage." She tilted her head. "You didn't answer the question."

Richard sighed, letting his eyes close now. "Stay till I'm asleep, please? You don't need to read." He wasn't usually like this, but he also knew she would, and without any demurral.

She squeezed his hand, just once. "You're worried about Gabe, aren't you?" His eyes opened, and she was leaning forward.

"How do you always know that sort of thing? I hadn't said." He let his eyes close again, revelling in the touch, simple as it was.

"Because I know you, remember?" She paused. "Not

about him being in London, but the ... what was it you said two days ago? The strain of it."

"That. He's going to be doing something tremendously challenging in a fortnight. Challenging is usually for people who are fully rested, who've been able to focus on preparation for months, who haven't been running flat out in a dozen places a week. I know how exhausted I am. I know how much he must be. And there are the things he wouldn't normally do. He's double scheduled himself at least three times I know about in the last fortnight. He spent an afternoon on his own after something went wrong in a meeting. I know his reports are largely overdue."

"More like two dozen places." Gabe did get around. It was true. Alysoun paused, and he let the silence begin to lull him. "I worry about that too. But I also know he's used to that degree of work. Of challenge. We've taught him well, I think. The rest of it - honestly, no one could keep it up like he has been, forever. Especially given how much he hates writing up reports. If that's the thing that slips right now, everyone will probably manage." Alysoun considered. "He said you'd suggested a secretary, and that he refused."

"He did. At some length. I'm right, but convincing him's going to be an effort. If you could figure out how to broach it again, it would—" Then Richard let out a long breath, because that argument wasn't what mattered. "I'm so proud of him." Richard had to say that much, because it was true. "I - do you think he knows?"

"I think Gil would say you should use words and tell him. Before the challenge. I am sure he knows, but I'm also sure hearing it will do you both good."

Richard let himself smile at that. "True." Alysoun generally was right about such things, and so was Gil. He'd find a time, if he and Gabe were ever in the same place and conscious at the same moment, which seemed a faint hope right now. Before he could say anything else, Alysoun patted his hand. "Sleep, my love. I'll wake you in time. I'll be in the library, looking at what we can find out. I'll give you an update when you're awake."

Richard nodded, and then turned over on his side, facing her, pulling the blankets up.

CHAPTER 10
NOVEMBER 27TH IN TRELLECH

Alysoun kept a smile on her face as the gathering finally began to break up. It had been three hours of uncomfortable chairs, barely more comfortable shoes, and keeping her expression blameless through the luncheon, the talk, and the social hour afterwards. She'd been making more of an effort to be at the necessary charitable events, even though she'd likely pay for it tomorrow in pain and exhaustion.

And then she'd need to make it through the day of Gabe's challenge. Which would, apparently, mean an evening or longer of sitting around in the Council Keep, waiting for whatever news emerged from the challenge chamber. Gabe was permitted to have whoever he wished waiting for him, and that included Rathna, of course, and his parents.

He'd apparently gone back and forth about Mason and Witt and Lucy Doyle. In the end he had asked them and they'd declined. Mason did not wait well, on average, and Alysoun wasn't sure, in this case, that Witt and Doyle would fare much better. Besides, all of them had work that needed doing - as did Gabe, who didn't have much choice in the matter. They'd all be happier with someone getting on with it.

She wasn't certain she would wait well either, but she was going to be there unless Gabe asked her to stay away. He hadn't, and he'd made it clear he wanted Rathna there. Not the children, though. Rowena and Anthony were at school. Getting them out for it would have been tricky, and bringing Avigail when they couldn't - and when they weren't sure what the outcome or reactions would be like - seemed unfair as well.

She'd been woolgathering, and missed half a sentence. "We'll see you on Friday, of course." That was Lysistrata Phipps, an old family, and in this case, aunt to Herana. "Quite a few of us plan to be there, and of course, a glorious celebration at the end of it."

Alysoun was grateful for decades of practice with the general social gladiatorial battles of this set, but this honestly was a bit much. She put the right sort of smile on her face, the one that looked interested. "Of course, I hope Herana comes through well. I will be there, of course, thank you for asking, and we're hoping Richard, as well, though it depends a great deal on whether he's needed urgently elsewhere. And naturally Rathna."

"Oh, but surely your Richard can spare a few hours. It's the done thing to make the proper show of it." It could be twenty minutes, as they experienced it, or twelve hours, apparently. Time didn't run the same in the challenge chamber, from what she'd got out of Alexander. "Trellech's been doing quite well so far, of course the magical protections are superior."

"The Guard tends to all of Albion. We've been lucky with Trellech, and safer, thanks to a number of people's hard work." Alysoun worked hard to keep her voice pleasant, and didn't quite succeed as well as she'd have preferred. "But London's had a horrible time of it. Richard was helping at Coventry, and then wherever he's needed."

London had been hit again the night after Coventry, Richard had been called out overnight, coming home at eight in the morning entirely drained. Many fewer deaths, thankfully, mostly casualties. The next two nights had been quieter. But then there had been two bombs quite near Veritas, and the night in the Great Hall with the sirens echoing through the walls.

"Well." There was that little sniff, the disdainful one. Lysistrata had one of those marriages with the couple in different houses in different counties. She had the Trellech one, of course. Her husband was somewhere near Grimsby, if Alysoun remembered correctly. "I suppose some people have to keep busy."

Some people took their oaths and obligations seriously. Alysoun wondered, for a moment, what that meant for Herana Phipps. Lysistrata had had a fair bit of the raising of her, since Herana's mother was prone to ill health. Alysoun certainly wasn't going to cast stones about health being a limiting thing, but she'd always made it a priority to give her children as much of her time and energy as she could. It had turned out well for them. "Richard takes his obligations seriously. He always has, of course, and I think that's a fine thing. Even if it means I don't have his company near as often as I might."

"Well." Another little sniff. "Is your daughter here today? I didn't see her."

Alysoun glanced around. She and Charlotte made a point of not sitting together at these things. It was entirely too good an opportunity to catch up on different bits of gossip. "She's over there, by the doors, chatting with some of the women she was at Schola with." That was Charlotte's usual mode, alternating between those women and people she knew less well. It meant they could split up the effort of a gathering like this, and Alysoun was delighted at that.

"Ah." It was another little dismissive sound. "Though I do like her frock." It was one that had been refitted from last year. Alysoun felt that war time was absolutely not appropriate for ostentation, even if materials were currently available. Charlotte did look particularly well today, though, an emerald green frock with gold and black ribbon for decoration. Quite smart, decidedly unique, especially in this room.

"I'll pass that along, of course." Alysoun could smile easily at that.

"It's just been such a flurry - I had to put off some of my own plans for my winter wardrobe this year, helping dear Herana. She had just so many fittings for her new robes for the challenge. The decorative ones, as well as the practical, though of course we wanted the practical ones to look as well as possible. So terribly tedious, having to have all the skin covered for the protective charms, and her hair up. She has such lovely hair, doesn't she?" Herana was, in fact, on the opposite side of the room, with an abundance of golden blonde hair currently in a modish pompadour. It seemed quite a lot of upkeep and fuss, honestly, though Alysoun thought the style did suit her face.

"I was just thinking the style suited her, the lines of her cheekbones." Alysoun nodded, making herself continue to be agreeable.

"I suppose your Gabriel has been busy with his own preparations? Robes and potions and training and all that."

Here, Alysoun had to stop herself from laughing. Gabe

had, with rare exception, kept on doing what he'd been doing, not just since the start of the war, but long before. He spent a great deal of time working, if he wasn't stretched out on some piece of furniture reading. There were regular intervals of pacing and debating with whoever was handy - himself, if no one else was. When he wasn't doing those things, he was probably on a horse, in the duelling salle, or in bed with Rathna. All three of which had a great deal to do with being part of a dyad, now she thought about that. She'd have to tell them both. They'd likely laugh and say they'd realised that a decade ago. "Oh, he manages all that sort of thing for himself, of course."

Another sniff. "One hears such queer things about the Penelopes." Emphasis on the queer, almost certainly. Alysoun had long since heard all the permutations of gossip about them, how people judged them. How the men were seen as less manly, how the women were unfeminine, how all of them made people just a tad uncomfortable in all the less sociable ways. Alysoun had long since decided she preferred the way the Penelopes of her acquaintance - these days, she knew most of them fairly well - went at a conversation. It was certainly not this stultifying mess she was in right now.

"Ah, but what do you expect me to say to that, Lysistrata, darling? Gabe is one of them, well respected, of course, and not just among their number." Not that it was easy to brag about him. Even the work he'd been doing for the Council was somewhat sub rosa, and much of his usual work was related to things that became cases for the Courts, one way or another. Just as Lysistrata seemed likely to say something else, they both spotted Charlotte approaching.

"Mama." Charlotte bent to kiss her cheek. "And

Mistress Phipps, I hope you're well." Charlotte had a knack for sounding pleasant in a wide range of circumstances.

"I was saying that was a rather striking frock to your mother, dear." Lysistrata settled into being an elderly woman of opinions. She had given it a lot of practice. "May I see it? Perhaps my dressmaker might manage something similar."

Charlotte made no comment, but obligingly stood back to do a slow turn. It would be a trick to duplicate it too closely. Charlotte knew precisely how to dress for the effect she wanted, but so many people did not realise that the trick wasn't transitive. That done, she folded her hands in front of her, looking entirely proper in a way that made Alysoun sure she was in a mood to be impish. Gabe was the one with the impulses, usually, but when Charlotte got that look in her eye, there was a particular kind of hilarity likely to come.

"Mama, I thought I might come back with you. Lewis won't be done until after tea-time, and I could get some time with my youngest niece."

Alysoun inclined her head. "I'm sure she'll be delighted to see you." It would be a kindness, with the rest of the household more than a bit on edge because of the challenge in two days. Even if Gabe was resolutely refusing to fuss.

"You must be very proud of your brother, darling," Lysistrata said.

"I'm not sure that proud is entirely the right word." Charlotte considered her words thoughtfully. "It's a bit like being proud of the sun for shining, isn't it? He will keep doing things, many of them quite consistently well. And I'm quite sure he doesn't need my pride in him. My teasing him and taking him down a peg, possibly. That's a little sister's job, even if we're both grown up now." She said the last part cheerfully, and Alysoun watched the realisation of what she'd actually said roll across Lysistrata's face. As it did so, Charlotte said, "Do you mind leaving now, Mama? We could miss the crush at the portal, and I do want to see Avigail for as long as I can."

"Of course. Do excuse us, Lysistrata. Let me just make my farewells, Charlotte, dear, can you get my cloak?"

Five minutes later, they were out the door, and ten minutes later, settling down in the library at Veritas. One of the maids brought the tea cart in, and Charlotte immediately moved to set things out. "You sit. I could tell you needed a spot of rescuing. Gabe told me to keep an eye out."

"When you conspire against me, I am both proud and worried, you realise." Not that Alysoun would argue. She nudged her shoes off, then pulled her feet up on the chaise and arranged the lap blanket to keep her warmer. "Tea and one of the scones, please. I'm not terribly hungry."

Charlotte smiled at the first part. "When Gabe and I conspire, you know we're right," she pointed out. "He said you've been holding everything together, and you're more tired than you let on, and you should let me fuss over you." She tilted her head. "Well, he didn't actually say that part, but he did that thing with his eyebrow, and I was going to fuss properly, anyway. How long do we have before Avigail's done with her governess?"

"About twenty minutes." Easy question first. "And what did he say about himself? He'll tell you things he doesn't tell me."

"You are Mama," Charlotte pointed out, but then brought over the teacup and saucer, another plate with a scone and a biscuit, and arranged the side table where they were comfortably in reach. "He said that the challenge will be what it is. He's as prepared as he's getting. And he thinks all the fuss he's hearing about people preparing is honestly a really interesting lesson in misassumptions. He intends to work up a lecture on it to the apprentice Penelopes as soon as he gets a chance. With charts and diagrams and evaluations of wasted energy."

Alysoun had picked up her tea, but she quickly set it down so she wouldn't send it flying. Then she was laughing, hard, the kind of laughter that shook her shoulders. When she caught her breath, she said, "On the whole, I'm glad I didn't know that before this luncheon. I'd have had a much harder time keeping a straight face. All right. Maybe I will worry a little less. Or try to."

Charlotte settled down on the chair nearest the chaise. "It's reasonable you worry. We all know there are risks, we don't know enough about what they are. You and Papa and Gabe are all much better at that set of maths than I am. You have a lot more practice with it. But it means worrying's, well, expected."

"Is that where the most recent story you sent over came from, then?" Charlotte wrote and illustrated children's stories, delightful ones, but often with some particular twist. The most recent one Alysoun had seen in progress, two weeks ago, when it was just sketches, had been about a young mouse who was terribly worried about doing something new. And the mouseling's mother had talked her through how when something was really new, it couldn't be measured properly. There were only guesses, and some of the guessing wouldn't be right. It had been a clever story, a kind one, but of course, now she could see the roots.

Charlotte ducked her chin. "Well, yes. My best work comes like that, leaning into whatever it is that I'm circling around. Might as well make the most of it." She shrugged. "I think Gabe's right, though. We're not going to find out more in two days than we do now until he's done. You're the first person who'd advise food and drink and as much rest as we can get." Then she frowned. "How has that been?"

"There were bombs north, at Gillingham, and at Dover last night. So we had the sirens." Neither were very near, but not very near didn't actually count for much with the sirens and alarms. "And I can't help thinking about everything else. The Patria, at the moment." A ship full of refugees had exploded in the port of Haifa. Men, women, children, who'd been desperately trying to get away from Germany's dangerous reach. They'd been turned away from the British who held Mandatory Palestine and sent off to, where was it, Mauritius?

Sometimes, Alysoun hated her country, or at least the people who claimed they ran it. She hoped that she'd have hated them just as much without knowing Rathna, without knowing the Jewish connections Rathna had made during own apprenticeship. But she hated how cold and brutal the British Empire in all its rigidity could be.

"Oh." Charlotte folded her hands into her lap. "Quite." She was silent for a long moment, before finally saying. "We can do the parts we can. And hope for the rest of it. And keep going, because what else can we do?"

"How did you get to be so wise, then?" It was one thing to say such things yourself. Hearing her child say it, seeing her children live it, day in and day out, whether it was convenient or not, that was a thing she'd never quite expected, somehow. And yet, both of them, in their own ways, simply set out to do what they felt was right, steadfastly.

Charlotte smiled. "You and Papa set a high standard. Both of you, don't you say it's mostly him. He does it more visibly, the Guard and the land and his fancy magistrate's seal. But you've always done just as much. And Gabe and I just, well. You set an example. And we seem to be setting our own, for the children."

Alysoun nodded. "I am, in fact, very proud of you both. Not the way people like Lysistrata Phipps mean. I'm proud of what you've chosen to do with yourselves, both of you. And how you know the right thing at the right moment. That's precious, isn't it?"

"I put a lot of practice in." Something in Charlotte's voice suggested she was thinking of something particular there, but Alysoun didn't pry.

Besides, just at that moment, there was a knock on the door, and then "Please can I come in, Grandmama, please, can I?"

Alysoun laughed. "Come in, Avigail." The door was flung open, though Avigail caught it before it could bang into the doorstop. As soon as she'd done that, she was flinging herself at Charlotte, babbling about what she'd learned that day. Could she show, please?

Charlotte was laughing right back. It let Alysoun lean back and listen to their cheerfulness and amusement. That, now, was a balm she could soak in forever right now, and she was glad of the chance to do so.

CHAPTER II
NOVEMBER 29TH AT THE COUNCIL KEEP

The Great Hall of the Council Keep was brightly lit against the dark of the night, with a sort of forced cheer about it that went badly with awkward nerviness on display. Gabe had arrived with Rathna and his parents precisely on time. It was six in the evening, near two hours after the sun had set. They were escorted to a small cluster of chairs on one side. Mama and Rathna looked lovely, Mama in a twilight blue frock and Rathna in a saree of teal green and gold. Papa was in uniform, of course, as were a number of other men there.

Glancing around, Gabe took in that each of the candidates had their own cluster, that his family was the smallest group, and that most of the Council Members had broken up into their own groups. Even Garin Fortier was there, though he sat with his brother Isembard, the two of them their own little island. Gabe could see Rhoe Belisama, Cyrus's sister, with a couple of others, including Vidya Acharya. Having more than one Healer on hand was likely sensible.

Cyrus and Mabyn stood up at the front, talking to Alexander. All three were in particular ritual finery, Cyrus in flowing robes of the Council purple, Mabyn in a dress that complemented it in a lighter shade. Alexander stood out in quite imposing robes of black and the deep luminous blue he favoured when he had a choice. Alexander broke off almost immediately to come and greet them.

"Lady Edgarton, Lord Edgarton, Magistra Edgarton." Alexander made a formal bow, pulling out his more Continental manners, something he had long since set aside when they were in less formal settings. "Do you need to change, Penelope Edgarton?" It was to be formality, clearly.

"I am all set, thank you." He saw Alexander's eyebrows rise, then a slight quirk of a smile. Gabe understood that other people had fussed over their clothing for this. He already had suitable clothing for the work he meant to do if he were allowed to do it. He had dithered for a moment about wearing one of his Penelope uniforms, the stark black and white, with all the enchantments built in.

He had decided, though, on one of his working suits, the kind of thing he wore when the uniform wouldn't do. Just as enchanted, it was made of a good weight wool tweed, lined with silk, embroidered and stitched with all the protective charms needed in his line of work. It fit superbly. He could move in it easily, and he thought the brown and the faint threads of deep green flattered him. He had his staff, his satchel, his working stones, his wand. What else did he need but the daily tools of his life?

As Alexander led Gabe to the front of the hall, Gabe saw part of why Alexander had been so amused. The other candidates were mostly far more, well, overtly magically dressed. Lilac Powell had duelling robes, tightly fit against the lower arms and with a split skirt. She wore the sort of trailing over-vest that was a decided disadvantage in anything like an actual fight, but he expected she'd be discarding that before things properly began. They were, of course, shades of lilac, which made for an interesting statement full of assumptions, in the way they went with the Council Purple.

Lycus Sisley was more sleek, all in the sort of black and charcoal grey tight-fitting silks and leathers that might restrict movement too far for the sake of style. Adrastos Rix was also in duelling clothing but in shades of blue-green, this one with a leather vest, breeches, and tall boots. He had a rather 18th century look that really wanted a hat with a feather to top it off. But the vest left gaps where an actual duel could have played havoc with his rib cage with a little skill.

Gabe could not help but imagine the sort of acid comments Livia might have made at the people who saw fit to fancy themselves duellists and try to claim her chair. She would have been just as competent at picking out the inadequacies in their stylings and, of course, far more vicious. He had no need to be nasty, such matters would tend to themselves, and besides, she'd have been horrified at him, too, though not his duelling.

Herana Phipps had clearly styled herself on an ancient sorceress, very much a re-imagined Celtic priestess in mode. Very much in the mode in the witchcraft groups he'd been around the past year, and he was sure that would horrify her. Her hair was streaming loose, a torc circled her neck, and she wore a deep green flowing robe and a flaring white cloak. Gabe flicked out a touch of magic, curious about the torc. Nothing unusual there, it must be a family piece, it had the general sorts of blessings on it. Her clothes were out of good quality wool-silk, but it would catch on approximately everything, if the conditions in the challenge got rough. She didn't look like she was used to managing them in working conditions.

The last two, Gabe had done some research about, as they came from more wide-sprung backgrounds. Warren Michaelton was an apothecary by trade, and he was wearing the protective gear of his profession. That included a leather apron, with elbow-length gloves tucked in the belt, and sturdy boots, trousers, and smock beneath it. Gabe approved, honestly, and gave the man a nod.

Maisie Wallace looked quite uncomfortable in her own robes, as if she weren't entirely sure how to manage them. She had a protective cloak over what looked like a flowing tunic, leggings, and a blouse. He'd have suggested she ditch the cloak, but he expected that was where most of the protections were. He glanced around the room, and spotted Hespasia Wallace, a contact from his existing work for the Council, sitting with a group of others. Maisie must be a niece or something of the kind, then.

Once everyone was gathered, one of the Council Members took their place behind each candidate. Alexander had mentioned this part, that the Council Member would lead them up to the door, and wait for them to escort them back, or see a Healer was fetched. Gabe had listened to the protocols and instructions, of course. Those said a lot about what the expectations were, and not just the spoken ones. It had been clear that all this escorting and show was a cover for the fact the challenge was outside of human control or ken.

"Be welcome to the Council Keep, all ye who would make the challenge to become one of our number. Be welcome, all of you, family and allies, who have come in their support. We welcome each candidate to ascend the stairs, in order of lot. The candidate will enter the challenge chamber, and face the challenge or challenges presented. We will know the successful challenger when they emerge, which might be first or last or anywhere in between. Until all the candidates have returned, all of us assembled will wait. You have the freedom of the public rooms and the courtyard until all return, and the staff will circulate to bring refreshments." There was a murmur through the assembled crowd, but the candidates knew this already and all of them nodded or looked ahead.

Mabyn came along the row of the candidates, having them draw a token each, a number painted on a stone from a jar that obscured the contents. Gabe drew third, and his had a seven on it, in bright purple. Cyrus waited until they all had one. "First is..." That would be Adrastos Rix. Cyrus went through the others in order, Lycus Sisley, Maisie Wallace, Warren Michaelton, Lilac Powell, Herana Phipps, then Gabe himself.

With very little fanfare, Cyrus and Mabyn led the way through the hallway at the back of the Great Hall, then to the door at the end. Up they went, a spiral staircase that climbed four flights before opening into a small landing. The stairs went up one more flight from there. Adrastos Rix went up first. Gabe took a breath and leaned his back against the stone of the stairs, half-closing his eyes to get a feel for this part of the keep.

He had an advantage on the others, really. He'd been here more than often enough to have some sense of the magic embedded in the stone, even if the portal knew him better than the rest of it. Alexander said nothing, all through, though he could hear the others giving last-minute advice here and there. Another went up, another, and when it was just Herana left, she sniffed at him. "You aren't taking this seriously at all."

Gabe raised an eyebrow, and didn't move. She turned away with a pointed snub that was wasted on Gabe. Bad judge of character, that one. Or very likely to be fooled by what she thought she knew, and that was going to catch her some day. Possibly today, who knew?

Finally, she went up with Silvia Warren escorting her. Gabe waited the last few minutes until it was his turn. There was a sweep of fabric against stone, and he knew it was time. Silvia swept back down past them to wait somewhere without acknowledging his presence. Alexander had said nothing all through, but as he brought Gabe up, he nodded, drawing something up in his hand from his pocket. "Your hand, Gabe, please?"

Gabe turned his hand palm up, curious but not alarmed. He did spare a glance to Cyrus, who looked somewhat beleaguered. Alexander pressed a silver token into his hand, an oblate shape, flatter at the poles, with a crescent lining it along one edge. It had a tingle of magic, but Gabe was quite sure it did not do anything in specific, not the way most of the candidates would have meant.

He bowed once over it, the way he would have over one of the family shrines. "Any last words?"

Alexander snorted. "See you in a bit." Very cheerful. Cyrus stepped aside, revealing a broad wood door with emerald green paint on it, and then opened it. Gabe nodded once more and stepped inside.

It took a moment for his eyes to adjust to the light. He found himself in the centre of a circular space perhaps ten feet in diameter, with the yew of the bushes - and they were yew, not boxwood - extending well above his head. It was likely a maze, he'd been in enough to know the feel of them. But just at the moment, he could see no breaks in the hedge whatsoever. Wherever the door had been, it was no longer there. He took a moment to look at the sky above him - both Rathna and Thesan would approve. There was no moon here, either. The night was truly dark, the stars sparkling with a vivid brightness.

Ursa Major and Ursa Minor were right where he expected them to be, Draco angling below them. He couldn't see the horizon proper because of the hedges. But there was Taurus, rising in the west, the great head of the bull peering over the hedges, with Mars right on the heart. He had not changed continents then, or days or times. Though admittedly, the continent had seemed likely to be stable in these particular circumstances.

Clearly, though, he had to get through the maze. He smiled to himself and said out loud to the air. "Are you giving me a puzzle you know I'll solve quickly?" He'd made something of a study of them, not just because of how they related to the magics of the land and of architecture, but because Charlotte had found herself in one unexpectedly years ago. Nothing responded to him, perhaps a slight ripple of a breeze through the yew.

Gabe shrugged, and considered, then called light to his hand as he reached with his other for the portable lantern from his satchel. It would hang from a clasp on the strap so he could have both hands free, and that definitely seemed a sensible idea. Now that he could see a bit better, he considered his options. There was no obvious exit, and that suggested a hidden latch or switch or something of the kind, but where? He took his time, walking the bounds of the space once, twice, then pausing at the end of the third, feeling for what he could feel. The ring on his right hand, the Fatae-gift, was warming, the way it did when it was active.

Gabe raised an eyebrow. "I wasn't sure what you'd think of it. Are you known here, then?" It had done what he'd asked from them, and - well, if tonight went as expected, he wouldn't need it again. "I am grateful for you."

He looked away from the centre for a moment, a sense of some bird passing between him and the stars, though he couldn't see any actual shape in the dark. When he looked back, there was a pillar in the centre of the space, made of what looked like burnished wood with a bowl in the top. Gabe could take a hint. The ring had been a gift for a specific purpose, a loan. It was as clear now to him as any words in English might be that it was no longer his to wear. He worked the ring off his finger, kissed it once, and then set it in the dish, where it promptly vanished. Across the circle from him, an arch rose out of the yew, branching over his head, and opening to a new path.

Gabe walked through, though without rushing. He listened for any new hint, any shift of wind or pressure, any change in the ground under his feet. The ground felt like November, too, even if the stars hadn't told him so. It had very little give. He followed the twists of the maze around and around, mapping it in his head as best he could, but it seemed unicursal. Besides, he rather thought the magical mapping methods wouldn't work here at all. Around and around, until he'd been walking for what felt like twenty minutes.

He came out into another clearing, but this one was paved in stone, with ritual markings on it. He stopped well before the edge of the stone, leaning slightly on his staff as he took it in. "Ralston's Second," he said. "Combined with a rather odd take on Hemington's Fifth. And there's two scribal errors, there and there. Come on, this is first year training. You know that, surely. I've taught it half a dozen times."

Getting across would be more of a trick, then, but it was the sort of trick Gabe worked out a couple of times a month, on average. He settled into the habit of it comfortably, observing first, then drawing out his working stones to see what resonated. The charms that didn't cause a reaction, first. But he had to pull out Thistlewaite's Third, Morrisey's Ninth, and a queer little bit of folklore he'd learned from Sorcha Macdonald up in Glencoe. He looked up at that. "If you wanted to remind me of my wife, you didn't need to bother. She's never that far from my mind."

That, now, brought on flashes of Rathna. Times he'd particularly loved her, first. Talking in the inn in Glencoe, for one, or her singing to the great stones beneath the mountains. The more personal ones, the moment she turned to him once they were properly married, and the way that kiss felt. The moments of their greatest celebrations, Rowena's birth, Anthony's, Avigail's. And of course, the most recent of the great joys, the moment when she'd stepped through the portal in July, come home safe. He hadn't found words for how good that felt.

But of course, the flashes changed. Joy by itself might be a motivation, but it wasn't much of a challenge, was it? Now it was all the moments where he'd felt the most despair. Some of those were recent, knowing she was in tremendous danger, and he could be of no direct help. Writing in the journal, hoping she'd write back sooner than later, that he'd taught her enough of everything he knew to be a help. The long hours she'd been in labour with Rowena, when all the reassurance in the world hadn't convinced him fast enough that everything would work out. And that stretch, before she met Mama and Papa, when he worried in the dark of the night that she'd run away from him and everything he was by birth. That she'd have been right to.

He took a breath, and moved his thumb to brush the ring on his left hand, the wedding band. Her people didn't exchange them, but she'd asked him, clear as day, if he wanted one. And he did. He wanted everything he could have of her as often as possible. She let him spread his wings and be himself, and loved him for it. As he loved her steadiness, her sense of proportion, the way her roots ran deeper than the world saw in an entirely different way than his own.

As he moved his thumb, the floor rippled and changed into a patternless expanse of stone. Then new shapes formed. A grid of seven by seven, of course it was sevens. Engraved symbols deepened on the corner squares, a chalice, a sword, a horse, and a ship. He snorted. "Really? We're doing it this way? I'd have expected some of the Thirteen Treasures, honestly. If you didn't go for the dragons." Not that there was actually a true count of them that he knew of, just a great deal of lore. No dragons, and that actually surprised him, given the history of this particular keep and the battling red and white dragons, never mind the green that had been haunting him.

Then he rocked back on his heels. "Also, I absolutely refuse to play the role of Arthur in this little game of yours. I may be a child of Kent, not of Wales, but I know a gwyddbwyll board when I see one. I know my legends, and I am having none of this one. Are we clear on that? This challenge is a dance with the land and the question of sovereignty, but I will not be herded along a path chosen for me. You have to know better." He did know his legends, too.

They were full of a noble knight or a king-to-be coming across a woman sitting by a board like this. In that context, the game itself was about becoming king, at least in metaphor, through the grace of marriage to her. "Also, I am loyal to my wife, and you wouldn't want me if I wasn't."

Gabe crossed his arms and waited. Nothing moved, not so much as a blade of grass or branch of the hedge maze. He'd heard small sounds, the ordinary ones, before, of birds in the distance. All of that fell silent. He didn't care, he'd keep waiting.

He could feel magic coiling around him. Little flashes of temptation came into his mind, real and vivid as the best memories. They were full of smells and sounds and touches, all the things that made the world real. The thing was, though, Gabe was used to his mind flickering like that. Day in, day out, unless he was intensely focused on something. He let them pass. He did not get caught up in them, he could wait them out. He had his focus, and that was to get through this challenge whole in all the ways he could.

Whatever magic was working on him tried again and again. It danced between the personal and the impersonal. There were the moments of time alone with Rathna - always a great delight, but he didn't need to be tempted. They would be there, so long as they both lived, or so he very much intended.

The visions of gold, of power, of people giving Gabe what he wanted, or what he was presumed to want, those weren't even a temptation. He knew perfectly well how many people would have done anything to touch and hold them. Besides, getting what he wanted easily wasn't good for him. None of those had any real weight behind them, he could shrug them off as easily as a fallen leaf.

Finally, as if it was one last attempt, there was a vision

of an older Gabe, but his parents were still alive, as if magic had halted their ageing. He loved his parents, dearly and richly, but that was unnatural. Besides, Mama and Papa would want none of that.

Finally, the visions and flashes faded, letting him get on with things. He cast two more charms, and this time, the path across the stone lit up. It was a matter of moving the pieces on the board here and there, making a space for him to walk through, and he could trace it with magic, then with his steps. He fed magic into it, until it glowed bright as day, the golden shades that Rathna particularly loved about her whenever she could. If he put a little extra energy into it because of her, well, that was all to the good in his eyes.

He made his way across the lit-up path, using his staff to make sure he didn't slip. On the other side, he paused to see how things felt as the game board disappeared. His ankle wasn't bothering him unduly, his bag was still balanced. He stopped to take out a flask of water and have a drink, but it hadn't been terribly long or particularly draining as such things might go. An open path lay ahead of him, and so he walked forward.

The next two dozen twists of the path had nothing terribly unusual. Statuary poked out of an alcove here and there, shapes that were animals rather than people, but not the Schola animals, by and large. There was a bear, but this had been an Arthurian place, before the Council, the bear wasn't actually a surprise. A colossal elk, what he thought was a lynx, though it was rather eroded around the edges, other animals that had disappeared from this island long since. Horses, a few times, but horses were near enough universal. Massive cattle, an aurochs, built on a scale that matched that giant elk.

Gabe came around another corner, and there was a

much larger clearing. Coiled around it, looping several times, was a massive black snake. He stopped dead. That was the snake that had risen up in his dream, and in nightmares, since. It was as thick around as Gabe's own torso, bigger in places, and the great head was more like a dragon's than anything else. The tongue flicked out. Gabe stayed back between the yews, not that he could really run if he wanted to.

He took a breath, forcing himself to set the shock aside. It wasn't an unexpected shock. He'd thought about this in advance. But that meant taking proper care. Being a Penelope meant he walked into rooms with all sorts of mind-twisting magic on a regular basis. He didn't know - yet - what was real, or what passed for real in this space.

Last month, it had been someone experimenting with hallucinogens. Back in, what was it, June, it had someone with a reasonably substantial sense of paranoia who'd loved fear-based traps. In March, it had been someone who'd had a quite annoyingly clever method of casting illusions. It had taken them a full day to disarm that one.

He ran through all those checks in his head, felt the magic spark in his fingers, the pricks and tingling that checked his body was with him. The flicker in his ankle, that anchored him, as much as anything else. A person could sink into the memory of an injury, and he did that now, to test everything else in his presumed reality against it.

Now, he cleared his throat, and said to a point roughly over the snake's head, "Oh, come on. I thought you were supposed to be subtle." He knew a great deal more now than he had at eighteen and terrified. This was a melanistic vipera berus berus, the common adder, the only venomous snake native to the British Isles. Likely female, as most of the melanistic adders were. Vastly larger than an adder normally was, many times over, but it was difficult to be a suitably imposing symbol if you were only about a yard long at best. Even for a snake.

The great head lifted, the tongue flicked out again and again. Gabe held his ground, making his breathing stay steady. The head rose until it was at Gabe's eye level. In Gabe's mind, clear as if someone were speaking in his ear, he heard a voice like the shiver of grass or a burbling brook, all movement. "Yes."

Gabe considered his choices, and then bowed, never taking his eyes off the head - or the fangs that were currently hidden. He was certain there were fangs. As he straightened, he cleared his throat. "I did not expect a conversation."

"No? When else would we have one? You are here. I am here. Of course." The sounds rolled around in his head, but with a remarkable lack of hissing, given the serpentine aspects of the being. Just that continuous rustle of movement, in all its forms. "The others wouldn't speak to me."

That was interesting information, and of course, now Gabe had to weigh it for accuracy and for reason. People said things all the time that informed more than they realised, but he was sure this snake - whatever it was - didn't say things casually. He wasn't entirely surprised. "I suspect they expected a different kind of challenge. Did you look like this to them?"

Now, instead of the sound of movement, there was a rolling laughter, the kind of chuckle that built and built, going on forever. Whatever else he'd done, whatever else this was, whoever else, it had a sense of humour. That seemed promising. The laughter rolled on until finally the voice in his head spoke again. "Oh, no." She gave a hitch of her tail. "Do you have questions for me?"

"Quite a few, many of which I am sure are rude, even if I'm not entirely sure which ones would be, yet." Gabe went for honesty. It seemed the best choice. Beings who could talk in his head, there was no point lying to them. Total waste of energy. Then, all of a sudden, he had one. "I would like to know about something my wife has suggested."

Now he'd surprised her. The tongue flicked out; the head lifted. "Yes?"

"Rathna argues that the Pact made a container, that we can work within that container in a way those in other places cannot. That we can use the shape of it to keep Albion's magic moving, eternally renewed like a magic cauldron, and to bring it to greater effect when needed."

There was a little shift of the coils, as if the snake was thinking. Then the hiss returned in his mind, almost laughing. "Your wife is wise, and you are wise to listen to her. And return to her." It was not a direct answer, but it was as good as one.

"Returning has never been the problem, no." Gabe couldn't help it coming out with a laugh and more than a bit of wistfulness. He wanted her to be here now, and she wasn't. "What is my challenge here, please?"

"So quick to leave?" That got another flick of her tail, a resettling of the coils. It wasn't threatening, there was no attempt to lunge or bite, instead it was more like Mama arranging herself comfortably on a sofa. "We have all the time you like."

Gabe sucked in a breath, then he gestured at the ground. "May I sit?"

"Sit? Oh. Yes." As Gabe sat, the ground smoothed under him, until he was sitting on stone paving, like the others he had seen, not the grass of the path. It was more comfortable, really. He pulled his good foot up under him, leaving the other out. "You do not wish to fight me?"

"You know better than that, surely." Gabe spread his hands. "Was that you, then, when I was eighteen?"

Snakes cannot shrug, they have nothing resembling shoulders. But there was a ripple, from the tip of the darting tongue down through the first loop of the coils. "Yes, and also no."

"It's a mystery, right." Gabe considered. "You know I've done my best to make peace with it, what that meant."

"I do." The voice had a considering note. "You do not have the hooks in your..." She searched for words. "In your magic, in your soul, in your self, that you did. That others do."

Gabe felt a certain pride at that. He had worked hard to come to grips with nearly losing his life, with everything changing, his whole sense of himself and his place in the world. He had not, though, been sure until this moment that he had done enough. Perhaps he had. "What may I do for you, then?"

"Do for me?" That made her laugh again, longer and louder this time, as if this were the funniest thing she'd been asked in centuries. "Oh, little one. Why do you think you could?"

Gabe held up his hands. "Opposable thumbs?" He wriggled them and earned another rippling laugh for his efforts.

When the snake had regained her composure, she set her head down on the grass, the brille on her eyes clouding for a moment. "I do not know what is needed. I know that something is."

Gabe considered his words very carefully now. "And I am here because I might solve a problem."

Brightly, the voice said, "Yes!"

He spread his hands out. "That is what I do. I see things that people do not understand, and I untangle them." He tilted his head. "It's been a very long time since you had a Penelope standing here. Far too long, I suspect. All sorts of things on the back of your shelves. Maybe nothing that is a big problem, but anything neglected can tangle in time." The snake twitched once, but said nothing. "I came here knowing I'd be asked to serve. Do I come back and talk to you sometime?"

"Oh, yes." The head lifted again. "If you would." Then she nudged her nose forward. "For now, mmmm. Touch me."

That, well. That would take all his courage. Having a conversation with her was one thing, but touching her nose, remembering the great maw of the snake's mouth on that horrible day, those were harder things. But he had done many challenging things in his life. He'd made oaths that called on his fears regularly. He could do this too. He would do this with courtesy and kindness. His mother had taught him that, and his father, long before he'd been tested by fangs.

Gabe took a breath to steady himself, failed, and took another that worked better. Then he held out his hand, and the snake lifted up to meet his touch. She was cool and dry under his palm for an instant. Then there was a brilliant flash of sunlight, the world turning around into a mirror of itself. A second later, he was stumbling as his feet were meeting paved stone and someone caught his left arm, holding him up.

Alexander stared at him, his other hand coming up to take Gabe's right elbow. His mouth opened and closed, as if he had no idea what to say. Gabe blinked, and could see the others from the Council, the ones waiting for their own candidates—

Gabe gasped for breath, more from the shock of the change than anything else. Then he smiled. He let himself beam. "She has a sense of humour, doesn't she?"

CHAPTER 12
LATER THAT EVENING

"Cover for me." Gabe almost hissed it in Rathna's ear. "Ten minutes, maybe fifteen."

She blinked. Cover for him, at a gathering where he was near enough the centre of attention, where everyone would notice he wasn't there.

"What are you doing?"

"Something at home. Need to be on our land for it. Please." No begging, just the raw need.

It was getting on toward midnight, and he'd been back for twenty minutes or so. They were still waiting on three of the challengers - Warren Michaelton, Herana Phipps, and Lilac Powell. Gabe had reappeared, looking as if nothing had touched him, but with a gleam in his eyes that Rathna knew meant he was rolling in magic and cleverness. It would all come bursting out at some point.

Two of the challengers - Adrastos Rix, Lycus Sisley - had come out quickly. They'd both needed rather extensive attention from the Healers present, but now they were bandaged up and tucked into chairs. Maisie Wallace had appeared just a couple of minutes before Gabe, after nearly five hours wait, but she looked baffled far more than any injury.

Gabe had accepted a glass of wine and a plate of things to nibble on, cheese and crackers and bits of sausage and such. He had said almost nothing in a way that would have worried Rathna in their younger days, and did not quite so much now. Sometimes, even Gabe needed time to think, it turned out. She had simply settled her hand on his left, and let him be, talking quietly with Alysoun and Richard about nothing of particular importance.

Then, just now, he'd stood up, offering his arm, with an almost blithe, "Let's get a bit of fresh air." In November, on the top of a rather tall bit of rock. She had not argued, however, that was foolish. He'd led her outside, into the courtyard, where no one was at the moment. It was quite dark, with all the lights hidden by curtains inside, thanks to the blackout. There were a few scattered shielded lanterns around the courtyard, casting just enough blue-tinted light to see the edges of the space.

She gathered her thoughts. "What do you need?"

"Time. Not long." He kissed her on the cheek, then paused and kissed her properly on the mouth. Then he spun on his good ankle, staff in hand, and ran for the portal, pressing his hand to the settings as soon as he reached it. She knew the patterns for Veritas as well as she knew the back of her own hand, and she held her breath as the portal flared.

Now there was the question of what she did. If she stayed out here, she would have a better chance of covering for him. On the other hand, she had come out without her cloak, and while she was quite good at warming charms now, there was only so far that went in a saree. It was not designed for this climate at all. But needs must, and so she made a small circumambulation of the courtyard. She knew the movement would help her keep warm, as well as keep an eye out for Gabe's return.

It wasn't until she'd gone by the entrance to the keep again that she felt someone just behind her and wheeled around. In the dim light, she could see Alexander's face, worried. "Is he all right?"

Rathna tilted her head and just waited. Gabe had taught her that, Gabe and his parents. She didn't know Alexander as well as some. She kept busy with her own work. She'd been gone much of the past months. And while Alexander had been impeccable about his respect for her and her work, they didn't have that much overlap in interests. But she also knew Thesan loved him, as she'd love another brother or perhaps an uncle, that the Carillons trusted him implicitly, and that he'd been a reasonable amount of help to Gabe.

Alexander waited for her response, then, after a good half minute, snorted. "Unfair question." Then, carefully, "Did he tell you?"

"Tell me what, Alexander?" Rathna braced her shoulders.

"Anything about his challenge." Alexander was on an edge of something, like one of the children insisting on walking along the top of a tall wall when they'd been tiny. "What did he say?"

"He hasn't said anything about that. He's thinking." This was entirely the truth. Whatever else Gabe was doing at the moment, he was thinking. He was always thinking, that was the point of a Gabe, and one of the many things she loved in him. Besides, what could she say? He's off communing with the land. That was likely true, in some form. Not only because he often was doing that too, but because he'd had that particular look about him.

"Do you know where he is, then?" Alexander looked around the courtyard but there were shadows deep enough to hide in, even if Gabe had been here.

"I do." She kept her voice steady. Alexander had power, he had fierce magic curled around him, he had authority here, second or third only to Cyrus Smythe-Clive. She wasn't entirely sure how their hierarchy ran. Before she had to figure out what else to say, there was a call from inside. "Alexander? You're needed." One of the staff came to the door then, holding it open as Alexander turned and ducked inside, leaving her out in the cold again.

She had glanced at her watch twice, making it more like twenty minutes since he'd been gone, when she felt the portal flare. Felt it, because it was a portal, and she knew what that burst of magic meant, down to her bones. Gabe stepped out, and the first thing she realised was that he was glowing. It wasn't terribly bright, but it was persistent.

"Gabe," she called out from near the door. "Come inside. The blackout."

He hesitated for just a second, as if something hadn't made sense to him, then held out his hands in front of him and laughed. A moment later, he'd crossed the courtyard to the door, and offered her his arm without explanation, sweeping her inside.

She had never had the sort of dreams and ambitions some girls apparently did, of sweeping down a staircase and having the entire room fall silent. If she had, however, they would have been fulfilled in this moment. They stepped into the Great Hall, and the entire room stopped and looked at them.

Gabe escorted her in, glowing brighter now, if anything,

even against the brightness of the hall itself. It was a golden glow, warm and comfortable, not the heat that burned. His arms came around her and he swung her as if sliding into a waltz, turning her around twice before depositing her on two feet again. Somewhere in the midst, he had slid his staff back into being a cane, and he used it now in his offhand, walking her over to his parents. Who were blinking, naturally.

Gabe bent to kiss her cheek. "Much better now. Let me see what people say." With that, he was gone, leaving Rathna staring after him. When she could turn away from the glow and the magic and the certainty that made him right now, she found Alysoun leaning forward.

"You're baffled too? All right. We'll find out soon enough, I'm sure." Alysoun was watching him closely now. Gabe had made a beeline for Alexander, saying something that visibly unsettled Alexander for a moment, before adding something else that seemed to draw a laugh. Gabe nodded amiably to the other challengers who had come down, but after a moment, came to go to one knee by Maisie Wallace's chair. She was sitting with a small group of people, not all of them directly related, Rathna thought. Maisie looked exceedingly startled, but nodded at something. Gabe leaned in close to her.

It was a kind of intimacy that most wives would be jealous of. It had all the sucking void of envy and unsatisfied want to it, except Rathna knew that whatever they'd shared, she did not want to stand in that place. She was made for different things; she knew it, and what Maisie had dared to do didn't take anything from her.

Gabe talked to her for a minute or two, before standing, bowing to the others with her, and sweeping into a circle of smaller conversations. He shared a few words here, a few words there. By the time he'd got through three or four of those, Cyrus Smythe-Clive had reappeared, standing in the space in the front of the room. Gabe turned, caught sight of him, and walked over.

Rathna had watched her husband walk so many times now. She'd watched how he moved when his ankle was paining him, and on the average Tuesday. She'd seen him in exhaustion and in jubilation. This was something else, and it took her a little to figure out what it was. It was a procession, where each step was a connection with the ground and the space around him, claiming it motion by motion. He'd been like that at their wedding and perhaps a handful of times since.

It was beautiful, a kind of patience that Gabe rarely had time for. She could watch it for hours, and yet knew she'd never have hours of it, not all at once. This procession was short. Gabe came up to Cyrus Smythe-Clive. He did not bow; he did not lower his eyes, instead he stood straight and tall, the cane just barely visible where it leaned against his hip. The two of them talked for several minutes, more seriously.

It ended only when there was some commotion from the corridor, and someone was bringing out Lilac Powell. Her fine purple robes were smudged all over dust and soot, and there were tidal marks of mud up past her knees, as if she'd been through fires and floods. The man with her had an arm under hers, which she looked entirely offended about. She caught sight of Gabe and nearly flew into a fury, before something stopped her, and someone led her into a back room.

Gabe got the tilt to his head when he was waiting for a key piece of information. Smythe-Clive said something to him, and Gabe nodded once, then turned away. It was very much the way he was when he and Mason and Witt were working, when brevity was a compliment. Gabe came back to them, settling in his chair, crossing the bad ankle over the good knee, and leaning back. "Pardon, my love. Mama, Papa."

His parents did not comment on any of it and certainly not the glow. This was not the time nor the place. They were all aware of listening ears. Instead, they settled into an agreeable conversation about a recent article in the Trellech Moon, the style of the reporting. It mattered, and it didn't matter at all, and that seemed to be what all of them needed. Somewhere in that time, the glow faded, slowly enough that she did not see it go so much as notice that it was gone.

Gabe was halfway through another glass of wine when Warren Michaelton appeared, looking not much the worse for wear, but tremendously tired. He was taken back to his seat - a small group that Rathna expected might be guild-mates or colleagues - and given food and drink.

It was perhaps half an hour before - finally - Herana Phipps appeared. She was leaning heavily on Silvia Warren. Her fine robes were in tatters, as if she'd had entirely too close an encounter with massive claws, thornbushes, or perhaps some of both. There was a long scratch along her cheek, looking more like a sabre duelling scar than anything else. She had what looked like branches in her hair, and the torc had twisted off her neck somewhere in the midst.

She collapsed to her knees near the front of the room, looking for all the world like a toddler about to have a tantrum. Not a particularly high-quality one, Rathna felt, with some experience in the matter. It lacked dedication to its goals, certainly. She was taken off by two of the staff, followed by Silvia Warren and Mabyn Teague. When they emerged five minutes later, Rathna strongly suspected someone had applied a silencing charm to Mistress Phipps. She had a strain around her that suggested it.

Only when she was seated did Cyrus Smythe-Clive take a large staff and bring it hard to the floor three times. People had not been talking loudly or much at this point - it was late in a long night - but everyone fell quiet immediately. "We thank you for your witness to tonight's work. Gabriel Edgarton, please stand?"

Gabe rose beside her, squeezing her hand once before he let it go.

"Welcome to the Council of Albion. We will be in touch about the practicalities in the morning. For now, know that all of you who have challenged have our gratitude for your efforts and willingness. All of you are welcome to challenge again, at such time as we have an open seat, if you wish." There was a round of applause and acknowledgement from the room, but no one said anything else.

Rathna knew there were other wordings of that, but this meant that while people might choose not to challenge, no one had been forbidden it. Sometimes they were. Sometimes people died, and Gabe had come to a theory that those two things might be somewhat related.

Smythe-Clive spoke again, concluding the evening, apparently. "We welcome you to find your homes and rest."

That meant a line of the Council Members coming by them in reverse order of seniority. Rathna was fairly sure of that, though she didn't immediately recall the entire list. A brief handshake, a word or two of congratulations, some with more welcome to it than others. Silvia Warren was seething, even Rathna could see that, and Garin Fortier looked as if he'd swallowed a bushel of lemons. But Malcolm Rolls was warm. Lettice Fowler and Desmond Belling, both of whom she knew through the Astronomers' Guild, had a pleasant comment for Rathna as well as for Gabe.

It did allow the others to pour out quickly, the unsuccessful challengers and their assorted family and friends, who would go off to drown their sorrows rather than celebrate. Alysoun did not do well jostled in crowds, and it was their family custom in larger gatherings to wait until most of the people had gone.

In this case, of course, Alexander, Mabyn Teague, and Cyrus Smythe-Clive brought up the rear of the line. "Gabe." Alexander held out his hand. "I look forward to whatever explanation of the glowing you feel you can share in due course. As well as the rest of it."

Gabe inclined his head. "Let me think about how to tell it. The meeting, then, next Wednesday? Do you need me to make time before then?"

Alexander looked at Smythe-Clive, then the other man shook his head. "We can skip your usual project meeting for the week, unless something particular comes up. I know you'll have some other adjustments to make. We'll be in touch tomorrow with the diary dates through summer solstice, a number of practical aspects. You'll want to give thought to what you want in an office here, you can move your things in any time starting next Thursday. We'll key you to the warding just before the meeting, if you could be here by six."

"Wednesday - or before that - you are welcome to use mine." Alexander put that in quickly. "And if you do wish to talk before then, I put myself at your disposal."

"I trust you'll pass along the relevant message?" Gabe

raised an eyebrow. Rathna at least knew that reference, that Gabe meant Geoffrey.

"Already have." Alexander glanced over at the doors. "We should let you get home now." There were the usual polite murmurs, gathering up cloaks, and then going through the portal. Everyone else had melted away, though Alexander walked them out to it without further comment. Rathna and Gabe went through first, then waited for Alysoun and Richard.

Alysoun waved a hand at them. "You go on ahead. Perhaps we might talk over breakfast in our rooms?" She'd likely not make it far out of bed in the morning, between a short night and the strain of the evening. "Gabe, you are all right?" That, now, had just a hint of the worry Alysoun had been refusing to acknowledge all evening.

"Adjusting, Mama, but it's fine. Different than I expected, but I expected that." He came to give her a kiss on the cheek.

Richard nodded. "In the morning. I need to be in by ten at the latest. Do you think we could manage half-eight?"

Gabe did some maths in his head and nodded. "I'm off-duty tomorrow, though I've reading to do. Isobel can go in as usual, I let her know by journal earlier." While he had disappeared, presumably, she hadn't seen Gabe take out his journal the entire time. They parted, then, with Gabe keeping a hold of her hand all the way up to their rooms.

"Bathe?" she suggested. He hadn't done a lot of strenuous duelling, she could tell that, but she also thought he'd be happier if he'd washed properly. "Do you need a potion?"

"One of the light ones." Gabe kissed her cheek. "Won't be long." She immediately heard the water running, and she spent the next few minutes getting herself ready for bed. Potion for Gabe, her own jewellery off and safely put away, the long length of saree silk folded over the hanger on her wardrobe to be cleaned and stored properly. She was in bed for perhaps ten minutes before Gabe reappeared, his hair lightly damp.

He advanced on the bed with that same processional step, though it turned into more of a prowl. "How tired are you, bright lady?"

She blinked. "Does it involve leaving the bed?" It would not be beyond Gabe to suggest a late walk or even a ride, though he tried not to put out the stable staff, at least.

"Oh, no. Not at all." He half-flung himself on the bed, discarding the dressing gown and stretching out beside her in a single movement. She realised he was decidedly rampant. "Not an imposition, then?"

She twisted, her hand resting on his hip, feeling the way his skin was under her fingers. "What did you have in mind? It was - I don't even know how to label tonight for us, never mind you."

"I'd like some reminding of how good we have it. What it's like to be buried in you, nothing but you in the world. How you make me laugh, how you take me as I am and help me do more." He rolled partly onto his back. "All the reasons, piled up together. Returning to you."

"Well." She knew she was going to say yes any moment. He certainly knew it, the way his eyes were dancing. "Am I going to get an explanation for why you were glowing?"

"Oh, yes. Tomorrow. Rather do it once. Do you mind, terribly?"

"Not if you give me something else to think about." That made him laugh, and then he had nearly pounced on her, nuzzling and kissing at her neck as his hands found her skin and began stroking and teasing. He knew just what she liked - more than that, what she was likely to want in this unsettled mood. Soon, his fingers had slipped between her legs, and she was moaning, giving herself over to the moment as completely as she could.

When he entered her, not too much later, it was far more rapid and active than they'd done in years. The heat and urgency of their youth, where it was only about how quickly he was thrusting, how her hips were rocking to bring him deeper. Her fingers clenched at his back, and that made him groan and then bury his face against her shoulder, hips hitching harder and harder until they both were flung into ecstasy, one almost right after the other.

In the aftermath, it took Rathna a long time to catch her breath, and by the time she had, Gabe was thoroughly asleep on her shoulder. He almost never did that. He was a considerate lover, as well as a skilled one. Tonight, though, she didn't begrudge him one bit. Rathna managed to lever the blankets up enough to cover them, even if he was radiating enough heat to warm the room itself, not just her.

She stayed awake for quite a long time, as it turned out. It was rare she got to see Gabe deeply quiet, and now he was. Even in sleep, he often moved or shifted, like something in him had to keep turning to look at what new thing had intrigued him. Now, though, he slept like a child, deeply and securely. Finally, she drifted off herself, nestled against him.

CHAPTER 13
NOVEMBER 30TH AT VERITAS

There was a knock on the door at half-eight on the dot. Richard came round to open it. Alysoun was still in bed, a shawl around her shoulders, even though the fire was going well in the fireplace. She'd taken another of the potions she took when she needed to be clear-headed, but she'd likely sleep a fair bit of the day once they had done the necessary exchange of information.

At least, Richard hoped for a significant exchange of information. He knew, with all his instincts, both innate and trained, that as soon as he set foot in the Guard Hall, he'd be surrounded by people. They'd be offering congratulations, wanting favours, all wanting to find out more. As a family, they very much needed to present a unified front to the world, and he needed Gabe to lay out what he wanted from that.

"Come in, come in." Rathna was in her usual working dress when she expected to be out and about, skirt and blouse and jumper. Gabe, well. Last night, Gabe had been very much in his own working mode, interchangeable with a country squire tending to his land, tweed suit and all.

Today, he was in a forest green kurta of fine silk, and wheat golden loose trousers beneath it. It was one of the sets he'd brought back from his second visit to India with Rathna.

Gabe remained entirely himself, all the time. It was not an outfit he wore outside of the house, usually. Wearing it this early in the day strongly suggested he was actually going to stay put. By the gleam in his eye, though, Richard wasn't sure about the well-being of the workroom. Staying home would at least make the immediate interpersonal diplomacy easier on Richard. He wondered how much that was weighing in Gabe's decisions.

Rathna had immediately settled on the small sofa Richard had pulled to face the bed. He claimed a chair, set so he could take Alysoun's hand. Gabe took the other end of the sofa, though he immediately leaned toward Rathna, not quite draping himself in her lap. Yet. Chances were good it would come to that within a few minutes.

"Eat something, please." Alysoun said clearly. "There's quite a spread." There was, the cart had a chafing dish with eggs, fresh toast, cheese and marmalade and a smidge of butter, fried mushrooms, sauteed greens, and one each of the chicken sausages Rathna liked. A lot of food, given the rationing limitations, but Richard was starving, and he was sure Gabe was more so. Gabe didn't grumble for once, but reached for a plate, getting food for Rathna and handing it over before making up one for himself.

"I let various people know last night." This part was Richard's. "Our usual. Gil and Magni are in at the Guard Hall, listening for the gossip along with the rest of it." Some people knew where they lived these days, but not that many outside the Edgartons' more intimate social circles, so that would be quite some use. And it meant no one would pry too hard just yet for gossip. Though of course, many people in the Guard knew that Richard had apprenticed with Magni. "The Carillons, of course, though Geoffrey said Alexander had already sent a note along."

"When is the interesting question there, isn't it? When I came out, or just before the official announcement." Gabe paused, a piece of toast halfway to his mouth.

"Documentation first, Gabe, then hypothesis." Alysoun, a little behind his shoulder, definitely sounded amused. "And I assume you've been on to Mason and Witt."

Gabe nodded. "Last night. Related to why I slipped out for a few, we'll come back to that."

"And I wrote the Leftons. Isembard was there. I didn't bother to write to Thesan as well." Richard was clear those two were as mutually informative as anyone might like. "She was holding down the fort at Schola, of course. Tricky to have them both gone the same night, unless it's truly urgent." Their older daughter had just started at Schola this year, and would be in the dormitory in any case, but their younger son was still living in their rooms. At eight, Leo was too young to leave alone for terribly long, even if at least half the Schola staff would cheerfully have had him for the night if needed.

"And we went up to see Avigail before coming down here." Rathna said. "Gabe has promised to have luncheon with her, and other amusements after. I have said that they're not allowed to explode things in the workroom."

"But there might be some experimentation with colours. I did promise to see if we could come up with better coloured powders for Holi this coming year. I have been a trifle busy, but that's no excuse, and it'd be an interesting lesson for her." Gabe spread his hands, amused.

Alysoun sighed, but it was her amused sigh. Richard twisted to pat her hand, then stood to arrange the bed tray for her and hand her a plate of food. "If you're all over shades of blues and pinks and reds at supper, I suppose we're forewarned." She considered. "Isobel?"

"Already off for the day. Witt has something she'll find interesting." Richard picked up the note in Gabe's voice at that. Or rather, more of it. Gabe had been sounding deeply contented so far all this morning, in a way that was more than a little new.

Then Richard considered something. "Any particular reason for the colours today?" He was slow off the mark at the moment. It had taken him near half a minute to spot that.

Gabe chuckled. "Something from last night, Papa."

"How did you get from your challenge to colours for Holi?" Richard had to ask, and for several reasons.

That got Gabe throwing his head back, a long and loud laugh. "Hemington's Fifth, one of the scribal errors from Erasmus Minor, the implications for fixatives, that thing Sorcha taught us about blaeberries, the way shed snake skin reacts in potions work, and stumbling into a patch of blackberries?" He laid out the chain almost casually. Long experience of his son had taught Richard how to follow it once it was laid out. But he would not have made half those jumps, even allowing for the fact Gabe had a vast store of obscure magical lore in his head that Richard did not.

Alysoun's voice came over his shoulder, very dry. "Are we advancing to the discussion of last night, then?"

Gabe waved his fork. "If you're about to tell me to eat my vegetables, Mama, I am working on it. Well, technically, fungi, but they're good for me too." Gabe was decidedly in a mood, then. A good one. A glowingly sunny one, though the actual glowing part had subsided well before they got back last night. He took another couple of bites.

Rathna was looking at her husband with amusement. "What do we need to cover today, then?"

"Enough that Richard can go through the Guard Hall and know what to say, first and foremost." Alysoun had worked that out, of course. "And then whatever else we'd find useful to share or avoid talking about. Gabe, love, I'm guessing there are some things you'll not be talking about yet."

Gabe swallowed, and then set his plate and fork down on the cart. "Some of it I'm not ready to, some of it really needs to be said to the Council first, and some of it - I don't know. Maybe never to anyone. I can't tell yet." He glanced from one to the other, ending up looking squarely at Rathna. "You don't mind?"

It was Rathna who answered first, and Richard was glad, all over again, that she understood this part of their lives. "You've always had things you can't talk about, Gabe. This is a new category, but it seems likely to be better defined from outside? Definable? I don't know what the word is."

Gabe leaned to kiss her, full on the lips, then did the shift of hips and shoulders that landed him with his head in her lap. He looked for all the world like a momentarily contented cat. Richard glanced back at Alysoun, who said agreeably. "Rathna's right. This is nothing new, for you or for Richard. You've always had cases you can't discuss. I've long since made my peace with it."

"And I know I don't understand half what's in your head, and I've experience with that feeling," Richard added. "Right. Out with whatever you're sharing."

Gabe grinned at him, the sharp grin that was near a salute, not that Gabe actually moved his hands. "Sir." Richard remained fascinated - as he had for decades now -

at how Gabe made that an endearment, not a stiff formality. It was a gesture at respecting Richard's own ingrained sense of formality and Gabe made it a gift, every time. Gabe considered for only a moment. "A maze, a handful of puzzles. I had a conversation with a particular snake." He shrugged, and Richard very much wanted to have already dissected his mien in those moments with Alysoun. Something had changed in the quality of the glass and mirror that was Gabe, and maybe Alysoun would have words to name it properly.

Rathna's hand was on Gabe's shoulder before any of them had any other reaction. "And the glow?" That was Alysoun behind him. None of them wanted to press directly about the snake, apparently. Richard expected Rathna might, in due course, as she had before, but even she wasn't bringing it up now.

"Ah. That. That's easier." Gabe shrugged his shoulder. The visible one. "I felt the bombing raid. There was one came down at Goudhurst. The edge of the estate proper. It'd have taken out one of the cottages and everyone there."

"It would have?" Richard had felt unsettled last night, but there were good reasons for that, even before the general unsettlement of the war and the relentless bombing. He couldn't have pulled that thread out of his feelings for all the world.

"Diverted it. No casualties, though I'm afraid one of the outbuildings is a total loss. Irving passed a note along last night when they checked on it." One of the villagers, up that way, and magical. Usefully in the Home Guard, so he tended to know what was going on quickly.

"Oh." Richard rubbed his face with one hand, then the bridge of his nose. He could feel a headache starting, just thinking about the implications. "Is that something you expect to be an ongoing role? Or just last night, fresh out of whatever it was with the puzzles and the snake?"

Gabe lifted up on his elbow. "You know, Papa." His voice was deadly earnest now. "You know I'd do everything I could for our land. And our people."

"I do. I always have." Richard tried his best to put all his own belief into those few words. From the time Gabe had become his heir in truth, Richard had had no doubts, not about Gabe's love of the land, not about Gabe's capacity. He worried a great deal - and more this year than perhaps all the years before - about what that drive would get Gabe into. But he had no doubt about Gabe's desires and commitment.

"I don't know yet. I'll have to see how it wears on me." Gabe lowered his head to Rathna's lap again.

"And the glowing?" Alysoun shifted behind him, sitting up and moving the pillows so she could settle her hand against Richard's back. He appreciated that rather a lot right now.

Gabe snorted. "It is not as if anyone has given me a guidebook, Mama. I did get the impression last night that the glowing was not the usual thing, and I'd rather upstaged the official announcement."

"You did have a number of glares in your direction. I needn't warn you to be careful of the Powells, the Sisleys, the Phipps, or the Rixes. Or their extended clans." Alysoun agreed.

"Not that I was much likely to be in more intimate settings with any of them. I did rather like the look of Michaelton, though. I should write and see if he'll chat in a week or two. And Maisie Wallace, I liked her very much." Gabe considered. "And I don't believe Lord Sisley much cares for Lycus, but he's serving somewhere overseas right

CELIA LAKE

now, so it will take a bit to find out where he stands. Isembard might be handy there, but I'll be cautious of the ones in Albion."

"The question about Maisie Wallace, love, is whether you've completely terrified her." Alysoun was back to sounding dryly amused.

Rathna shook her head. "Not terrified her. She was all alone with something she didn't understand at all, and she wanted it, and - I don't know what you said, Gabe, but it mattered." There was an iron steadiness in Rathna's voice, the kind Richard didn't tend to hear often. She didn't need to break it out for them, though Gabe and Alysoun had both helped her hone it over the years.

Alysoun took the - no, it wasn't a rebuke - the information in stride. "Pardon, Rathna. You had a better view of it, obviously. Gabe?"

Gabe stretched a little, rearranging himself. "Rathna has it right, of course. She got the strong inclination? I didn't have time to get into details. Anyway, that she should challenge again, as soon as there's another seat. I promised to talk through things with her. And help with less ridiculous clothing, she'd have been much more comfortable in something else."

"I did think that was an interesting contrast. You and Michaelton in working clothes, and everyone else in - well, I can see why Herana needed a dozen fittings, or thought she did." Alysoun shook her head. "Pity to see such fine workmanship only get one wearing, though."

That made Gabe laugh again, roll with it. When he finally quieted down, he managed to find more words. "Mama, you always have an eye for it. All right. I suppose that brings us to the hypothesis, and then to what we do about the gossip."

Alysoun nodded beside Richard. "Smythe-Clive implied that the Council would know, with that 'we', once someone was successful. But I note none of them came to congratulate you then."

"Not a word." Gabe agreed. "Though I startled Alexander somehow, I don't think that was it." He lifted his fingers. "Still thinking through what might have done it. I was a trifle occupied at the time with not falling down the stairs."

"We appreciate that you did not do the extremely challenging magical and mythological ritual and then break your neck on the way out, yes. It would have been a waste." Alysoun snorted at it. "Please continue to be sensible like that. When do you think they knew?"

"It's hard to tell with the Council," Gabe pointed out. "Ugh. And now there I am, in the midst of it."

"An inexorable outcome of last night's events, Gabe. Go on, your father does have to get into the Guard Hall." Trust Alysoun to keep an eye on the time.

"I think the Council knew, but they don't announce it for some reason. I want to know whose sadistic idea it was to make everyone sit around waiting. It's not like there was any ritual beyond the brief gesture at it at the end. We do normally like our chains of office and all that, don't we, as a people? I suppose some of that comes later, next week. When it's just Council. And more at Winter Solstice, though there must be a private part, before the public." Gabe shook his head, going on. "I mean, I'm not the ritualist Alexander is. Why is it like that? It's terribly broken."

That visibly reminded him of something. He lifted his fingers. "Digression. Rathna, love, I have it on excellent authority that we should treat your theory about the Pact and Silence acting as an eruv as reality."

Rathna blinked down at him. Richard could see she went entirely still, until Gabe murmured at her, something in Bengali. Richard only knew a few words of it, mostly the endearments and family names, but whatever Gabe said settled things immediately, and Rathna cupped his cheek.

Then Gabe picked up, as if there had been no interruption. "Though of the things that need untangling there, I admit it is actually probably fairly well down the list. For one thing, it doesn't come up all that often. Eight seats in the past decade, including me." Richard rather thought that he was trying that on, how it sounded when it was said out loud.

"So we should have some more information next Wednesday. Or you will, at least, whatever you can share. Do you know much about the meetings?"

"I need to ask Alexander a few questions about how they run, and exactly what the limits are on what I can say right off. The actual limits, not the customary limits, so I rather suspect it's more like whatever Cyrus lets me get away with," Gabe said. "But I can probably do that by journal, unless I need to get him to say something directly." He grimaced. "Bugger. I forgot I had something scheduled this afternoon. I need to remember to rearrange that."

Alysoun said, bemused, "You need a secretary, honestly, Gabe." Richard held himself still.

Gabe didn't argue, not like he had last time. Instead, he just shrugged, as if that trivial detail wasn't worth bothering with. The trick of it, he'd figured out at last, was that Gabe thought it'd be more work to tell someone what was inside his head. Also - and not entirely unreasonably - that no one who might want the job was going to be up to it. Gabe was not wrong, exactly, but Richard and Alysoun held out hope there was someone who'd find it just their sort of challenge.

Now, Gabe just forged on. "Right. Then. That brings us to politics, I think."

"Rathna, did you need more tea?" Alysoun was keeping an eye on everything, really, but it also served to give Rathna a moment to say something if she wanted.

"Please, if you don't mind. Gabe is being rather insistently present." Not that Rathna minded, obviously; her hand kept drifting to brush his hair. Richard took his cue and poured more tea into her cup. "Thank you, Richard."

"The other challengers aren't going to like you much. Are you involved in any cases where it might be a problem?" Alysoun was relentless, and Richard was glad of it. Sorting through this sort of thing with her was much easier.

"Mostly the Council work at the moment. We were thinking of having me consult on a case for Witt, but she can get someone else. That's one of the Rix cousins. Better leave me out of it. Dumping of alchemical by-products. Isobel can do the analysis work, probably, without being too closely connected. Loft can supervise; it's right up her alley." And Margaret Loft was not remotely connected to their family any other way than through the Penelopes.

"What sort of information do we want to give out, then?" Rathna considered. "I don't expect to be outside the Portal Keeper spaces too much the next few days, bar bombs disrupting a portal somewhere."

"But if that's the case, everyone's going to be too busy to gossip while you're there. At least with you." Gabe nodded. "Most of what I need to do right now is analysis, actually. I can go in and do that. I can bring some of it here. Depends on what's helpful."

Alysoun considered the options, her fingers tapping

along Richard's back as she thought. "Gabe, I think you want to make a public appearance sometime over the weekend, in Trellech. Assuming no crisis." She flicked her hand to knock lightly on the wood of the bedside table. "Supper out, with Rathna. Not me, I think, but you might see about Charlotte and Lewis. Other than that, we are all very proud and delighted. Gabe earnestly wishes to be of service in this, as in his other work, best wishes to all the other challengers. People will doubt all of it, of course, but they'll doubt everything we say. We can see about picking up further gossip as it comes."

"We can sort that out," Gabe agreed, before he added, more quietly. "Don't think I don't appreciate all the exertion, Mama. Can I do anything today to be a help?"

"Finish up with Avigail and clean up early enough to keep me company for tea." Alysoun had a ready answer there, if quite a common one when she got the chance. "In here, quite possibly, but we'll see if I make it to the baths and the library later." If she made it down to the baths, the library was rather more likely. And the soak would do her good.

"Of course, Mama." There were a number of things that pleased Richard about his son, but he thought that perhaps this was one of the greatest. Unlike so many families, unlike Richard himself, he loved his mother and let it show. He loved Richard too, though that came out differently. As Richard was trying to figure out what else to say, the chime on his pocketwatch went off.

"I should clean up and get along. Need anything brought back from Trellech, Gabe?" Richard shifted to set his plate down, then to stand.

"I'll take a look and let Mason know. She'll drop

anything off by—" Gabe considered the likely schedules. "Three?"

"Three is good. I need my office at four for a meeting. Go on. Walk Rathna to the portal. I want a word with your mother."

Gabe smiled, bouncing up sunnily. He paused by the bed to kiss his mother's cheek, offered another wave of his hand to Richard, and then gave his arm to Rathna. Richard waited until they were out the door and well down the hall before he turned back to Alysoun. "Is Gabe baffling you too, love?" He hoped so. Or he hoped not. It would be nice if one of them understood their son properly. On the other hand, it would be pleasant to not be alone with his bafflement.

"I think he's doing remarkably well." Alysoun said, patting Richard's hand. "And I am also baffled. We've time to work it out. Do you think you can manage the gossip now?"

Richard considered. "Be steadfast, proud of him, and don't say much? I think I can manage that." It did play to his strengths, after all. "I'll let you know what I hear, as always. I should be able to write a little over lunch, and half-three, and then supper?"

"Excellent. One more kiss, for luck?" Richard bent down to kiss her, taking his time about it. Luck, indeed. He was the most fortunate of men, to have a family like he did, and friends as well. Once he straightened up, he tore himself away to put on the last bits of uniform and head for the portal, or he was in fact going to be late.

CHAPTER 14
DECEMBER 2ND IN TRELLECH

"Mama, do you have everything you need and want?" Charlotte bustled around, distributing tea. Then she smiled, suddenly. "Well, achievable wants this afternoon? Tisane, yes. A biscuit apiece, yes, rationing being what it is, and some apples. Your notes, here. Lizzie, here's your cup, here's the rest of the food." She sat down herself in a swirl of movement, her skirts falling into place in a pool of green.

The three of them had claimed the library in the Edgarton townhouse in Trellech. For one thing, it was closer to where they'd been all afternoon than the Carillon townhouse. It also had fewer small children in and out than Charlotte's home - and fewer listening ears, given her younger two were nine and going on four. The staff here, as with the Carillons, were impeccably trained. Also, unlikely to be tempted to listen in, because the sound charms were entirely up to snuff. Charlotte had grown up thinking about that sort of thing, but her life now didn't involve it nearly as often.

They had spent a rather fatiguing three hours at a charitable event, the sort of 'sales for the troops' to support the Healing Temple that Alysoun felt was slightly ridiculous. She'd much rather just give money for the Temple's needs, rather than fuss around proclaiming about lace doilies, clothing for dolls, or various unimaginatively embroidered accessories.

She had been particularly caught in horrified fascination by a rather stunningly awful set of holiday decorations which mingled every vaguely winter holiday in Albion together in one glowing mound that included a ceramic dragon, a chimney, spiky branches meant to be evergreens, and a number of awkwardly placed lights. It had a charm that made a garbled noise every time someone walked by it until Charlotte had muffled it under a stack of tea cosies. No, not quite every holiday. It had been decidedly lacking a bull for Mithras.

On the other hand, it was important to make a showing, not only doing their part but being seen to do it. Charlotte had arranged things - she was on the committee this year - so that Alysoun had stayed in one place, and Lizzie had circulated from station to station. Charlotte herself had been nearly everywhere, making Alysoun think of an otter scampering in play, then bringing its friends along for the fun.

"I thought it went very well. There were no obvious arguments over the crafts," Alysoun began.

"No, just extensions of what was that, eight ongoing feuds?" Lizzie made herself comfortable in her chair. "Or did I miss one?"

"Three, Lizzie." Charlotte grinned. "I mean, besides my brother." She ticked them off on her fingers. "Stall arrangements, award for most festive centrepiece, and the winner of the award for best baked goods."

"Ah, well. I wouldn't have heard the details of those. Do tell, in the proper order." Lizzie didn't look offended, of course, rather entirely amused. "We must properly list our feuds, or where would we be in the world?"

It got a laugh from all of them. Better laughter than tears. Alysoun had played this social game for a very long time. She'd been bred and brought up to it. She hadn't wanted to land it on Charlotte's shoulders, but Charlotte honestly seemed to enjoy it in modest doses. And Charlotte wasn't a lady of the land, wasn't a magistrate's wife. She could dip in and out of it more easily. Lizzie hadn't been brought up to it, but she'd taken it on as surely as any other part of the life that came with her marriage. She had a deft touch in conversation that Alysoun deeply valued.

"So. The less personal feuds, then?"

Those took them twenty minutes or so, getting them through the first cup of tea, a round of food. None of them were terribly important, at least not at the moment. But all three of them knew that could change, often rapidly, depending on circumstances. Swapping what they knew, sharing the wealth of their knowledge and the tidbits they each knew, made things vastly easier. That brought them to the more complex ones.

"Did you see Margot Williams?" Charlotte asked, as they paused to consider their options. "Wasn't she abroad for quite a long time?"

"Her husband is a diplomat, he was posted to Paris. She entirely liked it there, but of course, now." Lizzie frowned. "I don't know if he's in Vichy, or if he's come home, too." Her nose wrinkled. "Not a pleasant man, though I've only met him once or twice."

"And her?" Charlotte leaned her elbow on her knee, leaning forward to take another biscuit. "She seemed very sleek. On the prowl for something, but I got the impression a charity fete is not her native environment."

"Not nearly enough men," Alysoun said. When Charlotte looked up, Alysoun waved a hand. "I don't know her well either. She was on the outskirts of your grandmother's circle for a while. Not close in, but not, hmmm. In competition. For one thing, she does enjoy the company of men a great deal."

"Ah. One of those. Flattery, flirtation, and finery." Charlotte put the label on it precisely. "Right. Lavendaria Newton was on about things again. She still holds a grudge, doesn't she, Lizzie?" Charlotte had the advantage of the fact that Lavendaria and her clan had not connected her to the Carillons.

"Still, yes. Honestly, it's been near twenty years. She's been married longer than I have." Lizzie looked more amused than upset. "She can't have Geoffrey. He's busy. Also not remotely interested in her. What was she on about this time?"

"Two insults about your frock, one about your hair, a bit of sniping about the quality of the woven goods on display. The usual, really, but she had a new knot of people around her, a couple of women I don't know well. Hebe Price and Glamoris Heddle."

Alysoun tilted her head. "What are their affiliations?"

"I meant to check the Gold Book. I know only some of it. Let me get it." Charlotte was the youngest of them, of course, that made sense. She brought the hefty copy of the most recent Gold Book back. "Hebe Price is niece to Randolph Price, who - wasn't he the one your Geoffrey skewered in the press last month?"

"Unusually, yes." Geoffrey Carillon did not usually take to such public modes. But he'd been directly called out on a matter of his horses, and not speaking up would be worse. "He wouldn't sell Randolph a horse, is the backstory." Lizzie grimaced. "Rufus wouldn't send a horse of ours to those stables. Bad care, bad fodder, they've lost two to foundering in the past year."

"So a personal grudge, with reason, not a political one." Charlotte flicked through the book again. "And Glamoris Heddle. Oh, she's married to Tessera Douglas's sister-in-law's brother." Which was convoluted as a sentence, but about par for the course when it came to Great Families feuding.

"They are all Fox to the core, and think far less of anyone who isn't. Which lets out both of you. And I am dubious because of my children. If I were a proper Fox, Gabe would be too, as well as Charlotte." Alysoun shook her head. "Why people can't think that there's good having a more diverse world, I have no idea. It's certainly more interesting."

"I've heard Thesan and Isembard's arguments on the houses," Lizzie said, considering. "And rather more of Alexander's rant on the topic. He's someone who was put in Fox, and it did him no favours, I think we all agree on that."

"Other than a certain amount of entry into the circles of people who are snobs about it, no." Alysoun frowned at that. "Though that brings us to the question of Gabe and the feuds, doesn't it?"

"It does." Lizzie shifted, pulling over her notebook. "Now, this is an imperfect cast of the net, for the obvious reasons."

"We're working at a remove from the Council, sometimes three or more, and also, there are other related factors." Alysoun nodded. "But anywhere to begin is better than nothing."

"As far as I can tell, there's five broad divisions of the Council themselves. Two generally positively inclined toward Gabe, two decidedly not but for possibly different reasons, and one set who seem to want to stay neutral, thank you. Mind, I got some of this out of Alexander last night, and the ground is rapidly changing. He doesn't hear all of it, of course, especially since he rather pointedly took Gabe's part in things, and the others on the Council know that."

Alysoun hesitated, feeling her fingers catch on her skirt for a moment. She wanted to ask about this, needed to understand it, but it was delicate, and she knew it. "What did Alexander say about Thursday?"

Lizzie took a moment, the kind of settling patient breath that Alysoun knew well. Then, very gently, she spoke, the words clear and precise. "Alexander is delighted. Not surprised at Gabe's success, but I think - this is implication, not explication - not entirely in the way Alexander expected. Something in that night startled him, deeply, but he hasn't talked about it yet with me. Or with Geoffrey."

"So not with anyone, then. Except maybe Smythe-Clive."

"Maybe. Alexander mentioned Gabe had been in touch about the parameters for the meeting." Here, Lizzie's eyes gleamed. "He'll be in a mood when he gets home, Wednesday, I entirely expect. To forewarn your household. I gather they're giving him free rein to speak."

"That's. That's unusual, isn't it?" Alysoun did not know how precisely how the Council ran things, though she was going to be learning that quickly, she expected. Gabe would want to talk through what he could in the future.

"As Alexander put it, Cyrus is quite aware they owe Gabe several large favours, and he has refused to call them in on his own behalf. Every time they've tried to even things out, he's asked for something of a larger benefit to Albion. Even bringing Rathna home in June. She's been everywhere, working on mending portals or shoring them up, since she got back. Cyrus has the sense to know it."

Alysoun nodded. Charlotte broke in. "Pardon, Lizzie. You call him Cyrus?"

"In private conversation, yes. A habit picked up from Alexander, partly, but also Smythe-Clive is awkward to keep saying. And - whatever he and Alexander were, they have sorted themselves out the last few years. Thankfully, or things would be entirely more of a mess." She flipped her hands palm up. "And Gabe told you what Geoffrey promised, yes?"

"That if Gabe succeeded, you and Geoffrey - Geoffrey, in particular - would be making an effort there. Not just yet, I assume." Alysoun had heard that nearly immediately.

"Not quite. But decidedly more of one at Winter Solstice, we're planning on staying until they shoo everyone home, rather than making our bow and going away as soon as possible. Geoffrey has plans to exert his charm, though he's still deciding exactly which directions to work." Lizzie shrugged. "Cassie's remaking a frock for me for the purpose, all very currently in mode."

"And are you thinking of making our connections more public?" Alysoun immediately added, "I can see the value both ways, though I'd want to talk it through at home, of course."

Lizzie laughed. "We came to the same conclusion. We should see about tea for everyone available in a fortnight? Enough time to coordinate plans, close enough to the event that we should have a good range of information."

"I'll check diaries when I get home." Alysoun agreed. "All right. So Alexander has made his affiliations clear. Who else is well-inclined?"

"Cyrus and Mabyn. Not that they're tipping their hands in public, but they've been clear about it in private. Malcolm Rolls also thinks well of Gabe, having seen his work the past year."

"Well, that's something. That diligent - if erratically timed - excellence does win some people over." Alysoun nodded. "Who else is inclined?"

"Vidya Archarya's the easy one. She likes Rathna, generally speaking, and she's in favour of a wider range of perspectives on the Council. Lettice Fowler knows Thesan fairly well, as well as Rathna, and she was inclined to take Thesan's advice to make her mind up for herself. Also, I gather Gabe helped with something she was working on a few years ago, and she found him impulsive but clever enough to make up for it."

"There's an accurate description of Gabe for you." Charlotte laughed at it.

"And Alcesta Romilly and Laodamia Noble are both newer to the Council. But Alcesta apparently had encouraging divinatory readings - I don't know the details, don't bother asking - and Laodamia thinks well of Mason, in particular."

"Gabe mentioned the Materia interests in common. And he can hold his own there."

"Which brings us to the more challenging ones. Silvia

Warren remains, apparently, entirely in a snit. Even Mabyn hasn't got very far with her, and the actual Challenge and how poorly Herana did certainly won't help." Lizzie shook her head. "That's one where I think the actual meeting may be telling. And of course it hasn't happened yet."

"No, but it's at least one where Gabe has a good idea what information she has." Alysoun considered the options there. "Is it because of changes in the Council, because Gabe is utterly unlike anyone Hesperidon would have approved of, or something else?"

"All three, probably. Silvia does think widely, from all I understand, given the opportunity. Her son's also married to Lillit Castleton's eldest. Not a family who approves of impulse and pleasure."

Alysoun coughed. "I remember when Geoffrey took her out. Lillit's the sort who wanted the kind of marriage that not only involves separate beds or sets of rooms, but separate houses in distant parts of the country. I gather the same is true of her daughter. It wasn't just men or anything like that. She didn't seem to take much pleasure in anything at all."

"I feel sorry for her, honestly." Lizzie said. "But I can be generous, having the benefit of Geoffrey's tastes in pleasure in all things as much as will fit into a day." She looked entirely smug about that, and well, she had some right to be.

Charlotte grinned broadly. "You and Mama have set an excellent example on that front. And Gabe and Rathna, too, honestly. Anyone else specifically cranky at him?"

Lizzie cleared her throat. "Garin Fortier. With some reason, and Alexander and Isembard are keeping a firm eye on that. I don't think it'd come to a direct attack, but Gabe should keep an eye over his shoulder. Garin's still, well.

Unpredictable is the charitable way to put it. He and Isembard had a massive row when Gabe put his name in." That was to Charlotte. Lizzie and Alysoun had talked it through thoroughly.

"Mama told me the outline. All right. That's not one Gabe's going to budge easily, if he ever does. Who else?" Bless Charlotte for driving them forward, really.

"Alexander had some intimations that neither Troilus Watts nor Godfrey Perran are terribly happy with it, but no specifics. Then we've got people who are rather setting their claws in against change. Probably the wrong metaphor, but Theo Carrington, Rhoda Morwen, Ivor Harris, and Ulric Monkton. The Morwens are hypocrites about it, mind, they've been on the cutting edge of every new fad for decades now."

"And whatever else Gabe means, change is a fair accusation." Alysoun could agree with that. Change that she suspected was much needed, from the various pieces she'd picked up, but people did resist it. "That leaves what, Kerran Pembroke, Desmond Belling, and Nonus Powell as neutral?"

"Oh, that's where it gets interesting. Nonus is Lilac's uncle, but he wasn't standing up for her. You noticed that. He begged off as too close to the situation, but of course, everyone's reading it now as having some other cause. That's what I was trying to find out more about today." Lizzie leaned forward, her eyes glittering now.

"Out with it!" Alysoun was amused. It wasn't very often that they got something really good out of these social obligations.

"I gather Lilac's had a hankering for the Council since her uncle succeeded at his challenge. But she was listening to a - well, Alexander put it as 'a lot of tosh' about what to do to prepare. She wouldn't listen to him, for one thing."

"And whatever happened to her in there, it seemed to involve a fair bit of mud. And smoke."

"There's a whole layer of her hair singed near to the scalp, apparently. Part of what I heard today was about sorting out the hairdressing. She hasn't shown her face in public since. But she's furious at Gabe for coming through it without looking like he'd done anything other than a stroll in the park." Lizzie paused. "It wasn't that easy, though, was it?"

Alysoun shook her head. "He wouldn't talk to us about it, other than the sort of entirely odd sentences where he could mean it six ways, and it's not clear yet which one's accurate. A maze, a few puzzles, a conversation." She waved her hand. "And then he came out and said he nearly fell down the stairs, so make of that what you will."

"That matches up well enough with Alexander's comments - not the more personal ones, he didn't share those, but Gabe reappearing - that they're probably both true." Lizzie said. "So, whatever it was, it had weight, but didn't do him harm."

"No, he was entirely bright eyed and bushy-tailed Friday. He stayed home, but that was as much to let the gossip bubble as anything else. And spend some time with Avigail, with an entirely legitimate reason to skive off for a day."

Charlotte snorted. "Mama, Gabe never skives off. He's doing six other things that also needed doing for his obligations. Though I admit, seeing to the education of the next generation covers a lot of ground. And we had a lovely dinner out with Gabe and Rathna Saturday night. He had quite a few people stop to congratulate him - we were in the little side room at the Lapin Bleu. You know how easy it is to have someone spot you and stop in."

"Which is why you chose it," Lizzie agreed. "Anyone behave oddly?"

Charlotte cocked her head. "I made notes, but nothing that seemed unusual. Lady Beaupres and her husband stopped by, which I thought a little interesting. They've skirted around Gabe in the past."

"That's an interesting connection - the current Lord's sister tried to entangle Geoffrey." Alysoun knew all about that. She'd helped Geoffrey untangle a touch of it. Edith Beaupres had found herself pregnant, by someone else entirely. Geoffrey had been careful only to see her in public, suitably observed. She'd gone to Canada for a year, come back without the child, married someone, and seemed quite happy with it, under the circumstances. Alysoun had never been sure what that meant for others with a certain amount of freedom.

"Something about an idea Gabe had proposed around Lammastide having more consequences than expected." Charlotte said. "They were talking around it - they knew me, but weren't sure about talking in front of Lewis, I think."

"We'll go gently around that at solstice, then," Lizzie said. "Thank you, Charlotte. That's very helpful for me to bring back to Geoffrey."

Charlotte nodded. "So. Anyone else?"

They consulted their various notes, but all shook their head. "That means we can settle into an entirely blissful discussion of embroidered goods and their uses in prolonging a feud. Three generations now, isn't it, for the Gascombs?"

"Depends how you count the cousins in. It might be

four. Did you ever hear the beginning of that, Charlotte? I got some of it, oddly enough, from your grandmother, while she was still speaking to me." That made a more enjoyable note to end on. The story had a dozen twists and turns and intermarriages. Someone could turn it into a saga of a novel, changing the names and details slightly, and have a best-seller, certainly.

CHAPTER 15
DECEMBER 4TH AT THE COUNCIL KEEP

Gabe waited in the hallway as patiently as he could manage. Actually, he felt remarkably patient, given the circumstances. He knew a great many things hinged on this next conversation, and no amount of planning would solve the problem. He would have to react in the moment, as quickly and surely as in an alchemical lab combining unknown substances thanks to an accident. Gabe had done that three times this fortnight already. At least he was in practice. Even if tonight, the dangers and challenges should all be words, not magic. Not that there was often all that much space between words and magic.

Today, he felt remarkably well rested, considering everything. There had been several bombs in Kent last night, but none very near them, with no unmendable damage. He'd been able to spend the night with Rathna, soaking in her company, and have a ride in the morning. The rest of the day had gone to working through a variety of notes and materials for his actual duties, as well as managing to solve a problem Witt had been chewing on for three days. His ankle was even behaving remarkably well, only the dull ordinary ache.

Alexander had been waiting for him at the portal, and had given him a brief tour of the Council areas of the Keep - bar the upstairs challenge chamber - while others set up for the meeting. He'd left Gabe in the hall to wait while they began things formally. It was not a long wait. In the end, it was maybe five minutes before the double doors opened, and Alexander came out to show Gabe in.

The room, the heart of the Council keep, presumably, was more or less what Gabe had expected. No large central table. Gabe suspected that put people too close together for comfort in some cases. And he himself was glad to avoid the obvious Arthurian implications. Instead, there was a ring of chairs around the edge of a large room, upholstered in well-worn and well-tended leather in a mix of shades of brown. A circular carpet covered the central space, woven and decorated with various magical plants and symbols.

Gabe thought it dated from the Norwich carpet makers of the 16th century, carefully preserved. It was heaving with magic, too, and not just the preservation charms. He desperately wanted to spend a few hours with it, to understand what it did, but he thought it was primarily for clarity of speech. Not a bad thing in a meeting room. The rest of the room gave that same feel of aged furniture, carefully tended and preserved with an eye to a long history, visible everywhere he looked.

Alexander did not take his own seat, instead gesturing for Gabe to stand in front of Cyrus's chair, at the centre of the wall opposite the door. It left his back to the door, and to the people with chairs in a good half the room, nearly two-thirds. Gabe did not like that at all. There were, Alexander had assured him, oaths about not attacking a fellow member of the Council. But Gabe did not know how much those were custom, or how well they would hold. He was sure the placement was deliberate, and he was equally sure it was unnecessarily adversarial.

However, he knew what to do. He approached Cyrus, bowing his head once, properly in the mode of junior expert to senior. "Council Head."

"We begin with the oath. Each of us has made this oath, reaching back to November of 1484, when first we were formed. These days, we take it in two modes, the original Latin, and in a modern form." Cyrus let the syllables of the original roll off his tongue. All quite understandable to Gabe, though there were, of course, shifts in pronunciation. Gabe repeated it, paying more attention to the shape of the oaths, the way they touched his own magic and his existing commitments, than to the precise words. He'd seen the words already, after all. Alexander had shared that much on Monday.

Then he repeated them, in modern English, with additions for current considerations, like the Official Secrets Act. There was nothing new here, and he could feel the Council oath slip in, weaving itself tightly into all the oaths he'd ever made. Gabe appreciated Cyrus's deftness with the magic. That was nicely done. It finished, as Gabe was aware it would, "And I swear on my magic, bound by the Pact and the Silence, to uphold my part and give my best to the work of the Council through flood, through fire, through war or famine, charm or glamour, no matter what danger might come to Albion." It was an oath he could make freely, and he appreciated that there was no hint of swearing to any particular person as head.

When it was finished, he raised his head, softening his eyes rather than focusing on Cyrus alone, so he could watch

Mabyn and Alexander's expressions. Especially Alexander's. He'd been sure the other man was reading how well the oaths took, now that he had the skills to do so himself. Alexander had a hint of a smile, a warmness Gabe had not entirely expected to see.

Cyrus broke the silence with an agreeable. "Be welcome, Gabe, as one of us. A toast." Alexander pressed a glass of wine into Gabe's fingers as Cyrus lifted his own. "May the Pact be honoured in all ways, may Albion prosper, and may Gabriel Edgarton bring gifts beyond counting to the Council's work." It was a tad florid, but Gabe waited for the echo of the toast - clearly traditional, no one stumbled over it - before lifting his own glass and drinking. He could feel the magic coiled there, a matter of sympathetic resonance, as he swallowed, as well as the quite respectable vintage.

The glass was plucked out of his hand as soon as he finished, and Alexander gestured. "Your chair is here." Next to Cyrus's left hand, which suggested that it was a common place for the newest. Gabe nodded, and placed his satchel there, drawing out a notebook and pen, but leaving the rest of his supplies tucked away.

Cyrus was still standing when he turned back. "You asked for the floor to begin. Please. Proceed." There was something in his expression that boded very well - Gabe thought it might actually be amusement. Or it might be a problem Gabe had not remotely anticipated. That was the thing with competent people who had a dozen reasons for doing anything. They were terribly hard to read. Cyrus settled in his chair, with Mabyn to his right, and Alexander to the left of Gabe's new place.

Gabe considered his options, then bowed to Cyrus and went to the centre of the room, pivoting slowly. In the process, he made eye contact with each of his new colleagues, or did his best to. Several deliberately did not meet his eye, and he made a note of who. Silvia, of course. Garin. But also Troilus and Ulric. Rhoda made a point of smiling back at him, but it was a sharp glittering smile full of risks and dangers. No surprises, at least. His mother's analysis was spot on as always.

Rhoda, Silvia, and several of the other women - though not particularly Mabyn - were wearing fashionable frocks, the sort they might wear to an afternoon gathering. Vidya had a golden yellow saree, and he thought that would be for knowledge and learning, as well as the coming return of the sun. The men were mostly in suits, tending to the more formal navy and grey and pinstripe, and Gabe was glad he'd chosen his better grey for the day. A few men and women had ritual robes on, suggesting they'd come from some other project, or intended to go right back to it.

Everyone had a small table that could be pulled across the chair to provide a comfortable writing surface, and most of them had notes out. The tables adjusted to a slant, that looked useful, and had a shelf where they could leave a journal or notebook until needed. Now that he could look around, there was a small drinks cabinet in the corner, and a space where a cart with food waited comfortably until needed. The charm lighting was also excellent, leaving no shadows but also not glaring.

Right. He had all the information he was getting for the moment. Time to begin.

"To be honest, I never expected to be standing in this place, coming to you as a colleague. You all know that Magister FitzAlan suggested I challenge, back in 1922, and I refused. You also know I have been leading work - essential war work, as it turns out - and reporting to Cyrus for the last year. When Alexander put the question to me, I wanted to refuse." There, that should be a nice start to putting them off balance.

Gabe took a slow turn, watching the expressions, giving them time to lean and murmur. He caught a glimpse of the grin on Alexander's face. He hadn't talked this through with Alexander. There were several points in here that Alexander did not know, and would not until Gabe laid them out. He was glad to amuse, however. When the muttering died down, he heard Silvia's voice, cutting across the rest of it. She knew how to use her pitch well, and he was glad she was picking up the cue he'd left for her.

"You didn't want to challenge? Don't be absurd. Why did you, then?"

Gabe turned slowly to face her, making a little bow. "I have, frankly, a life I treasure. A family who love me, work I excel at, constant challenge and amusement. Even in a time of war, with all the worries it brings." He spread his hands out further. "You all know I placed a particular condition on my challenge. I know that Cyrus, Mabyn, Alexander, and Silvia have told you." Another round of mutters and whispers followed, and he let them. "You also know the outline of what I did at the Solstice."

"You rode with the Wild Hunt, and you survived." That was Lucas, who was the other of the ritual specialists besides Cyrus and Alexander.

"I did. They bid me make three promises in return for their aid." Gabe held up his fingers, counting off. "That I ride through the night with them, and at that point, it was easy to agree to." He held up one finger. "That I give my all to convincing the relevant parties to collaborate in the magical working for Lammastide. I admit it feels shaky at the moment, but Hitler and his armies have not crossed the

Channel in force, nor do they seem likely to. Only the planes. And we've had what seems like excellent luck catching what spies have made the attempt. But I was already doing that, as well." Two fingers.

Another rustle, this one shorter. "And the third?" That was Cyrus, and Gabe turned to acknowledge him with a nod. He stayed facing that direction, though he took a few steps backward. That was both have his back nearer to the closed double doors and to get as full a view of the room as he could.

"They told me I would be asked a question I would desperately want to say no to. And that I must answer yes." He inclined his head to Alexander this time. "On August twelfth, Alexander asked if I would challenge. I don't know what he read in me then, but he postponed the question proper. I, though, knew what my answer had to be."

Watching Alexander was almost worth this utter round of nonsense. He saw Alexander's eyes widen, saw the entirety of the conversation in which Gabe had set out his condition play through in memory, and the realisation of how finely Gabe had sliced his wording. And Alexander had put something together now, perhaps about how the oath Gabe had made had shifted everything else. He could see Silvia out of the corner of his eye, and he knew she was making at least some of the same calculations. Gabe gave them a heartbeat or two. "But I could - and did - choose to make the answer my own."

It led so perfectly into what he wanted to say next, and since no one seemed inclined to stop him, he went on. "I am a Penelope. I began learning those skills, that view of the world, when I was quite young. Seven. Nine. Eleven. It depends where you count from. I have spent my life working with the cleverest, sharpest, most curious people of Albion. Women and men who share their skills unstintingly, in the service of Albion, of magic, and of the greater good. I have trusted every single one of them with my life, often several times a month."

He let himself smile, and let them see that these people here, skilled as they were, had not yet met that mark. "We do our work without a lot of recognition or respect. We're also quite aware of all the gossip. Several of our number make a point of indexing it thoroughly." He could see several people react to that, and oh, a part of Gabe did like to see them squirm, just a hair.

That was not his point here. "The thing we do more than anything else is share. No single one of us knows everything, no matter how much we wish to. There are always books we haven't read, rituals we haven't done, skills we don't actually have. It is a mistake, for example, to give me fine sewing, or expect me to do much with a list of information that requires hours or days of intense focus, unless it is very, very interesting to me indeed." He could mock himself, and he would. It set the right sorts of expectations.

"The other thing we do, the other thing we can't help doing, is untangling things we see before us. And my, do you have a lot that needs that." He went on, allowing no pause for comment here. "And so I came into my challenge as a Penelope. I brought all my skills to it, all my tools. The ones I use day in and day out. I came not to fight, but to look and listen and learn, and to see what happened." He shrugged. "Many people can fight. I'm quite good at it, actually." That got a little audible snort out of Alexander. Excellent. "But it was not what I needed to do to, up there." He gestured upstairs to the top of the keep.

This time, there wasn't a rustle, there was a silence.

Good, he'd got them caught up in the telling. "What I found was a maze, a series of puzzles. The first expected me to give up a power I held, the ring I'd been granted by the Fatae." He laughed, letting the ease of it show. "I'm quite sure most people would have found that hard to do, but it was never mine to keep. It was a token for a single act, now passed. It should go back to those great ladies."

It got a rustle of whispers, now. Giving up power was not something these people understood, nearly any of them. He had suspicions that Vidya understood it quite well, and that Alexander had his own unusual take on the question, as he generally did. But the rest of them? It was an utterly foreign thought, as if he'd insisted the grass was purple and the sky pure white.

"The maze led me to a second puzzle, one we use as a teaching tool, in fact. Nothing particularly hard there." He shrugged, and did not mention any of the metaphysical implications of those puzzles. Sometime rather later, perhaps, if things went better than he expected. "And then I came to the third challenge, and it's always the third that's actually difficult, isn't it, in our lore and our counting. Threes and sevens?" He'd given some thought to how to put this, how much to tell, and how much to hold back. "There, in an undeniably female form, was the land herself, the magic of the land. The one whose challenge I had answered." That was true enough, and delightfully ambiguous.

This time, he did leave time for the murmurs, because he wanted to read the reactions. He'd expected that at least a dozen of them had gone into their challenge as a fight, had succeeded, had been chosen as the best choice. He suspected a few had had something decidedly more mystical. "We had an interesting conversation, then."

Before he could say anything further, Alexander made a choking sound. "You - talked with her? And she answered?"

Ah. He had not realised the problems had run so deep. Poor Lady, to have gone for such a long time with no one to talk to. He would definitely have to see about fixing that, even if the conversations were inconsequential. Cyrus lifted his hand, and Alexander stopped. "Please, Gabe. Tell us what you think we need to hear of that."

Gabe nodded once in agreement. "She was not subtle, for the record. I had not expected a conversation, nothing in all the information I had suggested one was likely. But there I was, and flexible enough to move beyond the assumption to the reality." He added, after a moment's thought, "I ran through the usual checks to make sure it wasn't actually a hallucination or some trick of the Silence magic. It comes up every fortnight or two in my usual work." That, he could see, discomfited rather a few of them. The Penelopes had protocols for that for a reason, when they weren't sure they could trust their own senses. "She said the others wouldn't speak to her. I don't know if she meant the other candidates, or, well." He gestured at the room. "She was quite clear she had not taken the same shape with them."

"And then?" Cyrus kept his voice steady, and Gabe appreciated the skill that took. But he was leaning forward just a hair. His hands were tight on the arms of his chair, all the signs of someone who would tear the information out if it didn't come soon.

"She asked if I had questions for her, and I said - quite reasonably, I think - that I had many, but I knew some of them were rude. In the end, I settled on asking what my challenge was." He let himself shrug. "There is a matter in my past, and we spoke of that. That I had worked through those tangles in a way that was pleasing to her now. I asked, as one does in these situations, what I could do for her."

"And?" Now Cyrus's voice was strained.

"She laughed and asked how I could help such as her?" Gabe held up his hands and wriggled his thumbs again, in an echo of that moment. "I said opposable thumbs. And all they mean, really." There was a hint that whatever form the Lady of the land had taken, it had, perhaps, not been human. He didn't think most of them would notice just yet. Alexander would, of course.

That brought up a flurry of comments and people calling across the room, the kind of chaotic tintinnabulum that had too many notes to track. He took in what he could. He'd have to trust to memory - and Alexander's commentary - later, for some of it. Cyrus hushed them after perhaps thirty seconds, with a stamp of his foot on the floor that rang out like a true bell. Everyone quieted, thankfully.

"I am a Penelope. I untangle magics and solve problems. That is what she wants from me, and I am glad to give that. I have already offered that, with all myself. Before my oaths today, before my challenge, before agreeing to challenge. That is what I am and what I do."

"You're making this up." That was, oh, yes, that was Silvia. Though a second later, Garin echoed it.

Alexander's voice cut through the rising sounds. "When he walked out - and everyone there, including you, Silvia - can swear to it, Gabe said, 'She has a sense of humour, doesn't she?'" Gabe could hear the overtones in his voice, an echo of the way Alexander himself had taught him how to read oaths in someone's magic. He knew Alexander had been shocked by something, in that moment, but he also knew that something he'd said about that great Lady and her amusement had hit home in a way Gabe couldn't have planned if he'd had a century to do it. Now, there was a yearning there, just for a second, like Gabe had never heard in Alexander before.

The room went quiet. After a few seconds, Cyrus nodded. "I heard and remember. You succeeded. You have ideas, I am sure, of where to begin. Do any of them need to be addressed today?"

Gabe shook his head. "Many of the tangles have been there for a long time. The first part of my work is learning more about them, about the history. I have a great respect for history. It so often tells us how to avoid having the same problem again." His honest exasperation at the folly of humans got an uneasy laugh from someone. "Despite rumours to the contrary, I do not actually rush into every problem headlong without warning."

"If that is what you wish to share from your challenge at the moment, we can indeed look at time to discuss next steps in future meetings. I do know Alexander had a question."

Gabe nodded, then walked across the room to his seat. Someone had refilled his glass, and he took a few sips to wet his throat. He backed up again, making a slow turn in the centre, always moving sunwise, as he did out of habit.

Alexander waited until he was standing evenly on both feet, facing Cyrus and the others on that wall. "Why were you glowing, after? We know you left the keep for perhaps twenty minutes."

"Twenty-two, total." Gabe said, almost absently. He was horrible at time, more often than not, but his pocket watch had a timer on it for many reasons, and he'd triggered it out of sheer habit. Alexander raised an eyebrow, and Gabe considered the answer. "I have been my father's

Heir since I was twelve. I love our land. I always have and always will." He had a flash there, all of a sudden, the gripping fear of the other life and death in a land that wasn't his own, had never been his, and forced himself on through the moment of weakness. They'd read it, they'd know some of it.

"The glowing, Gabe." Now Alexander's voice was very gentle.

"I could feel there would be a bomb dropping near Veritas. The edge of our bounds, in fact. I diverted it. The glowing seems to be a side effect." He reached, instinctively, for that sense of the land, and then heard the sounds that made it clear to him he was doing it again. Ah, well, it wasn't like it hurt anything.

Alexander nodded. "This was the second time since you agreed?" He'd been at the first, honestly, not that either of them were going to mention those circumstances.

"Third. Probably." He was fairly sure now he had been during the challenge itself. "No one else has mentioned it. I was in London, a lot of the last fortnight." He gave a little shrug. "I have no fear of loving the land. Or of letting it show."

He got the sense, in the pressure of the magic around him, of several competing demands. The one that triumphed and came out first in words was "London? Why so much time in London?"

Gabe wheeled around to figure out who had spoken. Theo Carrington. "Have any of you spent much time in London, living there, other than Alexander? I know he used to have a townhouse near Bedford Square." Gabe caught the slight nod from Alexander.

There were many heads shaking no. "My wife and I lived there for a few years after our marriage, and she continues to have deep ties around the Spitalfields portal and market." Which all these fine folk likely ignored entirely. "Do you understand how a city works magically? How any city works magically? That isn't Trellech, I mean." Trellech was, in fact, unique.

"There are the portals and the magical streets, of course, but they're a fraction of the population. Even many of them have homes elsewhere. The magic's weak there, we all know that." He couldn't identify who that came from, someone back and to his left.

"The ones you know, maybe. But there are plenty of honest crafters and traders who live in flats or wherever they can get by." Gabe spread his hands, taking a few steps back to have the doors at his back and the best view of the room. "London's magic isn't the deep well of Schola, or this Keep, or Trellech. It's changeable as the river, isn't it? But that doesn't mean it isn't there. If London falls, we all fall. There will be no retreat to Trellech, or to this Keep, or whatever hidden family spaces you keep. London is the heart of the country, ours as well. Even leaving aside the libraries, the museums, the history, the treasury of knowledge and hard work that London holds."

Someone tried to stop him, but he soared on. "And here's the thing. I know now exactly what oath you all took. We are sworn to all of Albion, and that includes all of Albion's lands. The way I see it, it is our first responsibility to do what we can to keep things going. To keep bombs from falling when we can. To ease flooding, to make firebreaks. To stop an alchemy lab exploding and poisoning the streets around it. My father was at Coventry all through the night, well into the day. You don't see the Guard shirking that work, they know better." He tilted his head. "Yes, we all have other duties, things no one else can do. But when there is a bomb I can stop, I will. If that makes me shine with magic, so be it." Then he took a breath. "What I did that night won't work all the time. Maybe even often. But every bit matters."

The room fell quiet again. Out of the quiet came a sound, a strangled swallow, first. "You must be exaggerating." Ah. Garin. This needed delicate handling.

Gabe turned right to face him. Gabe had seen him, at Livia's funeral, a few times since, but he still wore unrelieved black. His face had an increasing gauntness, and his movements had the sharp jerk and eerie stillness of someone who moved from burning need and sank into exhaustion in alternation.

Gabe said the only thing he could in that moment. "Do you want to learn how?" It was a hopeless question, and Gabe asked it anyway. There had been two bombs near enough to Arundel last night, and Gabe could only imagine what it felt like to hear them fall and know yourself helpless.

Garin refused to answer. He looked away. Gabe let the silence draw out, let it be a blanket, hoping the gentle pressure would be something. After what seemed like forever, Garin looked back, and Gabe went to one knee. "When you're ready, I'll show you. Whatever I can."

Something changed in Garin's expression, and Gabe didn't know enough of the right scripts to read it. Before he could say anything else, he heard Alexander's voice over his left shoulder. "Can you expand, please, Gabe, what that might look like? You've told me a time or two, how you start reasoning out a puzzle from first principles and where someone began."

Gabe nodded, getting to his feet again, pushing himself up with the cane. Alexander had seen him do this particular party trick a few times, and Gabe had hoped he'd get the opportunity. "Garin, Lord Fortier, who holds Arundel. You'd have had Professor Lollard at Schola, of course, for Ritual. He was quite competent in a number of ways. You can see his touch on the work of most established ritualists of Albion, up through people a handful of years older than me. Now, mind, he didn't care much for Rathna, so some of this is personal, but I do think his approach is lacking." There was a murmur of commentary, and Gabe sailed on, ignoring it. Now he was far more sure Alexander had his back, rhetorically and practically, if needed.

"Professor Lollard heavily favoured a command-and-control approach in ritual, summoning whatever being to do your bidding. The lesser and greater summoning rituals, some kinds of elemental work, or the calling on the Royal Stars in the forms derived from Esteridge, just to give a few examples. But that mode doesn't do nearly as well with the land magics. There's a fair bit of evidence - not just my personal experience, which I would quite understand if you didn't trust on its own - that, in fact, it makes things rather worse. You cannot force a river to flow, nor a plant to reach for the sun. You can encourage, you can make conditions easier, you can charm. But force? It ends badly."

Gabe considered his choices here. "Have you read Phillida Wright's *The Spiral Stair: Building Upon Seasonal Rites?*" Garin shook his head minutely. "Madder's analysis of the Fifth Mode, or Mackenzie's 'Hunt and Horn', that looks to some of the older folklore for ritual anchors?" He didn't expect much recognition. These were out of the line of what Garin likely had spent much time with.

He thought about what might be more relevant to Garin's interests. "And hmm. You're an alchemist, 'Esse quam videri: an evaluation of astronomical implications for

Materia preparation' might put it in terms that you'd find closer to your usual work. There's a section that considers terroir." That title got a sudden shudder from Garin, entirely plain and visible, and Gabe wasn't at all sure why. Thesan had been second author on that, it was a perfectly fine article, and useful to purpose. "I can make a copy of a bibliography for you, and I know Alexander has copies of most of it by now, if your library doesn't."

He shrugged, and went on. No point in leaving the thing incomplete. "Now, you'd have had Professor Norton, like near everyone in this room, I believe. His alchemy's impeccable, of course, but he does like his structure. No colouring outside the lines, no making improvisations without working through all the consequences. And honestly, as someone who's cleaned up a lot of alchemical bad judgement, I appreciate that no end. But it does encourage a certain rigidity of thought, and again, that does not always suit the land. The Penelopes have stories from a century or so ago that would turn your hair white. We tell them as a caution to apprentices."

Gabe flicked his fingers and sailed on. "And then you apprenticed with Magister Hollowell. Extremely accomplished, he's turned out a number of the finest alchemists of the next three generations, yourself very much included. But again, following what has been done, without a touch of intuition except in the most rarified ways."

He took a step or two back. "So if you asked me what to do - which I understand you haven't, but Alexander has - I would suggest beginning anew, setting aside the old assumptions of how to learn the land magic. Approach it the way the world was when we were children, without predefined ideas. What makes sense from there is - I am a creature of impulse, I admit. But I've trained up three apprentices now, near enough, and helped with the training of quite a few more. Following where the impulse goes, thoughtfully, rarely leads me terribly astray. I appreciate the impulse to protect, to tend the land. And that is what we're all here for. Follow that, and I don't think any of us will go far wrong."

Off over his left shoulder, he heard a sound from Alexander he couldn't place at first, but it rapidly turned to a full-out rolling laugh. He'd only heard Alexander laugh freely a handful of times before in company, and he absolutely had not expected to find it here. It delighted him as much as the snake's laughter had, and all of a sudden, he was sure she approved of it now, too.

Gabe took another step or two back, so he could see both Garin and Alexander at the same time. Garin looked entirely uncertain what to do with this, like some other part of his world had shattered. Alexander stood, brushing past Gabe to come to one knee in front of Garin. He cast a circle of silence around him as he moved, so they could speak privately, and the sound of the laugh cut off abruptly. Gabe glanced at Cyrus, ceding the floor with a gesture and getting a nod.

"Refill your drinks, if you need." Cyrus's comment carried over the tumult of other conversations. Gabe took his own seat, sliding into it and finding it quite comfortable, actually. Excellent. He did not need unnecessary asceticism in his life. That was no good. A comfortable chair made long meetings far more agreeable. Everyone left him alone while they chattered. No one seemed to actually want to ask him questions.

He'd run through the possibilities with Mama, on Sunday, and how to play it. They hadn't been able to decide if people would poke and prod at him, or if they'd be unsure where to start. Gabe had laid bets on the latter, honestly, and he was amused to be right. Oh, they were glancing at him, and murmuring with each other, and none of them would do anything so straightforward as asking a question. He expected they'd need a bit more bravery and a bit more privacy to get there, that he should expect a series of invitations to tea or a drink in the coming weeks from a representative sampling.

After a couple of minutes, Cyrus cleared his throat, and Alexander straightened up, coming back to take his chair again. Whatever he'd talked to Garin about had been something of an improvement, and Garin was drinking a bit of wine and having a little something to nibble on. He looked very pale, but there was no help for that. It had needed lancing.

"That is the usual range you bring to analysis, is it, Gabe?" Cyrus asked the question clearly, and Gabe answered similarly, letting his voice carry.

"Part of a Penelope's training is learning how to do the evaluation of influences, and that often means tracing back through people's training. I did no particular preparation here. I do consider it a tad rude outside of an assignment. But of course, there's a lot of that sort of detail already in my head." He didn't want to get into the specifics here, but perhaps he would tell Alexander a particular piece of that soon. It'd almost certainly make Alexander laugh. Again.

Cyrus snorted. "It will keep us on our toes, I suspect. Which brings us to a necessary discussion for today, the solstice dances. Gabe, I gather Alexander's explained the basic outline."

Alexander had. There was a private ritual, just the Council, which Alexander felt was entirely too much by rote, but it did the job. The dances that followed, in public, progressed from more ancient forms into the swirls of the much more modern waltz.

Cyrus continued, "Is your wife willing to dance, or do we need to see about finding a suitable partner?"

"Rathna is quite glad to join me, and we believe we have enough understanding of the steps. Or will, by then." Alexander and Thesan - who generally partnered him these days - had promised a proper rehearsal, and Rathna found Thesan's offer very much a relief. From there, the conversation went on to other arrangements, working through the myriad details that needed to be set up.

Gabe had thought that he'd get swarmed with questions, after. But as it happened, they were just wrapping up, near to eight at night, when he got a summons on his journal. "Pardon, please do excuse me. That alchemical lab in London's still difficult and needs another set of hands again." They'd not have called him in if it weren't actually fairly urgent.

Alexander walked him to the portal. Just before Gabe stepped through, Alexander cleared his throat. "We'll have a lot to talk through when we get the chance. I look forward to it, truly."

Gabe grinned back at him. "You like me tweaking everyone's noses. Don't deny it." He read the truth of it in Alexander's rueful expression, just before he stepped through to the Southwark portal.

CHAPTER 16
THE MIDDLE OF THE NIGHT AT VERITAS

Rathna went to bed on Wednesday night wondering about Gabe. It had been a good day, in terms of her work and Ferdinand's. But of course, by late afternoon she was worried about how Gabe's first meeting as one of the Council was going. Her journal had chimed briefly, right at eight, to let her know he'd been called out to London, and had no idea when he'd be home.

That left her to finish a rather beautiful jigsaw puzzle with Avigail, a complicated one with a stained glass window that was quite a challenge. After that, Rathna read her a chapter, tucked her in, and tried to settle herself. It didn't really work, but reading in the library for an hour or two with Alysoun was pleasant, as always.

She fell firmly on her side of the bed, but she woke in the middle of the night, having taken over the middle, and there was no sign of Gabe. She frowned, and rolled over, blinking blearily at the lights over the door that would tell her if he'd made it back to Veritas or not. There was Gabe's light in his office. She reached for her watch, calling light into her hand to read it. Three in the morning. There was a chance he'd fallen asleep down there. He had a daybed; it wasn't unheard of. But even if he had, he probably wanted a blanket and a pillow wedged somewhere so he'd not roll onto the floor.

Right. Dressing gown it was. And she could make a mug of cocoa. If Gabe didn't want it, she'd drink it. They kept a small setup for it in the alcove on the ground floor, with the teakettle and a coffee pot for Gabe and whoever else wanted some. This was, at least, the sort of household where people sometimes needed those things in the middle of the night, and waking the staff wasn't to be thought of. She pulled on her dressing gown and slippers, grabbed her current book, and went padding downstairs.

By the time she'd made the hot chocolate properly, she was more or less awake. Oh, she was also doing the maths on whether she could get a nap in tomorrow, but she'd gone short on sleep before, and in far worse causes. She didn't have anything too delicate scheduled, fortunately; they were talking about longer-term tuning for portals near bomb sites, and that wasn't going to be solved in a day. It was, in fact, the sort of problem where the fuzziness from a short night might actually help a bit, free her mind. She picked up the mug and went along to Gabe's office, testing the door.

If he'd actually wanted to keep people out, it would have been locked. If he'd wanted to discourage someone coming in, she'd have felt the charm press against her, rather like a magnet repelling its like. None of that happened, so she eased open the door. What she found was Gabe pacing back and forth, half of a set of files out on his desk, in six or seven rough piles. He'd taken his jacket off sometime in the process and rolled up his sleeves, his hair trailing in wisps out of the braid down his back. She could see bits of dampness, from some fervent activity, or maybe being too near a fire, but it didn't seem recent.

He stopped, mid-step, with a suddenness that took her breath away. It was the way he sometimes shifted when he was duelling, when all his focus went to one place, and he was deciding what kind of threat it was. She held up the cocoa, like it was a white parley flag. Neither of them moved for three heartbeats, maybe four, and then he pivoted slightly on one foot, blinking at her, as if she'd completely derailed him.

"Rathna?" He rubbed at his face.

"Mmhmm. You weren't in bed, and I saw you were home."

"I didn't want to wake you." He grimaced, turning away with a little jerk of his shoulder. She'd seen him like this from time to time, but it had been a while since the last. The last she'd been home for, she suspected there'd been a couple of rounds of this while she'd been on the Continent. Maybe not quite this chaotic.

"Cocoa? I didn't put brandy in it. I know you've got a flask somewhere for emergencies." Rathna held it out.

Gabe leaned abruptly to reach into his satchel, pulling out a silver flask, unscrewing the lid and turning it upside down. Nothing came out except one tiny drop that Gabe flicked onto his finger.

"Let me refill that for you, then." Rathna held out her hand. "Go bathe. You'll feel better if you do."

It was a tricky thing, giving instructions to your husband. The family wedding vows didn't include anything about obeying on either side. But sometimes people - even grown adults, raising remarkably grown children - still needed to be told to do things. Gabe quivered there for a moment.

"Go up to bed. I'll be up in a couple. And let the staff know." It would be no good at all if someone startled Gabe awake in the morning, for either party. She went first to leave a note where they'd find it when they were up and about. In a few hours, ugh. Then she went to the library, where the open brandy would be, to refill the flask.

Finally, she came back by Gabe's office, tidying the piles into neater ones that weren't threatening to slide off onto the floor and create even more chaos. She knew better than to actually rearrange them, nevermind refile them. Richard's secretary could file them, if it had been a sudden tear without purpose. But it was just as likely Gabe would walk back into his office in the morning and find what he'd actually been looking for and needed precisely where he'd left it, even if that was in a heap.

By the time she got back upstairs, there were faint splashing sounds from the bath, not the sound of the taps running. Rathna looked for his cocoa, and he'd taken it into the bath with him. She poured herself a glass from the decanter up here. She tucked the flask back into place in his satchel before slipping out of the dressing gown and back into bed.

He took perhaps another five minutes, then came out, towel barely around his hips, strewing it on the ground as he fell into bed. Before she could do anything else, she realised he was shivering. Not with cold, exactly - the room was quite warm - but with something else. She knew enough about what to do with that, and pulled the blankets up, then pressed against him, offering as much pressure and steadiness as she could.

Gabe didn't say anything for a long time. The shivering got worse, along with the way she could feel him flexing his hand open and then closing it tightly into a fist, over and over again. She didn't move; she didn't let herself get impatient. It was the same as being with a tree when she was coaxing it to grow into a portal, or the stone or the water. She couldn't rush it, she could only be there.

She knew, too, not to move too much. She wanted to let her hand sweep against his skin, let her thumb rub and reassure the way she'd cuddled the children when they were little. And that wouldn't do here and now. It would make things worse. She'd learned that, long enough ago, it was an old friendly habit. Now was for peace and stillness, now was for letting Gabe take his time.

Rathna had heard the quiet chime of the clock twice by the time Gabe finally took a deeper breath and let it out, going near limp beside her. That was the cue she'd been waiting for. "Hey." She whispered it near his ear, careful not to blow too hard. She hated how that felt, when she was already sensitive, she knew he felt it more. "Need something to drink?"

He shivered once, but nodded, working to pivot onto his back and push up on one elbow. She extracted herself from the bed, going to fill a glass with water from the dressing table, bringing it back and holding it until he got a good grip. He drained half of it in a couple of gulps. "What time is it?"

"Near four." He winced, and she shrugged. "It is what it is. How long were you in London?"

"Eight to, um." Gabe grimaced again. "Two hours of work, an air raid, two more hours work, another two air raids inside forty minutes, and then we patched it together enough. Got back here a little before three?" He shook his head, the way he did when the time wasn't quite adding up correctly. "Acids. Nasty combo."

That made her wince. She knew enough to know how bad that could get. "Everyone all right?"

"Yeah." It came out more of a drawl than Gabe usually used, that blurry edge of exhaustion and lingering tension. Then he slumped back on the bed, and she had to grab for the water glass.

Rathna turned to set it down on the bedside table, then peered at Gabe again. She'd picked up enough of his inclinations by now to know that someone needed to poke at this, and the person available was her. Alysoun did it better, honestly. She'd had a lot more practice, especially when Gabe was this, what was the word? Reactant, like in alchemy, where everything he did might spark something new and poorly controlled. That wasn't right, but it was four in the morning. That was not her specialty, and she wasn't saying it out loud, anyway. Instead, she took a breath and went for the place that must be tender, whatever else had happened. "The meeting?"

Something in Gabe lit up. "I made Alexander laugh!" It had a sense of wonder to it, a flash of pure joy and curiosity and delight. Then he shivered again. "I said things to Garin. I don't know if he'll forgive me."

That could be any number of things, and Rathna knew it. She did her best to keep her voice steady. "What sort of things did you say?"

"That I'd teach him how to protect his land, if he'd let me." Gabe frowned. "No, that's not quite what I actually said. What I said was 'When you're ready, I'll show you.'" He let out a breath. "Huh."

"Something else caught your memory?" Gabe's memory was, on the average, fantastic, but every so often it hung up on something, like a sleeve catching on a nail, with the sudden jarring dangerous jerk.

"I thought I'd been sharper." He rubbed his face, then let himself relax a bit more into the pillows. "And then I laid out his training, and most of it's really good training. I mean, he's a better alchemist than I am."

"Gabe, love, you get distracted. This is, in fact, not good for alchemy." Rathna had pointed this out many times. These were dance steps they both knew well. It still made Gabe smile a bit.

"I'm good when it's interesting! But a lot of alchemy gets boring fast, doing the thing the same way so you get the same result." He shrugged, then patted the bed next to him hopefully. Rathna spent a moment nestling back up, propped on her elbow and the pillow so she could watch his face.

"What did Garin do? What did other people do?" That seemed like sensible information to start with. "I wasn't actually there, Gabe. You have to tell me what you saw. What you feel you can tell me."

It made him snort, and that was as reassuring as anything else. "I made Alexander laugh. That was when he laughed, when he heard me lay everything out, like I do. Like we do. But something I said made Garin flinch? I didn't know I could do that." The 'we' caught oddly in his throat for a moment, and Rathna made a note to come back to that. "And then Alexander talked to him, privately. One of the privacy charms. But Cyrus didn't seem upset with me?"

Rathna considered. "So that seems to be all right. And you can ask Alexander more about it when you get a chance. He knows you, he knows Garin, he can tell you if you were insulting." She waited, then.

Gabe considered, letting his eyes close, finally. Rathna settled her head on his shoulder, rearranging the blankets a little, and felt his arm come around her back. "There's an oath. That was fine. And properly done, it felt like it wove in neatly with my others."

"Neatly is good. Can't have dangling oath strings." It made him chuckle, and that was good, too.

"Then Cyrus gave me the floor, and I talked about why I made the challenge. The parts even Alexander didn't know, about what the Fatae told me." He'd told her, almost immediately once she'd got back from France, what seemed like a lifetime ago, and not just a few months. "That went fine, but my, Silvia is furious. A couple of the others weren't nearly as good at repressing their feelings as I'd expected." Then he blinked and sat up, dislodging Rathna entirely so she fell sideways onto her half of the bed. "Sorry, love. Need to write something down."

He flung himself out of the bed, trailing a corner of the sheet until he kicked it free, managing not to go down in a tumble of limbs. Gabe scrabbled in his bag for his notebook, got out a stub of pencil, wrote down three sentences, and got back to the bed at about the point Rathna had untangled the sheets again. He did at least look abashed. There he was, naked, flushed slightly with the momentary exertion, and it was very easy to fall in love with him all again. Not that she needed to. It wasn't as if she'd stopped at any point since Scotland. She patted the bed. "Idea?"

"Pretty sure the carpet in the Council chamber is enchanted so it's harder to cover that kind of emotion. Only if you're standing on it. And I'm not sure how many of them realise it. I caught charms for clarity of communication earlier. It's an interesting piece. I hope Cyrus will let me have a proper investigation of it, and then compare it to whatever records he's got."

Rathna laughed. "Oh, my. While you were juggling glass balls in the meeting, you spotted that. Come here, get comfortable." She waited until he was stretched out on his back again. "And then?"

"I talked about the challenge." He hesitated. "I talked to the snake. Not that I said she was a snake to them. But talking to her, that's the important part. And she talked to me. I think she hasn't had a conversation with anyone in a very long time, not with words. Symbols, maybe. I need to ask Alexander a lot of things now. But it was good. I'm in the right place. Only." His words ran out of steam.

"Only you're still getting the feel of it. And you're not sure what it means to be something besides a Penelope." Rathna laid out what she'd spotted enough of and hoped it helped.

He let out a long shuddery breath, the kind that meant she hugged him tight and nestled against his shoulder while he caught up with himself. "That. I've worked so hard on keeping ... keeping me moving in the right line. The right aim. Being Heir's easy. Love the land, let the land love you back."

"Easy for you, love, but yes. And you've been doing that all your life, even before you knew what it was, really. I have heard your baby stories."

It made him chuckle. "Papa would take me out and show me things when I was quite little. Or read me books. Even before he and Mama talked about that." He shrugged. "And I've been, being a Penelope is constantly new. But I've been doing that a long time."

"Do you feel that it's tugging your loyalties in different directions?" That was the thing Rathna had worried about, honestly. She'd not have been able to juggle those three different compelling demands.

Gabe took his time, letting his thumb brush against her shoulder, the way she'd kept herself from doing earlier.

Now, it was the perfect thing, the little repetitive movement that soothed them both. "No. That's what I meant about the oaths slotting in perfectly. It's all one goal, just different legs. A stool."

"A tripod's the most stable construction." Rathna knew her magical geometry perfectly well, and her engineering. They didn't make portals out of triangles because it was awkward to move through, but she still thought about the architecture that way when she could. "But it's odd, now, to think you're one of the Council, not just a Penelope. That - you caught yourself on 'we'."

Gabe nodded. "That. But I am. Challenge made, oaths made. I didn't flee into the night across the ocean in the interim. Not that I could."

"Given the land, no." Rathna said. "We know better than that. Was it all people being difficult?" She didn't want to press on the core of the meeting. She knew there were things he'd not be able to tell her, and especially that he was still working some of that out.

"Cyrus was remarkably relaxed about it? Gave me my head and let me go." Gabe's mouth twitched up. "He does have some experience with me."

"That's likely making things easier. And he knows everyone else. He can give you advice, or manage the meetings, or whatever."

"Yeah." This time, it was a softer sound.

"What else?" There was something nagging him still.

"Just. I'm behind in so many ways. I can't do this Council thing and everything else." Gabe admitting that he didn't have capacity was rather like the world shattering. And yet, Rathna had been waiting for this.

She shifted her hand, curling around him, to best feel his reaction in all the ways she could, how his magic responded most of all. "Richard has a point. Will you at least interview a few possibilities for a secretary if we find them for you?"

She wouldn't have got away with it a week ago, never mind a month. Now he sucked in a breath. "Since you ask." There was something there that was full of weight and depth, something far beyond the ordinary day to day of their marriage, as if he were giving himself over to the inevitable.

"Alysoun and I will put our heads together." Rathna was actually quite sure that Alysoun and Richard had notes on the topic ready to go. And perhaps a couple of candidates in mind who could deal with Gabe in all his roles and faces. If not, they'd face that challenge like all the others. Rathna reached to dim the charmlights, then nuzzled at his cheek. "Thank you, love. For not fighting me. Anything else for right now?"

"No." He let out a half breath, then the rest of it. "Think I can sleep now. Thank you, love, for helping me get the measure of it."

"You know me. Surveying a speciality. Next time, though, you can let me know you're in a state a little faster."

Gabe sucked in a breath and nodded. "Easier on both of us." That said, he rearranged himself, coiling around her, one leg over hers, his face in her breasts, the sort of hug that was half an octopus with ambitions. She was used to going to sleep like that, and more in the past few months than before. She stayed more or less awake, until she was sure his breath had evened off and he'd finally relaxed, before finally drifting off herself.

CHAPTER 17
DECEMBER 4TH AT ALEXANDER'S TOWNHOUSE IN TRELLECH

"Come in, the meal's in the library." Alexander opened the door, holding it to let Cyrus and Mabyn in. They'd made the decision to meet here. All of them had wanted to be a bit away from the Keep for this, for one thing. And Cyrus and Mabyn had had a nominally social engagement in Trellech this afternoon that ran to supper time, so it was convenient.

Well, except for Alexander, who preferred to be at Ytene for supper on Thursdays, but he could go out there when they were done. And he'd been in meetings all day, in half a dozen places. He'd started at Arundel, then the Keep, then a brief stop into Gabe's office in the Guard Hall, in hopes of catching him, then three other places, all private homes in Trellech.

Cyrus and Mabyn had both been here often enough to have their own usual chairs. Alexander had given instructions for an informal meal with finger foods and plates, rather than anything that required a table setting. He arranged things, they took their food while he sealed the wards as firmly as they would go.

When he turned back, Cyrus was watching him, the slight tilt of his head that Cyrus got when he was making multiple calculations. Alexander took his time making up his own plate and claiming his chair. "Silvia still in a snit, then?"

"A bit more than a snit." Mabyn grimaced. "We talked. It didn't do much good for either of us. Do you want the list?"

"Want is not precisely the verb I'd choose, dear lady." Alexander said, drawing it out in hopes of getting a little amusement from both of them. "Need, yes. Reach with grasping hands for, yes. Pounce on, oh, yes."

It did make Mabyn snort. "You could come up with it as easily as I did, I suspect. Gabe is getting above himself. He should have respect for seniority and how things have been done. He made a spectacle of himself, he talked about things that are not discussed, he threatens to break apart the Council."

That was much the list Alexander had expected, yes. "How does Silvia actually feel about it? Those are all the things I expected her to say, but that doesn't mean she feels them."

That one made Cyrus let out a bark of a laugh. "That," he added, "is what I asked. Good to know I'm better on the mark than I was."

Mabyn spread her hands. "Silvia has built her life on doing the approved of thing. She's very good, and it has, all told, cost her less than it cost me. It comes easier to her. And now, here's someone who threatens to break it all apart."

"I'd say, here's someone who offers to weave it all back together." Alexander pointed out. "A bit of unweaving first, to go back to where things knotted or pull out of season."

Then he considered his choices. "When it comes to tearing things down, that's what I'm for. That was what I was meant for, on the Council, one of the things." He held up a hand. "I'm getting ahead of matters. We'll come back to that."

Cyrus nodded. "All right. People first. You had Garin this morning. Who else?"

"Godfrey, Ivor, Lettice, Desmond, and I did get six and a half minutes with Gabe." Alexander said promptly. "Mabyn?"

"Silvia, Rhoda, and Theo." Mabyn's answer was just as a prompt. "Mostly Silvia."

"Which left me with everyone else. It has been a day. All right. Who do we actually need to talk about? Besides Garin and Silvia." Cyrus was doing his best to be systematic about it, and for once, Alexander wasn't going to interject just for the sake of it.

"Lettice and Desmond were unsettled, but I think willing to see what happens next. Godfrey and Ivor have some wrong-headed ideas, but we can see how they shake out." Alexander said. He thought all four of them needed more time, honestly. Though he'd at least got the information that Lettice and Desmond thought Rathna was a moderating influence on Gabe, and could she be encouraged to be more moderating sometime soon? As a professional compliment, it left something to be desired, but it at least gave a base to work from.

Cyrus nodded. "I got an earful from Troilus - quite similar to Silvia's bit, about him getting above himself. You know Troilus is a typical Horse like that. Standing out is to be feared and questioned and stamped out by that particular sort of mind."

"As a model for living among some of the most skilled

of Albion's population, it does leave something to be desired. We are all exceptional in our own ways, or we wouldn't be what and where we are." Alexander flicked his fingers. "I do wish he'd get over that."

"Not terribly likely at this late stage in his life. And he doesn't have Paulus to convince him otherwise, anymore." Cyrus shook his head. Troilus's brother Paulus had retired from the Council himself a year ago due to increasing ill health. "I won't be terribly surprised if we see him retire, honestly. Troilus, I mean. Sooner than later, if we keep giving Gabe his head."

Alexander's fingers went still, paused over his plate. "Was that in question?" He kept his voice as mild as he could, knowing they'd read all the danger into the mildness that might be needed. He could trust them that far, certainly. It was the question of how much further that was still a niggling problem.

Cyrus's chin came up. "Alexander." Now his voice was very gentle. "This is not a fight I am going to have with you. I will not. You hear?" Then he cleared his throat and went on. "I am convinced we need Gabe. I gave him his head on Wednesday for a reason. If I hadn't been convinced before, I would have been by five minutes into his bit of the meeting. If the rest of the Council can't deal with it, well. We'll work something out." He kept his voice calm and even, but Alexander had some idea what that was costing him.

Mabyn leaned to cover Cyrus's free hand with her own. "That. Silvia wants to fight about it. She wants to fight everything, and she's not used to wanting to fight like that. Not her kind of ladylike. I think she'll work through it. Especially once there are some results to point to." She swallowed. "I suppose that gets to me, then."

Alexander inclined his head. "Thank you for being so

clear, both of you. Your support for this. For Gabe." He swallowed once. "For me." A couple of years ago, he'd never have been able to say that. Even to them, even as tightly warded as they were right now in this room.

"Silvia's scared." Mabyn said, after a moment's silence. "If there is another way to do things, what does that mean? Does it mean Hesperidon was wrong? Wrong in critical ways." She flicked her fingers. "I know he was wrong about how he handled you, and I think that should be counted as critical. But Silvia hasn't brought herself to that, not yet. I don't know if she will. We're in waters she and I never charted before. It was just taken as a magnetic north that Hesperidon acted for the best."

"In the best of all possible worlds." Alexander winced. "That attitude leaves something to be desired. What's she going to do about it, do you think?" That was the key here.

"Be difficult. Talk to other people, convince them to be difficult." Mabyn looked up. "How do you think Gabe will handle that?"

"Honestly? I suspect like he did Wednesday." Alexander watched both their faces. "She called him a liar, flat out. He just dealt with it. Didn't let it get in the way of his point. We could use a lot more of the latter and less of the former."

"I did point out she'd been rather insulting," Mabyn said. "And that she doesn't have Garin's excuse for it. That's what I've got for now. I'll let you know what happens as she settles more."

It wasn't much, but Alexander hadn't expected there to be. Whatever there was, Mabyn had the best chance of getting it out of Silvia before it turned into a bigger problem. "Garin, then?"

Cyrus nodded, just once.

"Gabe - if I had to describe it, that would have been a

perfectly placed stiletto. Slipped in, neat as could be, no extraneous damage." Alexander spread his hands. "Potentially lethal, if something isn't done, but exceptionally skilled."

"If you're going to go down, better at the hands of someone skilled enough that you don't take extra harm in the process." Cyrus grimaced. "And what does Garin think about that?"

"Oh, he raged. We duelled. A planned one, not me fighting him down, thankfully, but he had to work out his thoughts that way. And Isembard wasn't handy, so he had to make do."

Cyrus grunted. "A strenuous bout, or?"

"Not as strenuous as it should have been, and he realised it too." Alexander rubbed his face. "There've been a fair number of bombs dropped near Arundel. In West Sussex." Garin's demesne lands. "He feels them. They give him nightmares. More nightmares, I gather, I got that part from Isembard. It's not like Garin told me. The idea that there was anything that might help, even a bit, floored him. The fact Gabe would offer it so easily, without conditions, even more. Garin can't help but see it as weakness."

"Gabe's weakness, not Garin's?" Mabyn leaned forward. "You know I don't entirely understand that mode."

Alexander shrugged once. "Both. But the idea of offering help like that is a weakness. Making yourself vulnerable by showing what you know, sharing it without conditions. It's not a mode Garin has ever had good experiences with, except a little from Thesan." Which made him smile with a curling amusement.

"What's that smile for, then?" Of course Cyrus caught it. Mind, Alexander had meant him to.

"I had to explain that to Gabe. Our six and a half

minutes. That article he mentioned, at the end of that bit? Esse quam videri?" They both nodded. "Thesan's second author on it, yes. It came out the year Isembard first brought her to the Council gathering that winter. Garin misinterpreted the results, without realising she'd been one of the authors. Rather badly, as I understand it. Near a year later, not long before their wedding, she brought it up at supper. I was there, and she did it exceedingly neatly, as part of a larger skirmish about Isembard's intelligence. It made Livia laugh, actually." That made him smile, just a little. There were moments of Livia he missed. "But it's a touchy point, and the perfect one in that case, and Gabe had no idea of that second part of it."

"He's got a real knack for hitting his marks, doesn't he?" Cyrus glanced at Alexander. "Nothing else about Garin for the moment?"

Alexander shook his head. "Though here's another example of it. You know the rug in the Council Room." Of course they did. "Do you know what it's actually enchanted to do?"

Cyrus frowned. "I looked it up. Clarity of communication."

"Gabe got that much as soon as he'd been on it for a minute or two. What he realised in the depths of this morning, apparently, was this. It's also charmed so that you can - if you are actually standing on it - get a much better reading of people's emotions around you. Standing there, putting yourself in the centre, feels like weakness. You're surrounded with too many people at your back. You know how all of us hate that. But it gives you a tool no one else has."

"And Gabe was there the whole time he was talking." Cyrus shivered, once, with the potency of it. "Luck? Skill?"

"Both. Always assume it's both with Gabe. Chance to make him stand there, skill to use it, even before he realised all of what it was doing." Alexander shook his head ruefully. "Mind, he's been doing that all along. That comment when he came out, as if he'd been on a pleasant stroll except for nearly falling down the stairs."

"What was it that surprised you?" Mabyn had been downstairs at the time, but Cyrus had obviously told her something of that.

"For one thing, he just appeared - I don't recall the door opening, and I was looking right at it. For another, the expression on his face. Similar to some of the truth-telling magic, you know the way it leaves people not quite here for a moment after? It had something of that quality." Alexander hesitated, then decided if he didn't say this now, he wouldn't. "Back to the rug. I'm glad he shared. I intend to put myself there next meeting."

Cyrus and Mabyn exchanged a glance. "To talk about your challenge, now Gabe has?"

Once more, Alexander considered how much better his life was with Cyrus as head. Not only that he was fast enough to put it together, but he said so, and saved them all time. Of course, if Hesperidon had still been Head, Alexander wouldn't remotely have made himself vulnerable like that. "Yes. Before I get into that, what was it that had you on the edge of your seat when Gabe was talking?"

"Besides all of it?" Cyrus shook his head. "No, I know what you mean." He let out a breath. "I can't believe the Land spoke to him. You and I, we've had symbols. Mabyn, too. Gestures. Flowering fields. Nothing that had words."

"And we're the ritualists, and Gabe isn't. I'd feel insulted only, well." Alexander spread his hands. He had, in fact, a suspicion about what form of the Land Gabe might have spoken to. He wasn't going to touch on that, even with Cyrus and Mabyn, until he'd had a chance for a proper conversation with Gabe about it.

"He didn't give you any hint of it, then." Cyrus considered. "He's a pleasure to watch, honestly. Confusing, sometimes, because he doesn't play by the rules we're used to. But he played that meeting like a skilled virtuoso. Me very much included."

Alexander chuckled. "I'm glad you're aware of it. He's clear on what his goals are, and he doesn't care they aren't what ours are. Except, of course, in the end they are. Or should be. We want to preserve Albion, the land magic, all that we're sworn to."

"And he bypasses all the politics and the tradition and goes for the heart." Mabyn said, considering. "That was one of the things Silvia couldn't get over. Why he challenged, if he didn't want the power. Never mind he said he had to or face the wrath of the Fatae."

Alexander had been giving that question some thought, but he left it for later. Another thing to discuss with Geoffrey first. Geoffrey would have a better grasp on some pieces of it, or at least know how to gesture at the spaces around it. "I didn't want power, you know. I wanted..." He let out a huff of breath. "May I tell you now?"

"Please." Cyrus responded immediately, setting his plate aside and leaning forward.

Alexander closed his eyes for a moment, running a prayer in his mind that this would all come out right, that the impulses of Set in him were mirrored properly, and it would remake the world. "When I came to my challenge, I had a great deal of hope. I'd been formed as a tool, I knew that. I'm not stupid, after all."

It made them both laugh, and that bought Alexander a

chance for a breath. One more moment before he did what had been unthinkable. "I went up, and the walls were sandstone, uncarved. I told you this much, Cyrus." Cyrus nodded, remembering the moment when they'd made an oasis of the challenge chamber, not so many years ago. "It was a featureless expanse. I couldn't see the edges of the room. I had to find my way through and figure out what way I wanted to go. There were mirages, shimmers on the horizon. I got turned around, and I knew enough to know the dangers of the desert, even though it's not a place I've ever spent nearly enough time." He'd had five months in and around Cairo, in his younger years, before his challenge, not even half a year. Not long enough.

Mabyn nodded this time, encouraging him to go with a little twist of her fingers.

"I went through puzzles and - well. Rather like Gabe's. They were there, it wasn't that they didn't matter, but I knew I'd make it through. It wasn't difficult, just took a little time and demonstrating my knowledge and skill." He could still remember them like they'd happened minutes ago, with a sharp acuity of memory, like nothing else in his life except Perry's death. That was to be expected, really. "And then I came to a place where there was a hollow. We talk of Aset, queen of life, mistress of magic, she of the beautiful throne." He kept himself from sliding into the ancient words. This time, at least. "At least I thought it was Aset at first. She came with a feathered cloak. Everywhere it swept, there sprung forth an oasis, water and green life."

He sucked in a breath and made himself keep going. "Only, somewhere in there, I realised that it wasn't Aset, it was the lady of this land, of Albion. The place I was born, the place I have made my home, even when it didn't want me. And that was the thing. The people in the land might not have wanted me, certainly did not know what to do with me. Some of them insulted me, many ignored me, a handful made me into a tool for their work and I let them." There, that was the hard part over with. The hardest part.

"She didn't care about any of that. There weren't any words. She didn't need them. I didn't need them. Just the land turning green, the touch of it making everything whole, showing me what should be, what could be, what would be, if I took just one more step forward. Set is lord of the oasis, and she showed me what that meant, and gave me a place to make my own."

He had to stop then, to take a shuddering breath. As he did, he heard Cyrus's voice, a reverent whisper. "And then you walked into that meeting, and Hesperidon slashed all of that hope to pieces." There was a pause, so slight it barely registered even to Alexander, then Cyrus said, "You'd have torn the world apart if anyone tried the same with Gabe."

Alexander's head came up. "Gabe didn't need it. Gabe - whatever else he is - he's never been wounded that way. The land and the king are one, is the old law, before the Pact. He's given blood and sweat and I'm sure tears. Over and over again. But he's always loved the land, and the land has always loved him back. He has always known it. I envy that so much. But we need that. More than ever, now. Even without his skills and his gifts as a Penelope, even without all the knowledge wedged into his head. That unbroken love. I can't give it. I don't think either of you can, either."

He watched them, the way they hesitated, the way they wanted to argue, and couldn't. The world had wounded them in other ways than Alexander, and they had all three of them mended a great deal. Alexander hesitated. "Gabe's spoken with me a little about what happened with his ankle. It's not that he's unwounded. Just not in a way that hurt his love of the land, somehow. There's a miracle for you. I know you don't believe much in gods, Cyrus."

Cyrus let out a sigh. "I am coming to think that it doesn't matter much if I don't, they still are in and of the world." He held up his hand. "That's a philosophical debate for some other night, with more leisure and also more wine in it."

Alexander laughed. "Fair, fair. I will look forward to the moment."

"I bet you will." Cyrus was at ease now with the idea that Alexander would pounce when he could. There was a silence that drew out then, but not uncomfortably. After perhaps two minutes, while Alexander finished the last of his supper, Cyrus cleared his throat. "I would like to tell you about my challenge, and as Head. But not tonight. It's getting late enough, and who knows what tomorrow will bring?"

"Fair." Alexander waved a hand. "I am holding to Gabe's good judgement here. Sharing is a gift, not a trade, not here and now. But I would like time to talk in next week's meeting. I don't know how much I will say, but some of it. What Hesperidon's choices meant to me. I'm sorry, Mabyn, that's going to keep Silvia annoyed."

"Spread it around, maybe." Mabyn sighed, but she seemed resigned. "No, I'll manage. You owe me another nice meal, though."

"Fair enough. I'll see what we can arrange." Being able to draw on Ytene's goods made that a titch easier. "For now?"

"For now, didn't you say you had a good story from last week, the one about the unfortunate stile and walking the bounds?"

"Oh, yes." That was, in fact, a funny story, one that should get them all laughing. It involved a stile out in the New Forest, an unfortunately located drift of pigs, and someone from the Home Guard with aspirations above his current station.

CHAPTER 18
DECEMBER 13TH AT YTENE

"Any other way you'd like to put off this bit of discussion?" Geoffrey kept his voice light. Alexander had turned up for tea, after apparently running around the country via portal in two large loops on Thursday and Friday. They'd had tea, a walk through the stables and the mews, supper, and now here they were in Alexander's rooms. Alexander had kept his public face firmly on, charm and erudition fervently on display, but not much at all in the way of emotion.

While Geoffrey was changing after supper, Alexander had gone off to his rooms. After a moment's reflection, Geoffrey had chosen to change into a dressing gown and pyjamas. The intimate mode, rather than the informal one, that was what he wanted. He had no idea where he was sleeping tonight, and that would be the more flexible choice. More comfortable too. In the meantime, Alexander had settled behind the desk. Now he had three, no, four piles of paper out, and was writing brief notes at the top. Geoffrey settled on the sofa, crossing one ankle over his knee, and waited for a response.

After perhaps forty seconds, Alexander looked up. Geoffrey had, in fact, been a tad worried, until that moment. There, though, was an impish expression, not the flat one that had come to haunt the corners of Geoffrey's quieter nightmares. "I don't know. A bit of fire watch. Seeing which of the Home Guard notice us? We do have choices."

"It is December. I have had quite enough conversations with the Home Guard for the week, and you are being perverse." Geoffrey shook his head, relaxing properly. "I want to talk to you, though. Your summary was again admirably concise. 'Went well' covers a lot of ground, not very informatively."

"If it had not gone well, I'd have been here right after." Alexander laid his hands on the desk, palms flat. "You do know that. That I come here when I need what comfort and understanding is on offer." He lifted a finger. "Which is in fact quite a lot. You needn't say it." Then he stood, pushing up easily from the chair. "Bed, I think. This wants dim light and a bit of space."

Geoffrey stood, letting Alexander go first. Alexander's bed was a fine place for this sort of conversation, indeed. They'd had many excellent ones there, over the past four and a half years. Alexander went off to change and do whatever washing up he felt needed doing, and Geoffrey adjusted the curtains. By the time Alexander came back, he was stretched out on the bed, leaning on his right arm, flipping through a book from the bedside table. It was, curiously enough, a book of folklore about Kent.

"A loan from Gabe. He promises me we can mock the foolish parts when I've read it, but he had a question or two about parallels to various points." Alexander had slipped into his own dressing gown, a deep blue and grey that suited him well. He found his side of the bed, then arched, and Geoffrey could hear a couple of joints crack as Alexander let out a sigh. "It's been a week. To follow the previous fortnight, which was not exactly an oasis of calm."

"You are a master of understatement, among your many other gifts." Geoffrey considered his tactical options and went right for it. "The meeting?"

"I owe Gabe a debt. Another debt, I really need to count them up properly. He softened them up nicely for me, with how he went at things last week." Alexander met his eyes. "No one was cruel. Surprised, yes. Awkward, absolutely. Silvia's still fuming, but about a wider range of options now, and that's probably for the good."

"Because you dared suggest Hesperidon was not, in fact, the font of all that was good and proper?"

"Oh, she'd still argue for proper, I think. But she does admit he was not always good. The rub of it is that she is convinced he had a reason for what he did, always. And I'll allow as how he probably did, but that does not make them good reasons or what's the word here. Complete reasons. Sufficient reasons."

Geoffrey nodded at that. "So, how did you begin?"

"We had some general business to take care of - there are a couple of specific petitions. There have been a few bombs that fell too near Fatae lands, and we have obligations on our side of things to stabilise the magic and all that." Alexander shrugged, and didn't go into that part. "Preparation for Solstice, and how we're handling various pieces of it." His mouth quirked up. "Thesan is partnering me, and not Garin." That was a signal win. Alexander had not been entirely sure how that was going to go.

"Who's partnering Garin?"

"Rhoe, actually." Cyrus's sister. "She knows the dances. She used to partner Cyrus before he and Mabyn made that tidy. And she's a Healer. She'll know if there's a problem that needs tending. Between the bombings, the shifts in the magic, Garin's general - well, he's not eating well, or sleeping, and that's no surprise."

"A Healer makes sense. A Healer who absolutely knows the dances, even better." Geoffrey agreed. "And she's hard to ruffle or insult. I'm sure it's possible to insult her, but Garin wouldn't know much about the things that actually would."

Alexander snorted agreeably. "That's a thing I wanted to talk through with you, actually. That and what I told them."

"And I've one for you, when you're done with those." They needed a bit of time to put plans into place, and there was just more than a week to work with.

Alexander rearranged himself, settling on the bed on his back, hands laced under his neck. Not looking at Geoffrey for the moment, but that was expected. "I don't know what I expected from telling them. It wasn't an epiphany, anyway."

"Have you been up to the challenge chamber since?" Geoffrey had wondered if that was where Alexander was, either Wednesday or Thursday.

"This afternoon, before I came here. You get ahead of yourself, Long-Striding One. Anyway, we got through the ordinary sorts of business, and Cyrus gave me the floor." He opened his hand, closing it again as if grasping for something. "I laid it out. The Lady, and her cloak of feathers. What meaning the stories I grew up with made of that. What my ties to the land here made of that. What it meant to come to the land as a lover." His voice cracked a hair at the last.

"I didn't know if you'd say that much." Geoffrey shifted,

leaning his fingers lightly on Alexander's forearm.

"It's Gabe's fault. He was very mild, actually, but he was sitting there, and listening, and after last week." Alexander let out a huff of a breath. "I'd say he's shaming us into good behaviour, but it's not shame at all. It's simply - ha, simply - and resolutely doing the thing he knows needs doing. It makes one want to do the same. He's as implacable as Livia, in his own way."

"You need him there." Geoffrey said, carefully, though he was thinking much the same. Had been, since it became clear Gabe was going to challenge for a seat. Not for the same reasons, exactly, but because Gabe brought a gravity with him.

"No one said anything for a little after. Twenty seconds, maybe. I didn't count the first few." Alexander let his eyes close most of the way. "And then I talked about coming into that first meeting, about being sent out as an attack dog. About how there had been no greeting, no welcome, precious little explanation. I could see how Laodamia and Godfrey were taking that one." Those were the two most recent additions to the Council before Gabe. The ones where Alexander had been able to offer them the explanation and welcome and ritual he'd been denied.

"The ones who've come on since you could change things a bit." Geoffrey said, because Alexander needed to hear it out loud. "Since you and Cyrus worked out how to trust each other. You to trust he wouldn't hurt you the same ways Hesperidon had, and him to trust that you had reasons for your caution."

"So many reasons." Alexander rubbed his nose. "I'd say uncountable, but I do actually have a list." It made Geoffrey smile. Words made things real to Alexander, written words. It was one of the precepts of how he saw the world, and one

Geoffrey agreed with entirely. "Vidya wants to have a chat when we can find a minute." She'd come on after Hesperidon's death, but when Cyrus and Alexander had still been in a careful detente.

"On the whole, that sounds as good as can be expected?" Geoffrey tried measuring it out carefully. It was tricky, though, when he hadn't been there, couldn't be there, had absolutely no desire to be there. Except that he always wanted more of watching Alexander at his best.

"We'll see what comes out in the next few weeks. Both Cyrus and Mabyn wish to talk about theirs, but likely not until after Solstice. A few people are still terribly offended." He shrugged. "I have a bet on with Cyrus that Troilus Watts will resign in the spring. I don't think he's up to the challenge Gabe presents to his worldview. Cyrus thinks he'll hang on until autumn at least."

That made Geoffrey snort. "So it's not that you disagree he'll resign, it's just about when." He considered. "I favour yours. He's not known for a flexible mind, is he?"

Alexander shook his head. "And well. Gabe's fairly sure that if Maisie Wallace makes an attempt again, she's likely to be successful. I'm not going to gainsay him. And we had an interesting crop this time. Mabyn has a few others she's sounding out for future opportunities, too. People she knows through Nora Martin-Baddock. Not Schola folk." He twisted onto his side to face Geoffrey again. "Which brings me to my second thing."

"Yes?" Geoffrey had less idea of what this topic might be.

"One of the things that offends Silvia - and I use that verb quite deliberately - is Gabe's attitude to power. And that's one I think I need to talk through with you. Possibly also Richard, but I'm starting with you."

"Now, there's an interesting parameter. Something to do with the demesne lands, then?" Geoffrey was pleased to consider this puzzle. Alexander did bring him the best ones.

Alexander shook his head. "No, about being born to the kind of family you were. And Gabe was. And Richard. Which is about the demesne lands, but not just those." Alexander's mouth quirked. "This is not one I know. I was born an outsider here, and will always be one. That it suits me down to the depths of my bones works well, but it makes certain things entirely opaque."

Geoffrey nodded. "You may ask whatever you wish, you know that." After a moment's consideration, he moved his hand to rest it on Alexander's and was pleased when Alexander threaded his fingers through Geoffrey's instead.

"Silvia is baffled because Gabe does not care about power. Does not care about the sort of power that comes with being on the Council, that is. He doesn't see it as a way to advance his family, or his own goals, or marry well, or make money, or any of that, either."

"He doesn't need the Council for any of that. He already has what he wants. Hasn't he said as much?" Geoffrey grinned broadly. "Oh, I can help a bit with this. You, at least."

"Please do. The better I understand it, the better I can shore up supports in useful places." Alexander squeezed his hand once.

"Now, mind. I do come at it differently. I never expected to inherit, so there was all my life, nearly through my thirties, where I assumed there would be some little new Carillon. There'd be a child of Temple and Delphina's, and I could go on travelling the world and minding my own business. And instead, here I am." He glanced around the room, felt the cloak of the family holdings and magic draped around the house, as it were. "I am very happy, but I didn't have that solidness when I was younger."

"Even allowing for the War bending your sense of the land magic." Alexander agreed.

"Just so. Now, there's Gabe. He's had a very good idea what he wanted to do with himself from the time he was tiny. Even early in his twenties, he had an incredible sense of self-possession. I first met him glancingly, when I was newly back and he'd just finished his apprenticeship. It caught my attention."

Alexander cleared his throat, and Geoffrey knew himself to be blushing. "For a minute there, I wasn't sure if he weren't offering a particular proposition. In front of his parents, mind, it was a very decorous sort of statement. But then he went off to Scotland and met Rathna. Besides which, that would be a bit too much complication, given how much I was relying on - and still rely on - Alysoun and Richard's good graces. Never mind the age gap, I am not actually inclined to that sort of thing."

"No, you prefer a suitably aged vintage." Alexander wriggled a bit into the pillows. It was the sort of delightful moment of relaxation that Geoffrey loved to provoke, when Alexander felt enough at ease to tease and let go of holding onto dignity so tightly.

"At any rate, Gabe knows who he is. He knows his worth. He is absolutely rock solid in his love of the land and his understanding of everything that means, like almost no one else of the generation between him and a bit older than me. Not having been in the Great War directly. And he's spent his adult life in work that values him, that challenges him, that keeps him curious and endlessly flexible. He has a wife he loves, a family who support him admirably even if they don't always understand him, delightful children..."

Geoffrey shrugged. "There's no power that can offer more than that. He's had some good luck, but he's done more to make his own happiness, I think."

"And that's utterly foreign to Silvia. To me, too. I envy him for it. Except I know it has pressures of its own." Alexander was considering something.

"Gabe's much better with it now - if you hear him do it, you can hear Alysoun coming through, actually, more than Richard. But I gather he didn't have many friends at Schola. Acquaintances, amiable enough, but no one close. His closest connections, besides Rathna, are all Penelopes, though they both spend a fair bit of time with the bohemian progressive set they found early in their marriage. But you don't join the Council to make friends."

It got a barking laugh from Alexander. "I certainly didn't. Join or get them." He hesitated. "Well. Cyrus and Mabyn. And Gabe now. But I'd never have thought that at the time, or until quite recently." He wriggled the fingers on his free hand. "I don't think Gabe's making too many enemies. Not out of the usual proportion, anyway. A bit more noisily than most of us do, but there's Gabe for you."

"I swear he can be subtle. You saw the fight. You told me about how he handled that meeting. Other men and women would have made it a duelling offence, being called a liar to their faces, and you were clear Gabe just swept by it."

"He didn't expect them to like him, and he had evidence to prove his claims. All right. I'll have more questions some-time, I suspect, but not yet." Alexander chewed on that for a moment. "Oh! I have something that will make you laugh."

Geoffrey raised an eyebrow. "Animal, vegetable, mineral, or magic?" he asked, the old childhood game. "First, though. The challenge chamber?"

Alexander snorted. "Mind like a trap. It was peaceful. Humming with it. Like a summer's day, even though we're nearly at winter solstice. There were bees in the background, getting about their work, there were birds, there was an explosion of garden flowers. I suspect I know a bit more about Gabe's challenge than he told. The details of it." He took a breath. "I talked to the Lady. I didn't see anyone. I didn't hear her speak back, but I felt her, in a way I—" He shrugged, once, shivering. "Feathers on the skin."

"Oh, Alexander." Geoffrey was overtaken with emotion. "Something healing, then." He made it a statement, not a question. "I'm glad."

Alexander was quiet for a long moment, then he ducked his chin. "I didn't know I could have that. And I don't know that I'd have dared that part, but for Gabe. Unexpected gifts. He brings the light with him, I think, that shows the way forward."

"That's an interesting image for us, isn't it? Especially in a time of blackouts." Geoffrey let out a sigh. "I hope it's a sign we'll make it through. There are days I have my doubts."

Alexander's hand shifted against his. "All of us do, I think. But one foot in front of the other. Make do. Keep going. We know how to do that, well enough." Then he shook his head, a quick little turn. "To answer your question, technically animal." Alexander was deliberately changing the subject, and Geoffrey didn't mind. "Gabe told me a bit about one of the exercises they do as part of Penelope training. I commented on his background on Garin."

"And?" Geoffrey blinked at this.

"One of their standard training exercises, early in the first year, is having the apprentices look at pairs of people. Often siblings, active in public, or parents and children, or close colleagues. How are these people alike and different? Drawing on public sources, plus a set of what's available to the Penelopes. School records, legal documents which include the apprenticeship agreements, and so on."

Geoffrey frowned for a moment and then started laughing. "Oh, Garin and Isembard must make quite a contrast."

"Very. Cyrus and Rhoe are also a popular example, apparently, and I'm saving that one for a good moment. Don't you give it away. Gabe said I could tell him when it was suitably timed. If you're very good, I'll do it when you're handy."

"I wouldn't dream of interfering." Geoffrey held back the comment he'd have made a few weeks ago, that it wasn't likely he'd talk to Cyrus privately unsupervised. "Troilus and Paulus Watts, I suspect? You could make any number of combinations of the Powells. Or the Howards or the Phipps."

"Just so. I gathered they've considered me and Philip, but there's not enough information in the usual sources to make a good one. I have offered myself as an object lesson where they can ask questions, sometime, when they next have new apprentices."

Geoffrey chuckled. "Oh, that one I'd like to sit in on. If you'd keep them off me."

"Of course, Nehkeny." Alexander hesitated. "You don't want them prying into your brother."

"It's not that. Well, it is. But I asked Gabe to pry. You were there." Geoffrey let out a hitched breath. "I know what happened, enough of it, the sequence of it. What I don't understand is why. Why Temple was so stubborn, what happened to make him neglect the land?" Geoffrey had a flash of that moment when he'd first come back to Ytene, after Temple's death, and seen the neglect. "I would have thought he'd be like Garin is, as Lord. Competent, even if he didn't have a feeling for it, or lean into that feeling. It was as if he'd shied like a horse."

"Some terrifying shape, and no way to know if it was some real threat or a deer." Alexander nodded, slowly.

"Just so. And that's the part I want to understand. I don't know if there's any way to, this long after. Temple didn't leave anything in writing. I've looked a dozen times. I even had Giles work through some of Delphina's household notes, but it's wisps of mist. She was worried about him, from 1916 on or so, and it just got more so, but she never says why. But if anyone can figure it out, I trust Gabe can. And I trust him to hold the necessary confidences."

"It must have been awful for her." Geoffrey looked up at the tone in it. Alexander, five years ago, wouldn't have known that feeling. Now he did. He knew what it was to worry about other people in that intimate way. Geoffrey was glad of it - and a tad sorry that the worry had to come along with the love. Alexander flicked his finger. "You had something to bring up?"

Which was Alexander deciding that going on along with this topic wouldn't be good for either of them. Geoffrey agreed, honestly. "I did. How do you want me to play things at the Solstice? I made a deal with Gabe. I intend to keep it. Would it be of use to you for me to have a public cordial conversation with Cyrus, or perhaps someone else? Bar the ones I'd really rather not, ideally. Exert my charm? Have me and Lizzie stay to the utter end of the evening, rather than sidling off just after it stops being rude? I am at your disposal for your plotting."

The breath went out of Alexander in a rush. "You mean it."

"I do." Geoffrey extracted his hand solely so he could

cup Alexander's cheek. "I'll talk it through with Gabe and his parents, too, but you first. Always you before anyone but Lizzie and the children."

Alexander considered. "You might bring Edmund this year, actually. He's old enough to appreciate it. And Gabe and Rathna are bringing Rowena and Anthony both, I believe."

"That we can likely do, unless Lizzie has an objection I don't anticipate. The rest of it?"

"I think that seeing you be charming, both of you being charming, would be delightfully confusing to a great many people. What's your goal, then?"

"The good of the land, the magic, the well-being of my loved ones and allies. What else?" Geoffrey let himself shrug. "But it is time to draw the falcons from the sky, and the horses in from the forest, and go to work, isn't it?"

"Your lips to the gods' ears." Alexander murmured. "Collaboration and resilience to get through the war and come out the other side. I'll think on it. Come up with people it would be excellent if you talked to."

Geoffrey let himself relax into the pillows finally. "I knew you'd have a list. Or produce one."

"Is that it, then? For the moment?" Alexander shifted to stretch along Geoffrey's side. "I read an article you'll like. You needn't move. I can tell you it from memory."

"That sounds like a fine evening. Want me to stay, then?" At the moment, Geoffrey very much wanted to fall asleep here. Partly so Alexander knew he was not alone with his world, not anymore. And partly because he wanted to hear Alexander's breath, whenever it happened, slip from watchfulness to trusting unconsciousness. A particular gift, a rare one, and all the more treasured.

EPILOGUE
DECEMBER 22ND AT THE COUNCIL KEEP

Gabe glanced at Rathna, as the surrounding conversations swirled into a new configuration.

He was feeling decidedly on edge for half a dozen reasons. There was an incredible melange of magic here, more than he'd noticed before. For all he'd been at the obligatory Council Solstice events with his parents most years since he'd become Papa's heir, it had an entirely different edge to it.

There had been the private rituals last night. Those had been formal, in a mode Gabe wouldn't have chosen himself, but that flowed impeccably. Cyrus and Alexander between them had made sure of it. Lucas was quite a competent ritualist in his own right, and everyone else knew their parts. That had been here, in the Great Hall, not up in the challenge chamber. Asking about that choice was on Gabe's increasingly lengthy list of questions for Alexander or Cyrus when he got a proper chance.

Now, they were back for the more public portion of the rituals. There had been the dance that opened the celebrations. That was a measured tread that ran from the older dances, out of the time of the Pact, then into the patterns of the country dances, then finally into the decidedly more modern waltz. He had found those took more attention for him, not from the dancing itself, but the swirls of magic. He enjoyed dancing with Rathna. They did not get a chance to do it often and he was not going to turn down any chance to have her in his arms or right at his side.

They were in their finery tonight, too. Gabe's suit was much as most of his suits were, though this time in a more formal black rather than the tweed he chose for most daily wear outside his uniform. The cloak over it, however, matched the waistcoat of the iridescent green that had haunted his dreams for the last year and change, though shades darker than that twist of dragon scales tended to be. Rathna had a saree, resplendent in the same green and with nearly as much gold embroidery as their wedding.

He felt they had made a grand show all round as a family. Mama had got Papa to wear something other than his uniform, and Rowena and Anthony had new outfits for the occasion. Rowena looked quite grown up, in a way that kept surprising him every time he caught a glance at her. Her hair was not yet up as an adult woman's would be, but that was near enough the only difference. She'd turn seventeen in January. He supposed her growing up was inevitable. Anthony was wide-eyed at his first event like this, but Mama was keeping him close and explaining who people were.

Rathna's fingers tightened slightly on his arm. She'd spotted someone or something from the other direction. "Love?" He murmured it in her ear, smiling generally at the people going across their corner of the room.

"Davis Fortnum." One of her colleagues among the Portal Keepers, and none too fond of either of them at the moment, most likely. He was still touchy about Gabe's having lent a hand with the Council portal back in June, and with Rathna because Fortnum's former apprentice was flourishing in Rathna's care.

"That is not the most challenging conversation we could be having." Gabe pointed out. "There's at least half a dozen more so in this room."

Rathna wrinkled her nose up. "No. But that's not actually much help given our last half-year."

"I've gone an entire fortnight without doing something out of myth and legend so far!" Gabe pointed out, hoping he'd get her to laugh or at least smile. "I'll probably go a month if we get through tonight, at least a month."

As he hoped, the corners of her mouth tugged up. Then she made a smile and nod. "Davis. You know Gabe, of course."

"Happy Solstice." Gabe said, the most neutral possible of the seasonal greetings.

"No Howard trailing along, Rathna?" Fortnum glanced around. Of course, he was the sort who'd use last names, even for his former apprentice.

"Not tonight, no." Rathna's voice stayed pleasant, of course, but Gabe could hear the tightness there.

"We brought our two older children with us, and Ferdinand offered to entertain our youngest, along with my own apprentice." Gabe said, keeping his voice even. "Very generous of him." Also, both Ferdinand and Isobel would have found this particular gathering complicated to navigate, if for very different reasons. A good reason to stay in was worth a lot to them.

"Ah. I'll have to catch up with him at some point." Fortnum nodded sharply. "I will say the portal's holding well."

That, now, that was absolute bait. Gabe wasn't going to take it. Fortnum wasn't unskilled in this sort of social duelling, but Gabe could handle it easily. "I knew you'd be the right person this summer. I made that clear to Cyrus and Alexander immediately, of course." Which all three of them knew, but it might be informative for eavesdroppers, and Gabe was sure there were some. He couldn't see behind him, not without various pieces of his kit that were decidedly not suitable for a formal social event. But he could feel a couple of people, close enough to hear and not quite close enough to make him truly jumpy.

Fortnum nodded once. "Good, you know your limits."

That, now, that was taking effort. Gabe restrained himself from laughing, funnelling it into a broad smile and his own fingers shifting against Rathna's. "It is a regular complaint from near anyone who knows me that I'm a tad fuzzy on the concept of limits, actually. But in this case, yes, I do. And I am glad to leave such things to the experts available." Which could include him. 'Available' was such a useful phrasing, really. Then he caught a glimpse of Alexander prowling and said, "Oh, do beg pardon. I should catch a moment with Alexander."

Fortnum glanced over his shoulder, and his posture immediately changed. "Quite." He nodded briskly to Rathna. "Perhaps we might find time for a thorough discussion in the New Year?"

She smiled agreeably. "Of course. I'm sure we can find a chance between our various commitments." Fortnum then turned and disappeared into the crowd.

Alexander joined them almost immediately. He was looking particularly resplendent in the deep blues he favoured, ritual robes flowing over his own suit. Gabe raised an eyebrow at him. "I am certain now you put the fear of something into Fortnum a while ago. Goodness."

"A decade, at least. I was a trifle sharp at the time. I let Cyrus and Mabyn make the arrangements this summer for a reason." Ah, that would be Alexander having been sent off to be the Council's attack dog under Hesperidon Warren. One more of those to lay on his grave and demand an explanation for, if only Gabe could. Not that he actually had any interest in necromancy. It was both intolerable as an idea and messy on every possible level. Let the dead rest, even if you wanted to shout at them. Perhaps especially if you wanted to shout at them.

Alexander was saying something, and he'd missed half a sentence. On the one hand, that made it clear he didn't actually feel at risk at the moment. On the other hand, it made having a conversation difficult. Alexander stopped, then, tilting his head. "Let me begin again. You did your parts excellently well, and Rathna, you are light on your feet. I am here to check that you don't need anything, perhaps glower at a few people, and tell you Silvia is unchanged. Thesan would love to catch you at some point, if you're all free at the same time, but right now she's waiting for Isembard and Garin."

Gabe nodded at that, thoughtfully. He looked across the room - he knew nearly everyone here, of course, though a fair number of them largely by sight and trained memory. Then his eyes caught on something specific, and he cleared his throat. Alexander turned, and there was a slow smile, something tinged with awe. Geoffrey and Lizzie were talking to Cyrus, chatting away as if there had never been any gap.

"Quite public, quite deft. Not that I'd expect anything other than skill." Gabe kept his voice low, watching Alexander's face. There was a deep delight there, before Alexander managed to hide it again. "I saw them talking to Rhoda a few minutes ago." She had not warmed to Gabe, not this quickly. But of the Council members dubious about him, she seemed at least plausibly willing to listen. Geoffrey had a long-standing interest in materia, one of her specialties, and he could be charming about that at great length and interest. "And Lord and Lady Winslow, of course."

They held Southern Hampshire, the next demesne lands east of the New Forest. Southampton had been hit heavily by bombing this fall, in multiple raids. Gabe knew Geoffrey had been lending support and helping coordinate, as he could, but making that visible here could only be a blessing.

Alexander nodded. "Perhaps we might catch up, in between the social obligations this week?" He considered, then tapped one of the passing staff on the arm, murmuring something in his ear. The man went off, promptly on an arc to where Gabe now knew the kitchens to be. "Rathna, I hope you're enjoying yourself as much as possible in an event where everyone is focused on Gabe and what he might do next?"

"You say that as if I'm not." Rathna laughed, though, and Gabe glanced at her, smiling. Letting his complete adoration and appreciation of her show was necessary politics at the moment, and it was also the easiest thing he needed to do tonight. Keep doing, though he did in fact have plans for more personal forms of adoration when they got home, assuming they didn't both fall immediately asleep. "People have been entirely polite, honestly."

Alexander, of course, caught the implications of that, and said cheerfully, "Do let me know if there's anyone I need to glower at." Outside the agreed on list. Not Silvia, for example, because glowering would not be helpful there. He considered, then made a few comments about various people who might be interesting conversational partners for a couple of minutes. Then the staff member reappeared, holding up a tray with a couple of cups of coffee.

"Gabe, you'll want one of those." Alexander took another. "Rathna, of course, if you'd like. Otherwise, Jacobs, I'm sure Cyrus could use a cup at this point to keep himself going." The man nodded slightly, waiting for Gabe to take his, before disappearing with the tray.

"Appreciated." Gabe lifted the cup. It would help him focus, he knew that. Next time, he'd know better how to pace the coffee in the evening against the ritual's ebb and flow. "I do have some things I'd like to discuss when we've more privacy. Wednesday, before the meeting, or some other time?"

"Short meeting on Wednesday. We could do it after, if there's nothing too demanding of our time?"

"You don't mind?" Gabe wanted to make sure of it.

"I'm staying in Essex while Thesan and Isembard are there." Ah, that explained why he wasn't as eager as usual to get to Ytene. That made sense. Though perhaps those patterns would shift again, now Geoffrey and Lizzie were being more visible in this space. He wanted to talk that through with Mama and Papa.

Rathna considered, then nudged Gabe. "They're starting up the music again. You could go offer Rowena a dance. She'd be thrilled. She's been practising hard. Entirely traditional, and in a mode people don't expect of you." They'd shared dances for the seasonal celebrations before, but of course never in this particular setting.

Gabe laughed at that. "Can't do the expected thing. Alexander, may I leave Rathna's temporary entertainment in your hands?"

"Absolutely." Alexander bowed. "I assume you've had your fill of dancing, then, but I can certainly be amusing. I'd say introduce you to people you'd find interesting, but I suspect you already know most of the ones I would think of."

Rathna glanced around. "In that case, let me introduce you to someone I think you'll find intriguing. Gabe, the Royces are here."

Gabe grinned at that. They'd be entertaining for Alexander for certain, and possibly a new experience. They'd got to know the current generation while living in London, but Nirin and Lise were both of excellent family, more than a tad eccentric in their interests. The tale of the two of them figuring out their own romance had been a chaos of misassumptions and talking their families round. "I'll come find you." He went strolling off in search of Rowena, making a bow. He whispered in her ear that he'd make sure everything went smoothly as he drew her out to the dancing.

If you enjoyed *Upon A Summer's Day* and would like to read more of this series, please sign up for my mailing list to get all the latest news and fun extras.

Your reviews (on whatever review site you use) are much appreciated, too!

Read on for more historical details about this book and an excerpt from *BOOK2,* the next book in the series.

AUTHOR'S NOTES

Welcome to the author's notes for *Upon A Summer's Day!* Thank you for joining me on this journey with Gabe and with Rathna, Alexander, Geoffrey, Richard, and Alysoun. I hope you've enjoyed it as much as I have. As always, my great thanks to my editor, Kiya Nicoll, for all their help brainstorming as well as editing, and to my early readers for their comments.

The title for this book - and the structure - have something to do with each other. The title comes from a Playford dance, *Upon A Summer's Day*. The name for this type of dance comes from John Playford's collection of dances published in 1651, *The English Dancing Master*. Various further editions came out into the 1700s, along with other similar books.

The book was an attempt to collect the various social dances for dancing masters in various locations around Great Britain. A number of historical re-enactment or re-creationist groups use them as appropriate. They were the dances of educated or well-off society, on the more decorous side, though some of them can get rather vigorous.

Many of the dances are done in sets of paired couples, repeating various patterns to music. You can find examples of many dances if you search on YouTube, as well as music and descriptions of the dances themselves.

"Upon A Summer's Day" is a dance based on groups of three couples, each of them progressing through a series of steps in sequence. Now, here's where I have to confess that when I was first working out which dance to use, I swear I found a variation where the couples changed places in the sequence. There's space for it in the music, where the first couple travels back up to their original position.

Can I find that now? No. Let's call it Albion's variation on the dance. At any rate, that also gives us the structure, with three couples, progressing through each portion, with a new couple ending up at the head of the line.

Partly, this sequencing amused me. More usefully, it allowed me to put Gabe's challenge where I wanted it to fall in the pacing of the book, with time to work through the aftermath rather than ending abruptly. I wanted to tell this part of the Gabe's life - and the larger arc of the land magic implications of the Land Mysteries - from multiple perspectives.

Having both people who know Gabe very well, and two who are amiably inclined but more distant, did just the trick. If you saw me talk about this on my newsletter, you may remember me saying this was supposed to be a novella. It decidedly outgrew that in the writing, and I think taking the space for that was the right choice as well.

Let's get into the discussion of the book itself.

Both *Old As The Hills* and *Upon A Summer's Day* deal with relatively early stages of the Second World War. As we get into the summer of 1940, various spies have been caught in Great Britain (from all historical accounts, very successfully. There will be a touch more about that in the upcoming Illusion of a Boar, but the history of those efforts is full of stories, some of them hilarious or almost unbelievable). As the book begins, we are also just about to enter the beginning of the Blitz, with more on that when we get to chapter 6.

Chapter 1 : We open with Gabe out on the family's lands in **Kent**. Gabe's mare is named Meliora, a Latin word that means either 'better' or 'honey', while Rathna's Madhup gets her name from the Hindu for "honeybee".

Chapter 3 : Winston Churchill made a number of notable speeches during the war. In this case, Gabe and Alexander are discussing his speech of August 20, 1940, where he's particularly praising the fighter pilots and air crews. "The gratitude of every home in our Island, in our Empire, and indeed throughout the world, except in the abodes of the guilty, goes out to the British airmen who, undaunted by odds, unwearied in their constant challenge and mortal danger, are turning the tide of the World War by their prowess and by their devotion. Never in the field of human conflict was so much owed by so many to so few."

The letter about **the snake and apricot** is taken from a real letter sent to the London Times by Eric Parker, a noted naturalist (as Gabe mentions). My thanks to my cover designer, Augusta Scarlett, for helping me track down an actual letter when I was casting about going "I can assume there's some weird letter that they can investigate in the Times, there always is..." and fighting with my desire to dive into a rabbit hole of research for something that would only be relevant for a sentence or three.

On the other hand, finding something that's real and historical is always a joy. This particular letter hit all the notes I'd been hoping for and them some. Of course there was a great deal of suspicion at the time about secret messages or unexpected communications meaning something dire. Thus, both the Council's caution and the results of the investigation are quite reasonable in context.

Chapter 4 : There was in fact a **bombing test range** just west of Ytene during the Second World War. It was being built during this period and not heavily used until later in the War, but it was used to test the damage from various bombs as well as other investigations. Not exactly the sort of thing you want close to your magical estate or your horses, but Geoffrey (and Lizzie) will muddle through. It does explain some of why Geoffrey is spending so much time with the Home Guard.

The **Home Guard** was formed May 14, 1940 after the invasion of the Netherlands, Belgium, and France. Originally known as the Local Defence Volunteers (but using the name "Home Guard" by July), they were uniformed but not officially military. While their role changed quite a bit over time, Geoffrey (as someone too old to enlist, but with highly relevant experience in the Great War and a thorough knowledge of the area) is an excellent candidate for an officer's role. Geoffrey's fifty-seven at this point. They were meant to help maintain order at home, respond to emergencies, and, in event of an invasion, to carry out plans to slow the enemy in a number of ways. The men involved were those who couldn't - for reasons of age, disability, or need to be in Britain for other employment reasons - enlist, but who still had useful skills or who were willing to learn them.

Chapter 5: While there had been fairly regular **bombing** raids in the United Kingdom from early in the war, they begin to pick up substantially in mid-August 1940. Generally, the UK considers the Battle of Britain to have run from July 10th, 1940 to October 31st, 1940, overlapping the Blitz running from September 7th, 1940 through May 11th, 1941. Originally, many of the targets were of a military focus, like airfields and harbours with significant shipping or shipbuilding. Over time, however (as we move into the Blitz), many more civilian targets took the brunt of the bombing.

Chapter 6 : One of my key research questions for much of this book was about where that bombing took place. Some I knew about, of course, like Coventry in chapter 9, and about the overall focus on southern England. My father was a schoolboy in Ipswich during the Second World War (and took some of his key exams in air raid shelters). My mother was enough younger and much further away (in Northern Ireland) that while they had many air raid warnings, almost no bombing occurred near her. She learned after the war ended that that was because the planes up to nearly the end of the war only had enough fuel to make it one way from the Continent if they ventured that far north.

Information about bombing in some areas was much easier to come by than in others. I kept finding fairly detailed information for London, or I'd stumble across a village history that had all sorts of specifics about that particular place. (Sometimes, this was down to which trees were destroyed.) This was helpful, but not everything I wanted, given that I had characters living in two different areas of southern England and responding to bombing in many other places (as both Richard and Gabe do in particular).

As I looked for answers, I kept finding references to a project published in 2019 called "Bombing Britain". Frustratingly, I couldn't get at the maps or data for a good while, just news reports about this exciting project that was now behind a paywall I couldn't get access to. Then I had a moment of brilliance and realised that if I dug through the Wayback Machine, I could get the spreadsheet file of the original data they'd used.

A bit of downloading and crowing about my delight at all this data later, I split things up into the groupings I needed. In this case, that includes the duration of this book for southern and southeastern England (the regions I cared about most). I also made separate tabs for a few other places. I then spent quality time with Google Maps vastly improving my knowledge of minor English place-names, to figure out which locations were key for my characters.

Thus, all of the mentions of specific bombs or air raids in this book are as accurate as I could make them, given the thousands of rows of the original spreadsheet. I was delighted to be able to do that, both because I think it's a part of history we don't think enough about, and because so many of my characters are deeply connected with the land.

London of course was a major target, and is the place with the greatest number of overall deaths by quite a lot. If you've seen photos of the Blitz, you've probably seen how some houses are entirely demolished, and a house next door might still be standing. Magically, of course, this can also cause all manner of problems, especially when you think of disruption to alchemical labs or to the energetic lines of the portals.

There were, however, also a number of bombs dropped in Kent in specific, and thus highly relevant to the Edgartons. Basically, there would be a raid with targets in or near London, and if there were bombs remaining when they turned back to Germany (or wherever they originated), the Luftwaffe would often drop the remaining bombs over Kent on the way out.

This means there are quite a few random sites in Kent and along the southern coastline that are not near any military target at all. So far as I can tell, the closest ones to Veritas proper are the ones Gabe discusses in chapters 12 and 13. I did not in fact edit history at all, though it is always possible I missed something in all those lines of spreadsheet.

In chapter 6, Alysoun and Lizzie also go in for a spot of **tasseography** or tea leaf reading. The meanings they use are me drawing from a book called *Tea-Cup Reading and Fortune-Telling by Tea-Leaves* by "A Highland Seer", published in 1920 and available from various sources including Project Gutenberg, since it's now in the public domain. As Alysoun notes, snakes are generally considered bad luck, but Gabe has an unusual relationship with them by this point in his life.

Chapter 8 : Here, Geoffrey asks for Gabe's help with a question that has bothered him since 1922 and the death of his brother, Temple. You can trace this story from *Bound for Perdition* (where Temple and Delphina appear), into *Ancient Trust* (a novella, available by signing up for my newsletter, that takes place immediately after their deaths) through *Goblin Fruit* and *On The Bias*, and into *Best Foot Forward*. The resolution of this mystery is coming in *Three Graces*, a novella where Lizzie, Thesan, and Alysoun tackle the problem and finally learn what happened. It will be out in December 2023.

Chapter 9 : I realised early in my outline for this book that I couldn't ignore the utter destruction of **Coventry**, but I also wanted to handle it in a way that both fit the book's focus and the characters.

If you do not know this bit of history, Coventry was the target of a massive bombing raid on November 14th. It was aimed at destroying the factories in the area. Many incendiary bombs were dropped from the evening of the 14th through to nearly sunrise the next day. As they dropped, they started many fires through the town, including destroying the mediaeval cathedral. The water lines failed fairly early in the evening, making it even harder to fight the fires or buy more time for people to get away. By the morning, much of the centre of the city had been destroyed. Over 500 people were killed, over 1000 were injured.

Richard, as one of the senior Guard, would of course have been in the middle of trying to help however he could. While magic (even the kind of not-obvious magic available under the Pact when people who haven't made the Pact are around) could do quite a lot, it isn't something anyone can maintain indefinitely. And as Richard says, it is tricky for the Guard to come and go to the same place, when they've clearly been elsewhere to recover their magic.

It's also here that we see a bit more mention of **rationing**. Rationing began in stages in Great Britain. First, butter, sugar, ham or bacon were all rationed in January 1940. In March, meat (by price) was added, initially allowing about a pound of meat a week a person. Tea was added to rationing in July, allowing for two to three cups per person per day at this point (the amounts allowed changed a bit during the war). As Richard and Alysoun are talking in this chapter, cheese is not yet rationed, that only comes in May 1941.

It was expected that these rations would be supplemented by meals at schools (for students) or canteens (for workers, including people involved in war work). People could also supplement from their own farms and gardens. In general, vegetables were not rationed, though a number of them became very hard to get. For example, most onions at that point were imports, and so onions became very expensive and scarce to buy.

Veritas has a home farm to draw on and therefore they are not limited to the one egg a week per person ration. Magical farming techniques allow them to continue the farm with somewhat less labour, while magical transportation via the portals allows people to be doing some kinds of war work and still return to Veritas to sleep (and handle the farm chores...).

We are handwaving some of the logistics here - they just don't fit in the flow of the story. Suffice it to say that they have some supplementation of the rations, but are using their resources carefully and sending their extra food to places like the Five Schools and the Temple of Healing. And of course, those things Veritas can't produce itself - like tea - remain rationed.

It's also worth noting that there was a significant restaurant scheme, and restaurant meals were not rationed the same way. People couldn't have meat with every course, or have significant amounts of jam or sugar or what have you. But you could have a full meal, with items that were rationed, without using up your ration card. Within Albion, rationing for the schools and those drawing heavily on their magic as part of the war effort is also handled a little differently in most cases, due to the extra demands magic makes on a person's body.

Chapter 10 : The sinking of **The Patria** is a tragedy in a war full of them. It sank on November 25th, 1940 while leaving Haifa harbour carrying Jewish refugees who had been turned away from Palestine due to not having immigration papers. The bombing was actually done by a Jewish paramilitary agency, seeking to disable the ship (though this was not known at the time Alysoun is mentioning it). 267 of the people on board were killed.

Chapter 11 : This chapter draws on a great deal of lore around sovereignty magic, particularly in some of the Welsh tales. In a number of tales in the Mabinogion, the collection of Welsh tales made in the 12th and 13th centuries and originally translated into English by Lady Charlotte Guest in the mid 1800s, there is a repeated scene. A young man - the hero, the one seeking sovereignty or kingship - comes to somewhere new. There, he finds a man sitting at a gwyddbwyll board, with a beautiful woman sitting nearby, and sometimes some other younger men who are likely her brothers. The hero must play a game and win in order to win the hand of the lady, who grants sovereignty over the lands through her gifts in marriage.

Gabe, of course, is both happily married and has no desire to be Arthur in this play. He knows better.

There have been some attempts at recreating gwyddbwyll as a game. We know it was a little like chess with pieces moving on a checkered board, but it's not entirely clear how many pieces or all the ways they move. The game does keep showing up in lore, however, and Gabe is obviously familiar with it in that context.

The rest of his challenge is largely explained in the text either here or in later chapters. If you'd like more of his original encounter with the snake, he explains his fall to Rathna in *The Fossil Door*. The extra (available through my newsletter) *Three Tales of Gabe and Rathna* includes "Three Times Told", where Gabe works through telling his family about that bit of experience. It also includes a series of scenes just after his fall from Gil Oxley's point of view. I will add that you'll be seeing a little more of one of the challengers in *Illusion of a Boar*.

Chapter 17 : The scene with Thesan pointing out the details of her article is in another extra, *With All Due Speed*.

I do hope you've enjoyed these author's notes as well! You can find more connections and information about different characters, places, and topics on my authorial wiki. My newsletter is the best place to hear about all my forthcoming books, current research, and other amusements. It's also the way to get access to those extras!

The next book in this series will be *Illusion of a Boar*, taking place in the run up to D-Day in June of 1944. It features four people we last saw as students in the 1920s, now all in their 30s: Claudio Warren (Silvia and Hesperidon's son), Orion Sisley (his long-time friend), Hypatia Ward, and Cammie Gates (both skilled magical specialists). It also has an appearance by Gabe, along with a few other people with an interest in the project. It'll be out in November 2023.

Again, please do join me on my newsletter to hear all

my latest news, and for more about what's going on in my other online spaces. You can also get more information about all of these people and their other connections on my wiki at bit.ly/celia-lake-wiki. My website at celialake.com has links to all of these things as well.

Also by Celia Lake

Land Mysteries

Best Foot Forward

Nocturnal Quarry

Old As The Hills

Upon A Summer's Day

The Mysterious Charm Series

Outcrossing

Goblin Fruit

Magician's Hoard

Wards of the Roses

In The Cards

On The Bias

Seven Sisters

The Mysterious Powers Series

Carry On

The Fossil Door

Eclipse

Fool's Gold

The Hare and the Oak

Point By Point

Mistress of Birds

Charms of Albion

Pastiche

Sailor's Jewel

Other stories

Complementary

Winter's Charms

Forged in Combat

Learn more about the world of Albion and future books at my website, celialake.com. Additional information linking characters, places, and timelines is available at bit.ly/celia-lake-wiki

Sign up for my newsletter to be the first to hear about future books and learn about fascinating bits of research. Happy reading!